Miss Davis and the Spare
Copyright © 2025 by Rogue Press. All rights reserved.
Published by Rogue Press

All rights reserved. No part of this book may be used or reproduced in any form by any means—except in the case of brief quotations embodied in critical articles or reviews—without written permission.

This is a work of fiction. Names, characters, places, and incidents are products of the author's imagination or are used fictitiously and are not to be construed as real. Any resemblance to actual events, locales, organizations, or persons, living or dead, is entirely coincidental.

This e-book is licensed for your personal enjoyment only. This e-book may not be re-sold or given away to other people. If you would like to share this book with another person, please purchase an additional copy for each reader. If you are reading this book and did not purchase it, or it was not purchased for your use only, please return to your favorite retailer and purchase your own copy. Thank you for respecting the hard work of the author.

Stay in touch through the C. N. Jarrett newsletter!

Miss Davis and the Spare

DAZZLING DEBUTANTES
BOOK THREE

C. N. JARRETT

To the quiet heroes I have met who provide mentorship to those who need it most.

And to the many amazing people I have met who incorporate charitable endeavors and love of our fellow man into their daily routine.

You inspire me.

PROLOGUE

JUNE 20, 1820, BALFOUR TERRACE IN MAYFAIR, LONDON

A small hand pressed against his forehead, startling him from his sleep. Richard Balfour's eyes shot open, and he suppressed a groan. "Ethan?"

"Papa, I cannot sleep."

"Is something wrong, son?"

"I miss Emma."

The Earl of Saunton sighed heavily as he sat up. "Let us go to the kitchen and see what we can find so we do not wake Mama."

Standing up, he scooped his little boy into his arms. Another night of coaxing his four-year-old son to sleep loomed ahead, but Sophia was expecting, and she needed her rest. Thankfully, Richard could sleep late as he had no early morning plans, but he missed his dawn rides. They were becoming a distant memory because of Ethan's eccentric sleeping habits.

Ethan rode atop his shoulders all the way to the

kitchen, where they enjoyed biscuits and milk. Richard smoothed his son's curls as the boy nibbled on a biscuit, his small legs swinging against the chair. "Perhaps tomorrow, we could write Emma a letter," he suggested.

Ethan's face lit up. "And draw a picture?"

Richard smiled. "Of course."

Satisfied, Ethan leaned against his father's arm, his biscuit forgotten. Richard pressed a kiss to the top of his son's head, gratitude swelling in his chest. Some nights were long, but these quiet moments, just the two of them, were fleeting treasures he held dear.

To his eternal mortification, Richard had been unaware of his son's existence until two months earlier. Having recently reconsidered his reckless ways, Richard had set his man of business to investigating whether his past actions had left any unintended consequences. He learned of his son the same week of his unexpected marriage in late April.

Ethan was the result of a brief summer encounter with a maid during a house party five years prior. Unbeknownst to Richard, the maid had sought refuge with her aunt's family in Derby, where she had tragically died in childbirth, leaving her aunt, uncle, and six cousins to raise Ethan with love and care.

Unfamiliar with children and their needs, Richard had swiftly arranged for Ethan to be brought to London in an effort to do right by the boy. But in his haste, he had not fully considered the consequences of uprooting a four-year-old from the only family he had ever known. The bustling warmth of a country home had been exchanged for the vast, unfamiliar townhouse in London—one with only Richard, his new wife, and his brother to replace the eight loving relatives he had left behind.

Determined to be a father who took part in his son's

life, Richard wished to make amends for his past mistakes. The governess he had hired was a capable woman, but she could not take the place of Emma, the cousin Ethan so deeply missed.

It was much later that morning when Richard finally rose. His first thought upon waking was that he needed to find a way to ease his son's troubled nights. Seated beside his wife at breakfast, he broached the subject, gesturing for the footmen to leave the room before speaking.

"Sophia, I must do something about Ethan's sleep. Since he has come to live with us, I believe I have had about three nights of unbroken rest in total."

Lady Sophia Balfour quirked a red-blonde eyebrow. "He woke you again last night? How did I not know this?"

"He did. In fact, he has woken me every night this week. But with you carrying our child, I have been taking him downstairs so we would not wake you." Richard sighed, rubbing his temple. "This lack of sleep is not good for him, and it is certainly not good for me. I feel as if I am out all night carousing, but with none of the merrymaking. And even I could not keep up such a pace in my heyday!"

Sophia grimaced in sympathy, sipping her tea as she considered the problem. "I appreciate your discretion in letting me rest. However, it is clear that you removed Ethan from the Davis family too abruptly, despite our efforts to ease the transition."

"When I made the decision, I did not consider that he was a small child with deep attachments." Richard exhaled, leaning back in his chair. "My father forbade emotions when I was a boy, so how was I to know that such sentiment existed? You must help me find a solution."

Sophia sighed. "I believe the mistake was having your man of business handle the arrangements instead of going yourself. If you had met his relations and spoken with them, the transition would not have been so harsh. He may be worried about this Emma he keeps mentioning, or there may be a bedtime ritual we know nothing about because we never spoke with her. The changes you imposed on him were simply too sudden."

Richard sighed. "I know I caused this problem. My old ways were dishonorable, and my attempts to repair my mistakes have been clumsy. If you are accusing me of being insensitive or inconsiderate, I will not argue."

The countess grinned. "We agree, then. It was not well done of you."

Richard sighed again, dramatically. "I will be the first to admit that this whole caring-about-other-people bit is new to me and that there was likely a clever way to go about this that would have eased the transition and been more considerate of all the parties involved. But I cannot change my past mistakes, bride, so I beg you—tell me how to fix it?"

Sophia giggled as Richard caught her hand and gave it an imploring squeeze.

"Stop, or I will not tell you how!" she teased.

He clasped both of her hands between his. "Never. Tell me how to fix this, or I will shower you with praise until you surrender!"

She gasped in laughter. "I think—stop, you rogue, I cannot think properly—we must invite this Emma Davis to join us in London. Perhaps we can offer her a Season."

Richard blinked. "Spend more coin? It is not enough that I gifted a healthy estate to the Davis family for their benevolence in raising the boy after his mother died. Now I must fund a London wardrobe for their daughter?"

"This Emma raised your son. She taught him to read

and how to play chess like a little champion. She nurtured his genius that you are so proud of. And what price would you place on your sleep?"

Richard groaned. "Any price. I will have my man of business arrange it."

"Nay, husband. That is how you arrived in this predicament. It is you who should fetch her."

"I cannot. Ethan needs me here, and I have several parliamentary commitments over the next few weeks that cannot be avoided. It is imperative we take action now. The boy has dark rings under his eyes, which he did not have when he first arrived."

"Then you will write to them yourself, and we will send your brother to collect her. The Davises are family now through Ethan, and your high-handed approach is precisely why you are losing sleep. Besides, Peregrine needs a project. I am disappointed that he has returned to his clubs and his ... less reputable company."

Richard huffed. "Confound it, woman! I hate writing long letters."

Sophia smiled serenely. "Husband, it will help you learn your lesson. Arrogance bears consequences, my love. Writing long letters and paying for a new wardrobe are your penalty.

CHAPTER ONE

"A real gentleman is always perfectly presented. Dirt on the collar is a sign of low breeding and will repel the ladies."

July 1801, the late Earl of Saunton to his son, Peregrine, on his sixth birthday after finding him playing with his tin soldiers in the gardens of Saunton Park.

∼

"Emma, Emma! We have news from London. It is about Ethan!"

Emma tipped back her head in dismay, one hand gripping the back of her bonnet. Her ribbons were twisted—again—and she was doing her best not to throttle herself by accident.

"News of Ethan?" she called back, straightening up. The rose garden at the Davis family home in Somerset was in full bloom, filling the air with the sweet, heady scent of damask and tea roses. The neatly arranged beds overflowed with blossoms in varying shades of blush pink, creamy white, and deep crimson, their delicate petals catching the golden sunlight of a warm June afternoon. Bees hummed lazily from flower to flower, while a gentle breeze stirred the leaves, carrying the fragrance through the walled garden.

Beyond the low stone wall, rolling green fields stretched toward the horizon, dotted with grazing sheep beneath a sky so blue it seemed endless. The warmth of the early summer sun settled comfortably on Emma's shoulders, but the occasional cloud drifting past offered momentary relief from its brightness. The hedgerows bordering the garden rustled softly with the movement of nesting birds, and a blackbird trilled a bright, cheerful tune from a nearby branch.

It was the sort of afternoon that begged for idleness, for quiet strolls along the pathways or leisurely hours spent reading beneath the shade of an old oak. But for Emma, the peaceful day was now interrupted by the news from London—news that sent a tangle of unease through her heart, despite the perfection of the summer around her.

Jane swung her head to find her, squinting against the sun that shone directly behind Emma's back. She hurried over, her expression perplexed. "What on earth are you doing?"

"I am attempting to trim these roses without hanging myself on these wretched ribbons." She gestured with the shears, causing Jane to wince as the sharp tip waved too close for comfort.

"I see. Perhaps I should take those from you before you put an eye out."

Emma sighed and handed over the pruning shears. She was not known for her grace, but she had yet to do herself a serious injury, and she intended to keep it that way. With her hands free, she straightened her ribbons and retied them before looking back at her younger sister.

"What is this about Ethan? Is he well?" she demanded.

"Our little cousin is now the son of an earl, living in a grand London townhouse! Of course he is well!"

Emma's lips pressed into a firm line. "Our little cousin is the illegitimate son of an earl we have never met. There is no of course. The arrogant jackanapes did not even have the grace to meet us before he snatched Ethan from our home!"

"By jackanapes, you are referring to the father and not the son?" Jane teased.

"Ha ha! Yes, the father."

"The father who gave our father this fine estate in Somerset, elevating our income and status in gratitude for raising his son?"

"The same man who forced us to leave our very nice farm in Derbyshire for this strange county, where we have none of our friends and neighbors!"

"And who provided us with a fine library, generously filled with books, which has kept you too occupied to mourn your lost friends and neighbors?"

Emma huffed in disgust but could not deny the truth. "It is a very fine library," she mumbled.

"Yes, it is. And if you were honest, you would admit you care for our new library far more than for any of your long-forgotten friends and neighbors. You love your family best, and we are all here with you!" Jane swept her arms wide, encompassing their home and gardens.

"Except for Ethan!"

Jane cocked her head before conceding the point. "Except for Ethan. But Ethan is with his father, where he belongs. The earl will provide him with the education and opportunities befitting a young gentleman of his birthright."

Emma did not venerate this unknown Lord Saunton, but even she had to admit she had lost no relationships that could rival the library he had gifted their family as part of their new estate. Still, she resented the man for stealing Ethan away and missed the little boy fiercely. His abrupt departure had left a hole in her heart.

If she were being truly honest, she would acknowledge that her little cousin now had far greater opportunities to learn and nurture his talents than their limited means could have ever provided.

But she did not want to be honest. She wanted to be resentful.

Lord Saunton had not even troubled himself to collect his own child, sending a carriage and a man of business in his stead. *Arrogant brute!*

"Now come inside and hear the news! It is quite exciting," Jane effused, grabbing hold of Emma's arm and pulling her along.

Once inside, Emma attempted to make her way upstairs to wash, but Jane mercilessly tugged her toward the drawing room, too eager to let her go.

"What have you dragged me in here for? Could you not have imparted the news of Ethan and Lord Arrogant, who stole him from us, while I cleaned up?" Emma demanded, before noticing the alarmed expression on her sister's face.

Then she saw her mother seated on the settee, the family's finest tea service arranged before her. Just beyond the wing chair facing the settee, a pair of expensive black riding boots came into view.

Emma's stomach dropped.

A tall gentleman unfolded himself from the chair, turning to face her. His silky, sable curls framed a strong, striking face, and his forest green cutaway coat was a perfect match for his piercing emerald eyes. He was, quite simply, an adult version of Ethan. One day, her little cousin would likely share the same broad shoulders, narrow hips, and chiseled jawline that—unfortunately—made her heart give an erratic little quiver. But with any luck, Ethan would not inherit the indolent, sulky airs of this stranger standing before her.

Wincing, Emma sank into a curtsy. "My lord ... um ... welcome to our home."

His gaze drifted downward, pausing at her feet. A sense of foreboding crept up her spine. Looking down, she discovered to her horror that the hem of her muslin gown was streaked with mud and grass stains from her work in the garden.

Tilting her chin back up, she caught a fleeting sneer of disdain before he smoothed his features into polite indifference.

Belatedly, he inclined his head in a brief bow. "Not Lord Arrogant, I am afraid. Just a mere spare. Mr. Peregrine Balfour, at your service. And you must be the famous Emma?"

EMMA WAS NOT what Perry had expected.

From his conversations with Richard and their man of business, Johnson, he knew the Davis family had Welsh ancestry, which perhaps accounted for the wild mass of black curls escaping from beneath her enormous straw bonnet. The hat itself was trimmed with an excessive number of tangled ribbons, as if she had attempted to tame the unruly thing and failed spectacularly.

Dark, almost black eyes peered up at him from beneath the absurd headpiece, filled with a mix of wariness and defiance. Unlike the younger sister who had collected her from the garden—a tall, graceful young lady—this girl was smaller, her frame boyish and slight.

Yet there was an undeniable energy about her.

She was all sharp angles and restless movement, as if she had been caught mid-flight rather than simply stepping into the drawing room. The state of her attire certainly supported the idea—her muslin gown bore clear evidence of a recent tussle with the garden, streaked with grass stains and smudges of earth along the hem. A stubborn dirt mark marred one cheek, though she seemed entirely unaware of it.

Perry resisted the urge to shake his head in astonishment. He had never met a young lady who looked quite so …untamed. Yet there was something compelling about her—a brightness in her eyes, a liveliness in her every gesture that hinted at a mind as quick as her tongue likely was.

And this was the girl his young nephew adored? The one who kept Ethan awake at night with homesickness?

He supposed he would have to solve that particular mystery himself.

Blazes! Perry could have throttled Richard for sending him on this ridiculous errand to rural Somerset. He strongly suspected Sophia's influence in the matter—his sister-in-law was forever insisting that he needed a project, whatever that meant—but this journey unsettled him. It stirred memories best left buried, of his father and of … her. The woman from the village. A past he had no wish to revisit.

Had it been up to him, he would have turned back in

Wiltshire and returned to London without a second thought. But Richard had been adamant—Perry must see this through. And, to his great dismay, he found he wanted to succeed. He wanted his brother to be pleased with his results.

Which was how he found himself standing in the farthest reaches of Somerset, facing a little hoyden with an indignant tilt to her chin and a streak of dirt on her cheek. *Heaven help me.*

His gaze flickered briefly to her ill-fitting gown, stained from the garden, with a bodice which hinted at feminine curves concealed beneath, before he forced himself to focus on her eyes—dark, sharp, and wary. A lesser woman might have wilted under his scrutiny, but this one stood her ground, staring at him expectantly. He realized, belatedly, that she had spoken, and he had failed to respond—too lost in his own thoughts.

Clearing his throat, he adopted an air of indolent amusement. "I apologize. I missed what you said because I was distracted by my handsome surroundings."

With a pointed glance at the grass-streaked hem of her gown, he offered a facetious smile, one visible only to her now that her willowy sister and mother stood behind him.

As expected, her eyes narrowed, darkening with suspicion. The other inhabitants of the room would detect nothing amiss in his polite words, but Emma had clearly recognized the subtle slight to her appearance.

Perry barely suppressed a grin. *At least she is quick.*

"Well, if you will excuse me, I shall just go freshen up."

"Not necessary. Let us enjoy an invigorating cup of tea together, now that I have come all this way to visit." Perry was uncertain why he was baiting the girl, but he found himself thoroughly entertained by the way her nostrils flared as she attempted to squash her ire.

"I must look a fright. I can return for tea in ten minutes."

"Not at all. The pleasure of your company is far preferable to your departure. Please ..." He held up his arm in a gentlemanly gesture, inviting her to take a seat.

A low growl rumbled in her throat as she complied, and Perry had to bite back a grin. *A trapped creature, this one,* he mused, watching her settle stiffly into a chair across from him. Had they been alone, he had no doubt she would have told him precisely where he could take his invigorating tea.

She fairly vibrated with repressed energy, and he was helplessly intrigued. How far could he push her before she exploded?

This afternoon's visit to Rose Ash Manor was turning out to be far more entertaining than he had expected.

Emma removed her gardening gloves, then reached up to unfasten her enormous bonnet. Setting it on a nearby table, she made a valiant attempt to smooth her disheveled hair. She failed abysmally. A few rebellious strands stuck straight up, defying her every effort.

Perry repressed a chuckle. He wished he could be present when she finally caught sight of herself in a mirror and realized how utterly ridiculous she had looked, sitting there sipping tea with the brother of Lord Arrogant.

Or, if she preferred, *mere Mr. Arrogant himself.*

Mrs. Davis poured a cup of tea and handed it to her eldest daughter before preparing another for their guest. The tea service was of delicate porcelain, patterned with blue forget-me-nots along the edges, a design that spoke more of sentiment than fashion. The silver spoons, though polished, were slightly worn, suggesting years of careful use rather than careless indulgence. A plate of dainty biscuits rested on a floral saucer at the center of the table, their golden edges crisp and inviting.

Perry took a sip of his tea and withheld a grimace. Ever since his brother had wed a couple of months ago, he had found himself drinking tea and nibbling biscuits far too frequently. Just more evidence that marriage wrecked a gentleman.

Emma watched him from the corner of her eye, suspicion still evident in her posture. It would seem she did not favor the aristocracy—though, to be fair, he had deliberately goaded her. She flung an accusing look at her younger sister across the table, and in his peripheral vision, Perry caught the girl mouthing something as he turned to smile at Mrs. Davis.

"I am sorry," was his best guess as to the covert communication between the two sisters.

Emma relaxed perceptibly into her chair. *Interesting.* He filed it away while considering how best to proceed, now that he knew the object of his mission was unlikely to be receptive to his invitation.

The drawing room, though modest, was warm and well kept. Sunlight streamed in through lace-draped windows, casting intricate patterns onto the floral carpet. The furnishings, though not of the first stare, were arranged with care—rosewood chairs with embroidered cushions, a walnut writing desk against the far wall, and a pianoforte in one corner, its lid closed as if awaiting an evening's entertainment. The room spoke of a home built on comfort rather than grandeur.

"I was just explaining to your hospitable mother that Ethan has been settling into his new life at Balfour Terrace like a champion," Perry said, taking another reluctant sip of tea. "The earl has hired a governess to help him continue the education that you began, and my nephew has convinced every member of our household to play a daily game of chess." He coughed lightly into his hand. "At least, on the days I am in residence."

He did not miss the faint grimace Emma tried to suppress. He could practically hear the tirade forming in her mind—something about idle gentlemen and their useless days spent in the pursuit of pleasure.

"A governess?" Mrs. Davis asked, her voice carrying a note of surprise.

"Yes, Lord Saunton hired a governess rather than the conventional tutor. The theory was that it would assist Ethan's transition if we emulated your daughter's presence as closely as possible."

Mrs. Davis appeared impressed with the strategy. "That was thoughtful of the earl. Ethan spent most of his day with the women of the household."

Perry smiled, then broached the reason for his visit. "There has been one ... minor issue since he joined us."

All three women straightened in alarm at the announcement. What was it about his young nephew that elicited such single-minded concern, not only from every member of his own household, but from this one as well? When Perry had been a boy, barely anyone had taken notice of him—except, of course, when his father had decided to tutor him, those excruciating sessions where Perry had wished to be anywhere but near the late earl.

"It is nothing serious," he assured the ladies. "It is just that he has trouble sleeping. He prowls the halls at night and wakes my brother every night."

Emma frowned, the expression deepening the shadow

of concern in her dark eyes. "Why? He has never done that before," she demanded, her tone heavy with censure.

Mrs. Davis, a cheerful woman with golden-blonde hair tucked neatly beneath a lace-trimmed cap, shot a reproving glance at her daughter. She was dressed in a pale yellow morning gown with delicate embroidery at the cuffs, her appearance tidy and composed, in contrast to her eldest daughter.

Emma, for her part, flushed and adjusted the sleeves of her faded blue muslin gown, which bore signs of wear along the seams. Though the color suited her dark hair and striking eyes, the dress itself was unimpressive—practical rather than fashionable. Perry could not decide if she simply had no interest in fashion or if she deliberately rejected such concerns.

She cleared her throat. "I mean ... What is keeping him up? Ethan always slept very well at our home in Derby."

"I am afraid it is all your fault, Miss Davis." Perry leaned back in his chair, watching as her frown deepened. "The boy misses you and worries after you."

Emma seemed to deflate, her shoulders slumping slightly. "I ... see." Her voice was quieter now. "We were very close. I have raised him since the day of his birth. His mother ... she did not survive."

Perry nodded, noting the way her fingers curled into her lap as though holding onto something unseen. "Most commendable. The earl is very grateful for all you have done for his son. He is impressed with the lad's manners and intelligence."

A pleased smile flickered across her lips before vanishing, her expression returning to its previously rigid lines. The young woman was clearly unhappy about his presence

—and resented, quite openly, the method in which his brother had taken Ethan from her life.

"Which is why the earl would like you to visit."

SHE FROZE with her cup halfway to her lips. Carefully, Emma lowered it back onto its saucer, then placed both onto the table, willing her fingers not to tremble.

She missed Ethan terribly. For the whole of his young life, they had been inseparable, their days filled with lessons, games, and quiet moments that had knitted them together like siblings rather than cousins. His sudden departure to London, to live with a father he had never known, had left a hollow ache in her heart—one she had not yet learned to quiet.

It was no secret that the boy was a by-blow, but the revelation that he was the natural-born son of a powerful earl had stunned her family. In gratitude for their care, the Earl of Saunton had gifted them Rose Ash Manor, elevating the Davises from respectable country folk to newly landed gentry. A generous gesture, to be sure.

But the arrogant lord had not even deigned to visit them. Instead, his man of business had handled the negotiations, speaking with her parents as if the matter were nothing more than a simple transaction. Papers had been signed, arrangements made, and Ethan had been whisked away in a waiting carriage.

Now, rather than calling upon them himself, the earl had sent his younger brother to Somerset as an errand boy to fetch her.

Emma folded her hands in her lap, pressing them together to still their restless energy. It seemed the great

Lord Saunton was content to issue commands from a distance, without ever troubling himself to meet the family who had loved and raised his son.

She lifted her chin, her dark eyes settling on Mr. Peregrine Balfour.

I would love to see Ethan.

Emma's hand slipped into the small pocket of her muslin dress, her fingers closing around the cool, familiar shape of a miniature tin monkey. Ethan had cherished the little toy, endlessly making it dance across tabletops and along the arms of chairs. But in the final moments before he had boarded the earl's carriage, he had thrust it into her hand, his small fingers curling over hers in quiet insistence.

"You keep it, Emma."

She had been too overwhelmed to argue, too consumed with holding back the storm of tears that threatened to spill. She had wanted to insist that it was his favorite toy, that he must keep it close. But the words had caught in her throat, and then—he was gone.

The carriage had pulled away, wheels churning up pebbles and dust, leaving her standing there with the tiny figure pressed between her palms while Ethan waved from the back window, his small face framed with anxious excitement.

Now, she carried the little tin monkey wherever she went—a silent token of the boy she had raised, a reminder of the laughter and late-night stories, of the countless hours spent teaching him his letters, and of the warmth of his small hand tucked into hers.

But life moves on.

Ethan had a new home, a new life, and she had no wish to visit London. Truth be told, she was beginning to love their new home in Somerset. There was much to do. She and her father were learning the responsibilities of estate management, transitioning from hardworking tenant farmers to landowners. It was a great challenge, one that required her full attention.

She would see Ethan when he visited over the holidays. That would be enough.

Would it not?

"That sounds lovely, but I am afraid I must decline, Lord Ar—Mr. Balfour."

Emma took great satisfaction in thwarting the gentleman. He might be as handsome as a Greek god, with his broad shoulders, striking green eyes, and an effortless grace that made his every movement draw the eye. And, yes, his powerful thighs were certainly well displayed in those finely tailored buckskins—though she would never admit to noticing.

But he was also more arrogant than she had envisioned the earl to be. Perhaps being the spare had left him with a chip on his shoulder, one that only added to the general air of entitlement that clung to him.

"Miss Davis, I do not think you understand." Mr. Balfour's voice was smooth. "The earl is offering to sponsor you for a London Season. He will purchase you a new wardrobe and provide a dowry of one thousand pounds."

Emma barely had time to react before her mother and Jane gasped at the news. It was a profoundly generous offer, the kind that would change the course of any young lady's future. But Emma did not want a Season. She had no interest in society's tedious expectations, no desire to waltz in glittering ballrooms or parade before landed gentlemen in search of a suitable match.

Wealth had its uses, of course, but she was quite content with their current circumstances. Eventually, she would meet a respectable, honorable man here in Rose Ash—perhaps someone in trade, someone unconcerned with all the new rules and expectations that came with being part of the gentry.

She met Mr. Balfour's gaze with steady resolve. "I am afraid I must decline. Please enjoy your journey back to London."

With that, she made to stand.

"Mr. Balfour, how remiss I have been!" Mrs. Davis interjected smoothly, her warm smile as unshaken as ever. "You have been on the road for days, and all we have offered you is tea and biscuits. I shall have the housekeeper arrange sandwiches immediately." She turned to Emma with a pointed look. "Emma, dear, do you care to attend me?"

Emma's heart sank. She recognized the forced brightness in her mother's voice—never a good sign. A lecture in the hall was surely forthcoming. Pasting on a smile, she rose and followed Mrs. Davis from the drawing room.

The moment they reached the corridor, her mother spun to face her, grasping her hands with gentle urgency.

"Emma, it is a generous offer, and I implore you to consider it."

"I do not wish to go to London," Emma insisted. "It is noisy, overcrowded, and stifling. I have no desire to marry a gentleman of the *ton*—nor even the gentry!"

Mrs. Davis's usually warm, round face was drawn with concern. She tucked an errant blonde curl behind her ear, her ice-blue eyes serious. "I shall not force you, but you burn your bridges every time you open your mouth. It would not hurt to learn a little diplomacy, Emma. The world is a lonely, brutal place, and we are fortunate to have such a large, loving family."

Her voice softened as sorrow flickered across her

expression. "Look at what happened to my niece. Kitty was in respectable service until the earl ruined her and left her with child." She paused, her hands tightening around Emma's. "She was fortunate that your father agreed to provide her with a home, despite the disgrace. Many husbands would not have been so accommodating, but your father is a good man. For my sake, he weathered the scandal of it all. He deserved this estate after the sacrifices he made." A deep sigh escaped her lips. "Even now, Ethan could be in a foundling home, raised by impersonal strangers."

Emma swallowed, guilt settling uncomfortably in her chest. "I am sorry, Mama, but I do not wish to have a Season. It would be a disaster. I cannot dance, despite Jane's best efforts, and we both know that I am woefully unskilled in polite conversation. It would all be a horrendous failure. I wish to stay at home."

Mrs. Davis studied her daughter carefully, her expression unreadable. "Emma, I only want you to find a young gentleman of your own. So that one day, you may know the joy of raising your own children. Watching you with Ethan ... You would make such a wonderful mother, my dear."

Emma dropped her gaze to her shoes, where the muddy hem of her skirt mocked her with its unladylike evidence of her earlier gardening.

It was her deepest desire—to raise a family of her own. To love and nurture a child, to know the same simple, unbreakable bond she had shared with Ethan. A child who could not be taken away from her, whose unknown parent would not suddenly appear to claim them.

But a Season? The scrutiny, the rules, the endless expectation to smile and charm men who cared more for dowries than for hearts? No. She would be a disaster in high society. She knew it, and so did her mother.

"I cannot go," she murmured. "I would be an utter failure."

Mrs. Davis was silent for several moments, her searching gaze unreadable. Then, with another sigh, she reached out to smooth a curl behind Emma's ear.

"I will not force you to accept the invitation," she said at last. "Though I am disappointed to see you allowing fear of failure to make your decision. You are usually so courageous, Emma."

Emma resolutely studied the dried mud clinging to her gown, pretending she had not heard the gentle rebuke in her mother's voice.

Mrs. Davis reached for her daughter's chin, tipping it up so their eyes met. "As you like. But do not be rude to the earl's emissary. Lord Saunton has been exceedingly generous to the Davis family, and through his benevolence, we have secured a brighter future for your brothers and sisters. I expect you to summon some deportment and address the earl's brother with respect, young lady."

Emma nodded, pressing her lips together. She knew she had a tendency to be too forthright, too sharp with her words. It was why she had never been courted in Derbyshire or in their new Somerset town, why she had few friends outside of her family.

But quelling her tongue for the duration of Mr. Arrogant's visit?

That, at least, was not too much to ask.

Perry sipped his tea and offered a polite smile to the younger sister while Mrs. Davis took Emma to task in the hall. Jane Davis was undeniably lovely, with refined features and a graceful manner, but Perry had long learned to avoid innocent young ladies. He had no interest in finding himself ensnared in a marriage he did not seek.

Strangely, though, it was not the elegant Jane who commanded his attention. It was her older sister—the one who had been glaring at him moments earlier, her dark eyes flashing with barely contained ire.

Emma Davis was a contradiction—brash and untidy, yet sharp-witted and fiercely loyal to the boy she had raised. The impulse to provoke her, to see how far he could push before she lost the battle with her temper, was almost overwhelming.

Perhaps it was simply exhaustion. Travel wore on a man, after all.

Perry reached for a biscuit, swallowing it in two bites. *That must be it. I am merely tired and hungry from the road.*

Mrs. Davis and Emma reentered the room, resuming their places at the tea table. Emma perched on the very edge of her chair, her posture stiff, as if she were moments from bolting. In contrast, Mrs. Davis sank onto the sky-blue sofa with an air of practiced ease.

Despite his general disdain for country life, Perry had to admit that the Davis drawing room had a certain charm. It was warm, lived-in—a place meant to be occupied rather than merely displayed. Books teetered in small piles on end tables, inexpensive but tasteful ornaments adorned the shelves, and cheerful landscape paintings hung upon the walls.

It felt like a home. Something Perry himself had never truly experienced but sentimentality had no place in his task. Richard had charged him with a mission, and Perry intended to succeed.

When he had protested—rather colorfully—against making this trip to Somerset, his brother had appealed to him in an uncharacteristically earnest manner.

"I need your assistance, Perry. You are a man accustomed to getting what you want. I need you to turn that charm on the Davis family and obtain their agreement to send their eldest daughter to London. I will send Sophia's lady's maid with you for propriety's sake on the return journey. This is an important family matter, and I must send a relation I trust to handle it."

Why pleasing his brother gave him a sense of purpose, he did not fully understand. But when he had assisted Richard with his own difficulties back in May, after his unexpected wedding, Perry had been surprised to find himself enjoying the role.

Not that he would ever admit such a thing to Richard's wife. *Sophia had already declared that I need a project, and I will not give her the satisfaction of being correct.*

Still, she might have a point.

Which was why success was imperative. Richard needed him, and Perry would not fail. His brother had been right about one thing—Perry always achieved what he set his mind to.

And so, as Emma settled back into her seat, Perry scrutinized her expressions, noting every flicker of resistance, every glimmer of defiance.

He had formed a conclusion.

She was not motivated by personal gain, nor by ambition. She did not seek elevation within society.

No, Miss Emma Davis was driven by something far stronger.

And now that she was seated once more, he intended to make her an offer she could not refuse.

CHAPTER TWO

"Females are purely ornamental. When you forget this truth, you will uncover the need to drown your sorrows in drink. Here, take a sip of my brandy. It will help you forget the silly chit."

July 1802, the late Earl of Saunton to his son, Peregrine, on his seventh birthday after finding him climbing the trees of Saunton Park with the daughter of the stable master.

~

"Before I forget, my brother wrote you a letter, Mrs. Davis."

Perry drew the neatly folded missive from his breast pocket and handed it to Emma's mother. From the corner of his eye, he caught Emma shifting in her chair, her hands clenching into restless fists in her lap. *Ah. So the little minx is displeased with the earl.*

He suppressed a smirk. It seemed rather churlish to resent a man who had gifted her family an entire estate—

including the comfortable drawing room in which she now sat. *Ungrateful chit.*

Mrs. Davis carefully unfolded the letter and began reading, her expression thoughtful. By the time she reached the end, a small, satisfied smile curved her lips.

"Well ... what does it say?" Emma's caustic tone drew a sharp look from her mother.

"The earl extends his apologies for how he handled the matter of retrieving Ethan," Mrs. Davis replied patiently. "He admits he is not well-versed in family affairs and that his new countess has pointed out his error in handling such a delicate situation with so little sensitivity. He realizes his actions caused some distress for Ethan—whom he is very fond of and impressed with—and he seeks our help in easing the boy's transition."

A barely audible growl came from Emma's direction. Perry did not need to strain his ears to recognize the words *Lord Arrogant* muttered beneath her breath. He ignored it, though the temptation to laugh was considerable. *Richard will be most amused by his new title when I inform him. In fact, I may take to calling him that myself.*

Mrs. Davis turned back to Perry with a polite, measured expression. "I appreciate his lordship's consideration and the thought he has put into this matter. However, I am afraid Emma has decided to remain here at Rose Ash. Perhaps she can compose a letter of advice for the earl, along with a letter for Ethan to reassure him?"

Perry had anticipated resistance from the moment he had laid eyes on Miss Emma Davis. She was, after all, a woman of strong opinions and little inclination to be swayed.

Which was why he had been observing her so carefully, not unlike a strategist preparing for a battle.

She might not care for fine gowns, grand ballrooms, or the lure of wealth and status, but there *was* something she valued beyond reason—family.

And so, with the confidence of a man who knew precisely how this game would end, Perry leaned back in his chair, waiting for the perfect moment to deliver the one argument she could not refuse.

"That is a pity, Mrs. Davis. I would have enjoyed escorting your daughters to see the wonders of our great city. And the modiste our family uses—her creations are sublime. Every young woman dreams of owning such gowns, of attending glittering balls and dancing the evening away in the arms of charming gentlemen."

Perry paused for effect before adding smoothly, "My brother is exceedingly protective of his family. Only the most distinguished of gentlemen would be introduced to two such important ladies."

As expected, Jane leaned forward in excitement. "Ladies?"

Perry feigned an expression of innocent surprise as he turned to look at Jane. "Did I fail to mention that the invitation was for both of you?"

Jane inhaled sharply, her face alight with excitement. She turned to Emma, clasping her hands together. "Emma! This is so exciting! A Season in London! I have always dreamed of waltzing in a grand ballroom. Please, we must go!"

From his right, Perry felt Emma's heated glare, burning with barely restrained fury.

She knew. She knew she was caught, that the trap had been laid too carefully, too thoroughly. He could almost see her mind working, scrambling for an escape route. But there was none. He had measured her correctly—she might resist for herself, but she would not deny her sister something she so clearly longed for.

"Jane," Emma began, her voice tinged with desperation, "I am sure we can request the waltz be included at the next local assembly—"

But Jane was already lost to the vision Perry had painted for her.

Time to deliver the final blow.

"Not to mention how disappointed the Duchess of Halmesbury will be when she learns she will not be sponsoring you both," he added casually, sipping his tea. "She was quite looking forward to it."

Or she would be—just as soon as she was informed.

"A duchess!" Jane nearly squealed, her excitement spilling over as she jumped to her feet. "Mama, where did we put the trunks? Perhaps I should start packing before dinner!"

Emma sputtered in protest, but Jane did not hear a word of it.

"Oh! Should I take my fashion plates? No—of course not! London will have far newer designs than the ones I have collected!"

With that, she clapped her hands together and rushed from the room, leaving Emma, Perry, and Mrs. Davis behind in bemused silence.

Emma shot Perry a murderous scowl, her hands clenching as if she were contemplating whether she could get away with throttling him. Swallowing a smile, Perry ignored her and turned to Mrs. Davis, who, to his great amusement, appeared to be holding back her own smile.

"Well played, Mr. Balfour," she said, her voice tinged with amusement. "It would seem my eldest daughters will leave with you in the morning—provided my husband agrees. Would you care to stay for dinner?"

A moan of protest erupted from his right. "Mama!"

Mrs. Davis turned to Emma with a placatory expression. "Admit when you have been outwitted, my dear. My advice is … do not play chess with this gentleman. His talent for strategy surpasses your own, young lady." Then, her tone softened. "Or would you rather be the one to stand in the way of your sister—your closest friend in the world—embarking on the adventure of her dreams?"

Emma turned her glare on Perry, dark fire smoldering in her black eyes. "Jane was not included in the invitation—admit it!"

Perry let a slow, condescending grin spread across his lips. "I do not know of what you speak. Lord Saunton was quite explicit that your sister should accompany you under the same terms I put forward."

Her head whipped back to her mother. "Mama, I do not wish to go. Speak to Jane—make her see reason!"

Mrs. Davis gave a polite but firm frown. "Attempt to stand between Jane and a new wardrobe fit for the peerage? I would not dare. It is out of my hands, I am afraid."

"Then she can go alone!" Emma declared desperately.

The cheerful mother suddenly grew stern. "Absolutely not. You are to ensure nothing happens to Jane. You are the responsible one, Emma. I expect you to look after your sister and see that no harm befalls her. She has only just turned eighteen—she does not understand the ways of the world as you do."

"But … but … I am not that much older than her!"

"You are more—" Mrs. Davis hesitated, searching for the right word while Perry watched, highly entertained. "—

mistrustful." Perry nearly choked, forcing his laughter back at the appropriateness of her selection. "Besides, this visit will be good for you. You spend far too much time buried in your books and toiling in the garden. It is time to experience the world."

Emma's lips parted, as if she had a retort ready, but then her thoughts played out across her face—resistance, frustration, reluctant understanding—until, with a dramatic slump of her shoulders, she surrendered. "Yes, Mama."

Perry had never been more entertained in his life.

He had succeeded in his mission, and the fact that he had just neatly doubled the planned expenses on behalf of his soon-to-be-very-vexed brother only sweetened the feeling of victory.

Timing his final move perfectly, he leaned forward, meeting Emma's livid gaze with a triumphant one of his own—well aware he was provoking her—before turning to smile at Mrs. Davis.

"And I would love to stay for dinner, Mrs. Davis."

PERRY PERUSED the books in the manor's modest library while he awaited the descent of the large Davis family for dinner. In keeping with the style of the drawing room, the space was attractively furnished, the shelves well stocked with leather-bound volumes that suggested both refinement and curiosity.

The family had good taste.

Except, perhaps, for the eldest daughter.

Emma Davis had an unerring ability to dress in the most unflattering colors and styles, more akin to a governess than a young lady of the gentry. It did not appear to be for lack of funds—the younger sister was well turned out in dresses only a few months out of fashion, likely sewn from patterns copied from long-traveled fashion plates. Perhaps she was adept with a needle?

And yet, despite her regrettable wardrobe, Perry still could not quite shake the memory of Emma's—*ahem*—impressive figure from his thoughts. The boyish young woman had some pronounced curves trapped within her ill-fitting bodice to fascinate even the most tepid of gentlemen.

Most inconvenient.

Clearly, he needed to return to London and visit one of his agreeable widows before his mind wandered further down this absurd path.

Behind him, light footsteps announced an approaching presence. Seconds later, the library door thudded shut.

His lips quirked. *Ah. A confrontation. And a private one at that.*

Taking his time—because he knew it would aggravate her—Perry slowly turned, letting a sardonic smile stretch across his face.

"Miss Davis, what a pleasure to see you."

Emma stood just inside the doorway, her arms folded tightly across her chest.

"Why are you doing this?"

"Doing what, exactly?"

"I made it clear I did not wish to journey to London with you, and yet you deliberately maneuvered me into it."

She had at least taken the effort to clean up. A fresh gown replaced the garden-stained muslin, and her hair had been vaguely styled. She appeared fractionally less wild than at their first encounter.

But not by much.

The gown itself was tragically outdated—likely fifteen years old, its voluminous fabric billowing around her slight frame and buttoned primly up to her chin. As for her hair ... the thick cloud of dark curls looked as though it had been piled atop her head in a battle she had barely won.

Perry resisted the urge to sigh.

Richard had better not get any notions about Perry having a hand in refining the little hoyden beyond delivering her to Balfour Terrace. Polishing Miss Davis into a lady fit for society would be nothing short of a herculean task.

He tilted his head, feigning innocence. "Miss Davis, your mother believes this trip will be good for you. Do you not wish to meet eligible young men?"

"What is the point?"

Perry frowned. "All young women wish to marry, do they not?"

Emma snorted. "Let us be honest—none of the young gentlemen of London will have any interest in courting me."

Perry's brow furrowed. *Well, that was unexpected.*

For all her fire and defiance, Emma Davis lacked confidence.

To his great irritation, a peculiar sensation—something uncomfortably close to concern—settled in his chest.

"Emma," he said, his voice steady, "the earl will ensure you are ready. He will purchase you the finest gowns, provide you with a lady's maid, and arrange tutoring in anything you need to master. My brother will take care of you."

She did not respond immediately. Instead, she studied him, her dark eyes searching his face as if she were looking for the catch.

For the first time since he had arrived in Somerset, Perry found himself wishing he had chosen his words more carefully.

"Do you not understand? It will not be enough." Emma's voice rose with uncharacteristic urgency. "I am happy with my life. When I step into society, I feel unkempt, ridiculous. People see me as a child. A poorly dressed one. Then I open my mouth, and I see their discomfort—their need to get away from me. And then there is you"—she flapped a hand in his general direction—"the very pink of the *beau monde*. Flawless in your attire, perfect in your etiquette. You and your priggish friends will make sport of me—the silly country mouse who does not know a pleat from a ... a ..."

She gestured wildly at her own gown, struggling for words.

It was painfully obvious that she was wholly illiterate in matters of fashion.

"*Gros de Naples?*" Perry supplied smoothly.

Emma froze, staring at him with her mouth slightly agape. "Is that a real thing?"

He shrugged. "I suppose you will find out when you visit my brother's favorite modiste."

Her expression darkened. "Do not mock me. I asked you a direct question! And why would your brother have a favorite modiste?"

Perry felt a flicker of shame. *Well done, idiot.* That was hardly an appropriate subject for an innocent young miss—even if she was a little wild.

Clearing his throat, he drew a steady breath. "I misspoke. Formerly his favorite modiste. It is now frequented by the new countess and her cousin."

Emma eyed him, suspicion lingering. "I see. So it is true the earl has reformed?"

"He has."

"It is most indiscreet of you to inform me of such matters."

Perry stretched his neck unobtrusively, attempting to relieve the discomfort creeping up his spine. "My brother's ... affairs ... are well known. As is his recent marriage and reformation. His regard for the countess is infamo—" He barely caught himself. "I mean ... famous."

Emma tilted her head, considering this. "He married her for love?"

Perry suppressed the urge to roll his eyes. "He did."

"He must have changed drastically since the time our cousin, Kitty, knew him, then." Her tone was rhetorical, so Perry remained silent.

Emma exhaled, some of her earlier fire dimming. "As to your friends, I shall allow no one to snub you, Miss Davis," he said, his voice steady. "This truly is about helping Ethan adjust to his new home. My brother and the countess are earnest in their desire to take care of your young cousin."

She met his gaze then, and something in her dark eyes unsettled him. There was a depth to them, a piercing intelligence that set his nerves on edge. She was studying him, as though peering past the carefully constructed façade he presented to the world.

He had no wish for her to see the darkness that resided there.

Emma nodded slowly. "So, we shall call a truce, then?"

Perry smirked. "Hmm ... I do not know about that, Miss Davis. You are such a delight to tease, and it is a long journey back to London."

Her eyes narrowed into slits of pure animosity. "Pretentious buck!"

"Now, now," he tutted. "Name-calling will not get you far in the drawing rooms of the *ton*. You will need to learn subtler methods to put your foes down if you wish to succeed."

A ghastly smile—one of restrained, murderous politeness—curved across her lips as she sank into a curtsy so deep it was nearly mocking.

"Mr. Balfour, you are an astute man. I am sure you know precisely what you can do with your *subtler methods*."

With that, she strode past him, chin lifted high.

Perry bit back a laugh.

"Much better, Miss Davis. Much better," he called after her in an encouraging tone, as if speaking to a young child.

The only indication that she had heard him was the sharp, guttural sound of frustration just before she slammed the library door behind her.

Emma stood in the stable yard of Rose Ash Manor, tugging her thick carriage dress closer against the early morning chill. The soft pink and gray of first light dappled the sky, casting a muted glow over the assembled carriages.

Two carriages.

Two!

What extravagance!

Breathing into her freezing hands to warm them, she watched as the footmen secured her and Jane's trunks to the roofs of the earl's splendid vehicles. She had already met the countess's French lady's maid and Mr. Balfour's valet—*I cannot believe he has brought an actual valet along to collect two country lasses from Somerset!*—and the presence of the maid only confirmed her suspicions.

Jane had not been part of the earl's original invitation.

No, Mr. Arrogant had extended the offer to maneuver Emma into accepting against her will. Why else would a female servant have been sent, if not to act as a chaperone on the return journey?

Turning, she found Mr. Arrog—Balfour eyeing her with an expression of unvarnished horror.

"What?" she snapped, scowling at him.

"I have never seen anyone dress in that particular shade of ... mud."

Emma gritted her teeth. "It is very serviceable. And nothing ruins a gown like a long, dusty carriage journey."

"Serviceable?" He repeated the word as if he had never heard it before in his life.

"It is rude to comment on my attire in a derogatory manner."

He shrugged, entirely unrepentant. "It is rude to comment on rude behavior."

Her blood boiled. *Please, Lord, grant us fair weather so that we may reach London with all due haste!*

If the skies remained clear, the journey would take two days. If it rained ... heaven help her, she could be trapped in a carriage with him for nearly a week. In that much time, she would either throttle him or fling herself under the wheels just to be rid of him.

"It is simply that your sister looks so fetching in blue velvet, and with your coloring so similar, you would surely—"

"Mr. Balfour!" she snapped. "Is this how society behaves? Comparing one sister to another—to her face?"

He rolled his eyes. "As you wish. Clearly, the decision to

wear a gown in the precise shade of damp earth is your prerogative. Far be it from me to interfere with such a ... bold choice."

The innocent smile he flashed her only deepened her ire.

Yes, Jane looked lovely. Jane always looked lovely.

Did this idle dandy think she did not know that?

Emma had attempted to wear the same colors, the same styles, only to find they did not suit her at all. Jane was tall and elegant; Emma was ... realistic about her short, boyish frame.

There were no illusions that she would attract a gentleman of the *ton*.

Since Ethan had left, she had longed for a child of her own. But to have a child, she would need to find a husband.

And what man would look twice at her?

The notion was laughable—and it was insufferably vulgar for Mr. Balfour to discuss her failings so openly. The best she could hope for was a respectable match with an honest tradesman, someone who would not mind marrying into the gentry.

Someone who would not sneer at serviceable gowns.

At last, the trunks were secured, and the footmen began assisting the passengers into their respective carriages. Jane climbed in first, disappearing with a flash of blue skirts into the plush interior. The footman then turned to Emma, who accepted his assistance, carefully lifting her mud-colored skirts as she ascended.

Once inside, she took in her surroundings with quiet disbelief. The leather squabs were butter-soft, the thick rug beneath her feet plush enough to sink into.

She had barely settled into her seat when movement at the door caught her eye. Emma squeaked in alarm.

"Are you traveling with us?"

Mr. Arrog—Balfour—ascended the carriage steps, wholly unconcerned by her distress.

"I assumed you would ride …. or … or … travel with the servants!"

He settled into the seat directly across from her with an insufferable smirk. "Nay, Miss Davis. As I stated, the journey is long, and you are entertaining. So I shall sit here and watch you."

"Mock me, you mean?"

He shrugged. "We shall see where the day takes us, shall we?"

Emma scowled at him before pointedly turning away to stare out the window.

Lifting a hand, she waved to her family gathered outside, their figures growing smaller with each passing second. Her round, cheerful mother, her swarthy father, her three brothers—and little Maddie, the youngest, who bounced excitedly on her toes. They all waved enthusiastically, their expressions full of encouragement, but within moments, the carriage took a turn in the winding drive of Rose Ash Manor, and they were gone.

The sun had barely risen, and already she was on her way to London for a Season.

She could scarcely believe it.

She had tossed and turned the entire night, her stomach twisted with trepidation. She knew—knew—she would be a colossal failure. But if Jane found a suitable young gentleman, and Emma spent time with Ethan, it would all be worth it.

At least, that was what she kept telling herself. Over and over.

The carriage turned onto the main road, the turnpike

that would lead them out of Rose Ash. Emma's heart sank into her shoes as she imagined her arrival at the Earl of Saunton's grand townhouse.

With a heavy sigh, she reached up to untie her bonnet—just as Jane did the same. They caught each other's gaze and giggled at the synchrony before setting their bonnets aside on the seat next to Mr. Arro—Balfour.

Zooks, Emma, you must learn to call him by his name before you accidentally address the earl himself as Lord Arrogant.

Jane rummaged through the basket she had brought along, producing her embroidery frame. As she lifted it onto her lap, Emma saw the beginnings of a perfect rose, surrounded by curling vines and a tree in the distance.

Their new home.

Emma sighed. *Trust Jane to commemorate Rose Ash Manor in delicate stitches.* She had always envied her sister's talent. Her own fingers, utterly hopeless at needlework, had long ago resigned themselves to more practical pursuits.

Resigned, she leaned down and pulled a book from her own basket, settling back into the plush squabs to find her page.

Across from her, a groan of disapproval sounded.

She looked up, narrowing her eyes.

Mr. Arrogant was staring at the cover of her book as if it personally offended him.

"You cannot be serious," he said flatly. "A text on animal husbandry—on the road to London? Are you expecting to find herds of sheep wandering through Mayfair?"

Emma scoffed. "We both know Jane is the one who will find a wonderful gentleman, at which time I will return to Rose Ash and resume my familial duties. Running an estate requires a vast store of knowledge, and as we had little cattle in Derbyshire, I am expanding my understanding. We now have more livestock, so I intend to see that the estate prospers. There is a fortune to be made in supplying wool to the local textile industry."

Mr. Arrogant—*no, Balfour*—swiped a hand over his face in evident dismay before rubbing the back of his neck.

"Have you ever considered," he asked dryly, "that your ... challenges with men might stem from your decidedly unladylike pursuits?"

Emma stiffened. From the corner of her eye, she saw Jane's fingers still on her embroidery frame. Then, with practiced ease, her sister carefully rolled up her work, retrieved a shawl from her basket, and folded it into a makeshift pillow. Without so much as a glance in their direction, Jane leaned back into the corner of the carriage, propped up her head, and within moments ...

A soft, ladylike snore.

Emma clenched her teeth. *Of course.*

Jane had always possessed the enviable ability to sleep whenever and wherever she wished. But Emma knew her sister better than that—Jane had no desire to overhear this conversation. And so, with what could only be described as expert skill, she had exited it entirely, leaving Emma alone with him.

Lifting a hand to smooth her curls, Emma caught the flicker of disdain that crossed Balfour's face.

Her fingers stilled.

Her hair was frowsy. *Again.*

She could not help it. Jane's hair was sleek, impossibly silky, while Emma's was a wild mass of rebellious curls. They were both dark, but it seemed insolent to compare her unruly mane to Jane's perfectly arranged tresses.

Egads!

The differences between herself and her sister had

never truly troubled her before. But since meeting Peregrine Balfour, she had become uncomfortably aware of them. Seeing herself through the eyes of a polished buck—one of many she would encounter in London—had given her an unwelcome taste of what was to come.

Jane, I hope you appreciate what I am doing for you. Because every single moment of this journey will be excruciating.

Shaking her head, she looked back at her book, determined to ignore the obnoxious nobleman until they reached the inn for lunch and a change of horses.

Across from her, Mr. Peregrine Balfour smirked, stretching his long legs comfortably before him.

No man had ever infuriated her as much as this one.

And before this journey was over, she might actually do him an injury.

CHAPTER THREE

"No young woman of real worth will ever accept a mere spare. But take heart, my boy—there will always be a widow or two willing to ease your disappointment."

July 1803, the late Earl of Saunton to his son, Peregrine, on his eighth birthday, upon noticing the boy's interest in the squire's daughter.

Perry did not understand his desire to be close to the ridiculous, yet fascinating, Emma Davis. Something about the young woman fired his blood and made him feel invigorated.

He had planned to ride his own mount as they made their leisurely way home, but had instead been drawn into the carriage, where he had now watched her read for the past two hours, surrounded by the faint scent of chamomile and wildflowers.

There was no arguing that he was behaving like an

untried youth battling his first infatuation. She had delicate features, a sweet heart-shaped face, and those large black eyes that seemed to look directly into his soul. He should know. They had been the subject of his dreams the night before—dreams he was not eager to revisit.

Emma also possessed the same luminous skin as her sister, smooth and glowing. But it was not the younger sister who had captured his imagination. He could only be grateful Emma was so entirely oblivious to fashion and the finer points of dress. Fortunately, her mud-colored carriage gown dulled her otherwise warm coloring, and its many layers and tucks left little to distract him.

And yet ...

There was something disarmingly endearing about her earnest expression as she licked a finger to turn the page, her focus utterly fixed on the dry text before her. Perry found himself almost envious of her dedication.

He considered following Jane's example. Her sister had fallen asleep not long after they set off and had remained in peaceful repose ever since.

Perry's sleep the night before had been anything but peaceful.

The coaching inn had been noisy, the sounds of distant footsteps and slamming doors echoing through the thin walls. But worse than the noise had been the dreams.

He had dreamt of Emma. Not in the way that usually troubled his rest, but in a different, more unsettling way. In one moment, she was dancing with him, her face lit with laughter, her hand warm in his. In another, they were seated on a garden bench, engaged in an intense argument that somehow left him smiling before he had leaned down to capture her lips with his. And still another dream found him waking beside her in some future time, with her tousled curls spilling over the pillow, her sleepy voice teasing him about something clever and absurd.

The dreams had been far too vivid. And far too pleasant.

He had awoken restless and oddly wistful, the vision of her cheeky smile refusing to leave his mind and the softness of her mouth still present on his lips.

Across from him, Emma stirred, as if sensing his thoughts. She raised her hands to unfasten her outer gown, clearly intending to remove the heavier layer in favor of the lighter muslin beneath. The idea unsettled him far more than it ought to. It was much easier to forget her womanly form with the hideous carriage dress to hide the generous curves of her bodice.

"Keep it on!"

She turned, startled by the sharpness of his tone. "Why? The morning has been warming up, and I wish to be comfortable."

Perry scrambled for a reasonable explanation, schooling his expression into a lazy smile. "We shall stop at an inn for luncheon shortly. As you said, the roads are dusty, and I imagine you wish to keep your day gown pristine."

Emma tilted her head, as if considering a retort, but after a moment, she sighed. "You are correct. It would be pleasant to wash up and change properly. You finally concede that the carriage dress is serviceable?"

He nodded absently, though he had not truly registered what she said. He was simply relieved she had left the gown in place. She was the least ornamental female he had ever met, and yet ...

He scowled out the window. Where had this vacillation come from? *You are a buffle head, Balfour.*

Before he could stop himself, he barked, "You really ought to find better reading material!"

Well done. Why not just set a match to gun powder?

From behind the edge of her book, large black eyes narrowed. "What, pray tell, did you do to entertain yourself on the way to Rose Ash?"

"I rode my mount and enjoyed the country air."

A triumphant smile played across her lips. "I knew it. You are in this carriage to be close to me."

"No—I—" He floundered for a reasonable explanation. Anything but the truth, which was that he wanted to be near her.

"Admit it, Mr. Balfour. You have made it a sport to irritate me."

He reclined back into the squabs with a faint smile. "Irritating you is considerably more entertaining than riding."

Emma rolled her eyes and returned to her book. "Would you care for something to read, Mr. Balfour? It appears you are in need of occupation."

Perry considered it. Reading would be preferable to thinking. He gave her a terse nod.

Emma marked her page with a ribbon and leaned forward to reach her basket.

His eyes darted away. The carriage dress remained as unflattering as ever, yet somehow the grace of her movement still managed to stir his awareness. He gritted his teeth. *Get a hold of yourself.*

"Here you go."

He looked up to see a green volume with gold lettering being thrust into his hand.

"*Pride and Prejudice, Volume One?*"

"I have the other two volumes when you are ready. It is a delightful book about *etiquette*." Her emphasis was unmistakable.

"You have read a book on etiquette?" He blinked. "And now you expect me to read a romantic novel?"

Emma's jaw set. "As you wish, Mr. Balfour. It is either a romantic novel or a text on animal husbandry."

He eyed the weighty tome she had been reading earlier with a grimace.

He sighed in defeat. "I shall read the novel."

Emma returned to her own book and leaned back into the corner of the carriage, content to ignore him once more.

Perry opened the volume and read the first line.

JANE DAVIS WAS at that age when she was a strange mix of giddy girl and astute young woman. Emma could not decide which version had just spoken, as she stared at her younger sister, mouth agape.

"Have you gone mad?"

Jane merely shrugged, continuing to plait her hair in preparation for bed, her expression infuriatingly serene.

They had stopped for the night at a comfortable coaching inn. Once again, it was clear that Jane had not been part of the original plans for the return to London—evidenced by the fact that they were sharing a chamber that had clearly been reserved for Emma alone when Peregrine Balfour passed through on his way to Rose Ash.

The weather had been mild, the pace unhurried. Mr. Balfour, it seemed, had planned for a leisurely journey, which Emma had to admit she appreciated. They had paused for a pleasant midday meal earlier in the day, and this evening's accommodations were the finest Emma had ever seen in an inn.

A cheerful rug covered the polished floor, and a large

bed awaited them—plump with clean linens and thick counterpanes. One of their trunks had been brought up by the footman, adding to the sense of ease and comfort.

Still, none of it settled Emma's thoughts. She turned back to Jane, who was now humming as she tucked the end of her plait beneath her nightcap.

"Jane!"

"I stand by what I said." Jane adjusted her nightcap, entirely unruffled. "Mr. Balfour continues to tease you because he is smitten."

Emma shook her head in disbelief. "But ... but ... he is him, and I am ..." She gestured helplessly between them, waving her hand back and forth as if that explained the enormity of the gap.

"Emma," Jane said gently, "you are a unique woman. Despite your tragic neglect of your appearance, you are quite comely. And Mr. Balfour cannot seem to stop looking at you."

Emma scoffed. "That is absurd. Mr. Balfour is a handsome second son of an earl, with a healthy annuity, I am certain. He could have any young lady he wished. He teases me because it amuses him. He as much as said so."

"I do not believe that is what I am witnessing," Jane replied calmly.

Emma turned away, arms folded across her chest. "Jane, he is clearly experienced with women. And I am ... no one."

"Women, perhaps," Jane allowed. "Ladies, not so much. And certainly not intelligent, forthright young ladies of honor. More like—" she wrinkled her nose, "—widows, if I were to hazard a guess."

"Jane!" Emma hissed, appalled.

"Well, I cannot say for certain, but it is clear he has not

spent time with anyone like you." Jane fluffed her pillow. "And that may be precisely the reason he cannot look away."

Emma blinked at her sister, a faint flush rising to her cheeks as she stared at her younger sister in amazement. Jane truly believed her words. Not only that—but the very subject of her remarks suggested she was not quite the naïve young miss Mama had implied the previous afternoon.

A flash of pride bloomed in Emma's chest as she studied the beautiful, composed young woman before her—so full of grace and wit. Jane was going to excel during her Season. That much was certain.

Then, as swiftly as the sentiment had formed, Emma recalled the ludicrous notion that Peregrine Balfour might be infatuated with her and promptly stamped her foot in outrage.

"This conversation is absurd! Mr. Balfour—nay, any gentleman of the *ton*—would not give me a second glance. And if he were enamored of intelligent young ladies of honor, it would be you he was mooning over, not me!"

Jane, undeterred, simply folded the end of her plait and tied it neatly with a ribbon. "Emma, we are two very different personalities. There is something about you in particular that calls to the gentleman."

She met Emma's gaze steadily. "I know when a man is looking at me with interest—and I assure you, Mr. Balfour is not. It is you who has captured his attention."

Emma narrowed her eyes. Jane had gone mad. There could be no other explanation. The stress of an unexpected London Season among the elite had clearly unbalanced her and robbed her of all reason.

Jane continued serenely. "If you yourself were not so infatuated in return, you might notice the signals."

"WHAT?"

Emma clapped a hand over her mouth in horror.

Had she just howled?

In a public inn?

Lud! What was the matter with her?

Nay. What was the matter with her sister?

Emma's concern for her sister's mental state deepened. Perhaps she ought to insist they return home. She had no notion how to care for Jane if something had truly gone awry.

This conversation was so far removed from anything she had ever experienced, Emma briefly considered whether she, too, had been driven mad by this ill-advised journey.

Jane, unperturbed, sat down to remove her slippers. "Usually, if you think a man is of inferior intellect," she said mildly, "you politely rebuke him and walk away. But Mr. Balfour is an intelligent and worthy adversary, so you argue with him. You engage him. His wit has clearly earned your admiration."

Jane looked up, her tone perfectly reasonable. "The more he bests you in conversation, the more fascinated you become. It does not hurt, of course, that he is one of the most attractive men either of us has ever laid eyes upon. I think you shall be married long before I, Emma."

She stated it with such startling calm, as though she had not just delivered a pronouncement of such profound absurdity that the family might have to lock her in her room lest the neighbors suspect madness and summon someone from Bedlam.

"MARRIED?" Emma gasped.

The very air had been knocked from her lungs.

Fisting her hands at her sides, she drew in a fortifying breath. "Jane, are you quite well? Did something disagree with you at dinner? Are you overwhelmed by the pressure of this journey?" She reached forward to feel her sister's forehead. "We will finish the journey and then I shall ask the earl to send us home with a promise that we shall return later—after we have had time to prepare properly. We might find a tutor to assist us, and you can have time to rest—"

Jane laughed softly, rising from her seat. She took Emma's hands in her own, her blue eyes searching Emma's face.

"He is not at all what I would have predicted for you," she said gently, "but he is interesting, and I am positive you will work out your differences."

Emma frowned. "Jane, Mr. Balfour is not the marrying kind. He is a gentleman who—who—" she floundered, "—engages in scandalous pursuits. You have seen the gossip columns. You have heard the whispers about him and his brother. He will never settle down."

"The earl did," Jane replied, with infuriating logic.

Emma huffed. "The earl has a title, Jane. He needs an heir. Once that is accomplished, all pressure is lifted from his brother to procreate. Mr. Balfour will most likely never marry. There is nothing—nothing—about his conduct that suggests he is in want of a wife."

She took a breath, her voice rising with indignation. "Consider *Pride and Prejudice*—'*It is a truth universally acknowledged, that a single man in possession of a good fortune, must be in want of a wife.*' Well, he has no fortune of his own! He is the earl's dependent!"

Jane smiled serenely. "Indeed... consider *Pride and Prejudice*."

With that cryptic remark, she dropped Emma's hands. "Time for bed, I think."

"You napped all morning!" Emma objected.

"And embroidered all afternoon," Jane replied breezily. "All that fine needlework and travel has quite taken it out of me. Which side would you like to sleep on?"

She climbed into the bed without awaiting a response, tucked the counterpane around her with practiced ease, and within seconds, her head sank into the pillow as she released a soft, huffing snore.

Emma stared in disbelief.

Damn Jane and her uncanny ability to sleep like a carefree babe.

How dare she make such outrageous declarations—suggestions of affection and marriage, no less—and then simply close her eyes and drift off as though she had merely discussed the weather?

Emma paced the room, her ire at full staff, muttering beneath her breath as the full strangeness of their conversation replayed in her mind.

Yes, Mr. Balfour was the most handsome man she had ever laid eyes on. That much was indisputable.

But that did not mean she admired him.

And what utter rot about his intellect impressing her!

The man was a buffoon.

Yes, his emerald eyes made her want to drown in their depths, but that was a customary response to an attractive male, was it not? Entirely involuntary. Unimportant.

His words, however, made her palms itch.

He fired her blood in the worst way, making her want to

grab him by his broad, arrogant shoulders and shake him until ... until ... until—

She stopped mid-step, chest heaving.

Until what, precisely?

"Oh, lud!"

Emma dropped into the armchair in the corner of the room and lowered her head into her hands, overcome with mortification.

Until he kisses me like he means it.

The horrifying truth reverberated through her mind.

She was nothing more than a shallow, feather-brained young woman whose head had been turned by a tall, perfectly sculpted specimen of manhood—without the least consideration for the odious personality housed within.

She was going to hell.

Nay, I am already there.

The very idea that he might feel the same inexplicable yearning to embrace her in return—as Jane so blithely suggested—was beyond comprehension.

Physically, he was flawless. A Grecian statue come to life. And she was ... a country mouse with hair like a bird's nest and the fashion sense of, well ... a country mouse.

Emma snorted into her cupped hands.

Developing an infatuation is robbing me of my intellect. Even my analogies have become redundant.

This could only lead to heartbreak.

Hers, not his.

He would never know of her absurd feelings. It would be humiliating—excruciating—for him to suspect. If his mockery was aggravating now, it would become intolerable if he discovered she harbored any sort of attachment.

Emma groaned aloud.

What was she to do? She had read enough novels to know this never ended well for the foolish heroine.

She would not be some poor girl who dared to aim too high, only to be painfully snubbed for her presumption.

She would not be Icarus, hurtling from the sky for daring to fly too close to a man carved from sunlight and smugness.

This requires a healthy dose of realism, Emma Davis.

Yes. That was the only way forward. She would focus all her energy on preparing for the Season. She would keep her head down, make no spectacle of herself, and do her utmost not to be considered a fool.

She would help Jane find a suitable young gentleman—one worthy of her sister's grace and kindness—and once Jane's path was secured, Emma would return at once to Rose Ash.

There was no question that Jane would attract notice. She always had. In Derby and in Somerset, gentlemen had admired her, though Jane had yet to show interest in any of them.

But Emma?

Emma would avoid Mr. Peregrine Balfour with military precision.

Once they reached London, he would vanish into his clubs and idle pursuits—just as she expected—and she would be free to return to her natural state of mind.

All she had to do was not engage with him.

Avoid him at all costs.

Surely that would be simple enough.

∼

The next morning, just before midday, Mr. Balfour laid the final volume down on his lap with a contented sigh.

Emma glanced up from her own book.

"Did you enjoy the novel after all, Mr. Balfour?"

Wonderful, Emma. So much for your solemn vow not to engage.

"It was excellent," he said. "Truly a masterpiece."

Emma tilted her head, eyes narrowing in surprise. "Truly?"

It was her most beloved novel—her comfort during long winters, her solace when the world seemed to hold no prospects. To hear him echo her thoughts was ... startling.

"Mr. Darcy," he mused, "was most astute regarding the troubles of a gentleman."

Emma frowned. "What do you mean by that?"

He turned toward her, all lazy charm. "That Bennet flibbertigibbet was entirely unsuitable. A gentleman of such class and distinction ... to be brought down by such a snare. Quite lowering."

Emma leaned forward in disbelief. "I am not sure you understood the—"

"—the troubles of managing country mice? Oh, I assure you, Miss Davis, I am intimately familiar." He gave a mockingly tragic sigh. "The story is a heartbreak, truly. A romantic tragedy."

"Tragedy?"

"That a man of Mr. Darcy's consequence should be dragged down in station by a family so far beneath his own. All those sisters, and the embarrassing mother—"

Emma shook her head in disbelief. "Mr. Bal—"

"He should have escaped when he had the chance," Mr. Balfour interjected airily. "Once he learned of the sister's elopement, that was his opportunity. And he blew it."

Emma, to her dismay, made a rather unladylike squeaking noise. "That was not—"

"And what a prideful, ill-mannered young woman this Elizabeth Bennet was," he added, sounding almost offended.

Across the carriage, Jane calmly set her embroidery frame down on her lap and reached out to place a soothing hand over Emma's tightly clenched fist. "Each reader takes away their own interpretation of a story, Emma."

"But—"

Mr. Balfour looked genuinely confused. "Have I said something you disagree with?"

Emma's spine straightened like a snapped ribbon. "Mr. Darcy was insufferable!" she burst out.

"I do not understand."

"He was arrogant and pompous! He refused to dance at the Meryton assembly, which is the duty of every gentleman of good character. And his first proposal—do not even get me started—it was insulting! He spoke of how unsuitable she was while asking for her hand!"

Mr. Balfour gave an exasperated shake of his head. "Darcy could hardly encourage the notion he would marry a silly chit from the country. He was a man of substance! And I would argue it was rather honorable that he offered for her instead of proposing the—ah—more customary arrangement for a woman of her situation."

Emma gasped. "You mean—as his mistress?"

Perry gave a negligent shrug. "It would not have been unheard of."

"It is a comedy, Mr. Balfour. A beautiful love story!"

He leaned forward, eyes glinting with challenge. "It is a tragedy. A cautionary tale of what becomes of a man when he fails to keep women in their proper place."

Emma's brows arched. "What place is that?"

"Women," he said loftily, "are purely ornamental. When a man forgets that, he finds himself drowning his sorrows in drink. Speaking of which"—he glanced out the window—"I could very well do with one now."

"ORNAMENTAL?"

There was no denying that last was a shriek. Emma was so furious, she half-contemplated leaping across the carriage to pummel the arrogant idiot with her fists.

But then—

A strange expression crossed Mr. Balfour's face. Not smugness, not amusement ... but something oddly unsettled.

Emma's fury stuttered. He looked stricken.

"I apologize," he said quietly.

Her mouth fell open. She had thought her outburst had shamed her, but it appeared Mr. Balfour had been inspecting himself—and found something wanting.

"That is something my fa—" he hesitated. "Something someone once said to me when I was a boy. I did not realize it had taken root in my thinking until I heard myself repeat it aloud. It was ... appalling."

He drew a steadying breath. "Miss Davis. Miss Jane. Please accept my apology. You are both lovely young ladies. And more than that, you have been ... remarkable company."

He reached up and tapped on the roof of the carriage.

The carriage gradually slowed to a halt.

When it stopped, he opened the door and descended the steps.

"If you will excuse me," he said, bowing politely, "I believe I shall ride for a few miles."

Without another word, he closed the door gently and disappeared from view.

Emma and Jane turned to stare at one another.

"I think the gentleman hides a dark youth," Jane murmured.

Emma groaned aloud. That was the last thing she needed—to begin empathizing with the devil who both taunted and tempted her so.

"Please do not tell me I must now care about his point of view," she pleaded, sinking back into her seat. "I ... I thought about what you said, and I admit it—I have grown attracted to him. But Jane, it is a disaster! The very first man to attract my admiration is wholly unattainable. And worse still—we do not even like each other." She covered her face with her hands. "Now he is having some grand revelation about his erroneous thinking. This is already such a pickle!"

Jane broke into a wide grin. "What an adventure this is turning out to be!"

"Jane!"

"Well, I am highly entertained. There is a gentleman who clearly needs a woman's influence in his life. Did we not read in *Debrett's* that his mother died when he was only four or five years old? That is Ethan's age, Emma. Poor man. What if he had no one like you to guide him?"

Emma groaned again. "Please do not make me sympathize with that impudent man! His ghastly teasing has already made me nervous enough about appearing in London society. And now, besides being attracted to the rogue, I am beginning to feel concerned for his well-being." She closed her eyes in dismay. "Next I shall imagine I am in love with him—that I could somehow save him from his troubles—and then my torture shall be complete."

Zooks, Jane's sentimental whimsy is going to get me into trouble!

Jane ignored the outburst entirely. "I think I understand why he is so intrigued. There is no woman more capable of influence than you, Emma. Look at the way you cared for Ethan when Kitty passed away. And you were just a girl—younger than I am now!"

Emma softened slightly. "Thank you, but—"

"Though," Jane cut in, "even I must admit your conduct these past two days has been most unbecoming. Quite unlike your usual even temperament. When do you intend to allow Mr. Balfour to meet the real you?"

Emma stared at her sister in disbelief. "Never, Jane. There is no future for the two of us. I have admitted my attraction, but if Mr. Balfour harbors any interest in me—which I very much question—I would be nothing more than a novelty. A curiosity. The moment a more alluring woman enters the scene, he would immediately lose interest in the strange little rabbit he was sent to fetch from Somerset. He is a polished member of the *beau monde*, a fashionable buck of London society. I am merely an inelegant bluestocking from the countryside."

Jane tilted her head. "It all sounds so eerily familiar," she mused, her voice light with mischief. "Almost as if it were the plot of a grand romance." Her gaze flicked meaningfully toward the book Mr. Balfour had left on the opposite bench.

Emma followed her line of sight, scowling when she saw the third volume of *Pride and Prejudice*. She snatched it up and gave a dismissive humph.

"Our Season in London is not a work of fiction, Jane," she muttered. "In the real world, such an ill-matched couple could never find their way to a fortunate marriage, you sentimental goose."

Jane leaned back with a contented sigh, her smile lingering. "Perhaps not a novel," she said softly, "but that does not mean your story cannot have a remarkable ending."

Emma rolled her eyes. "Now you sound like Mama."

"I shall take that as a compliment."

Emma clutched the book to her chest and turned toward the window, her reflection faint in the glass as the countryside rolled steadily past.

She would not imagine a future that could not exist. She would not let herself yearn for something foolish. She would be practical, poised, and protect her heart.

Still, in the faint shimmer of glass, she caught sight of herself—and wondered, just for a moment, what a woman like Elizabeth Bennet might have seen when she looked back.

The carriage hit a rut, jostling them gently. Jane stirred, glancing toward the window.

"We must be nearing the city," she said.

Emma nodded. "Yes."

London loomed ahead, with all its glittering promise and peril. She would face it. With dignity. With purpose. And, if fate allowed, without giving her heart to the green-eyed rogue who had, thus far, made a mockery of her common sense.

CHAPTER
FOUR

"Always maintain a good relationship with a talented modiste. Purchasing fine gowns for a reticent lady will ensure her lasting affection."

July 1804, The late Earl of Saunton to his son, Peregrine, on his ninth birthday, after the boy came downstairs in search of his dog and instead discovered his father in the drawing room, entangled in a compromising situation with the neighbor's wife.

∽

Under any circumstances, Perry hated to be reminded of his father.

The late Earl of Satan, as he was known in private memory, had been the worst kind of *roué* imaginable. The dark events held at Saunton Park and Balfour Terrace alike … well, there had been a significant cleaning effort when his brother inherited the title.

Perry had borne witness to every interminable year,

month, week, day, and hour of the old man's slow descent into madness, courtesy of the pox he had contracted from his indiscriminate vices. His lone parent's death—finally—during the year of Perry's seventeenth birthday had been a mercy.

The very moment Richard inherited, he had turned to Perry and asked, plainly, what he would like to do now that their father was gone.

Perry had never known such utter joy.

Their tyrant of a father had kept him imprisoned within the Satan—*Saunton*—household throughout his entire youth. While most boys went off to Eton or Harrow, as Richard had, Perry had been confined at home under the watchful eye of stern tutors and his father's insidious whims.

It had been a twisted sort of apprenticeship. The old man had taken a perverse delight in educating his youngest son in what he believed to be the true methods of a proper gentleman—methods always delivered under the influence of drink and in the shadow of sin.

It had been hell.

So when Richard gave him a choice, Perry had immediately applied to Oxford, where his brother was still finishing his degree.

It was the first taste of freedom he had ever known.

He made friends. Chose his own schedule. Laughed without fear of reprisal. For the first time, he was the master of his own life, no longer merely the unloved son of a cruel and lascivious nobleman who, in Perry's mind, ought to have been jailed.

For that alone, he would always be grateful to Richard.

Which was precisely why Perry avoided all memories of

their father as if the very hounds of hell snapped at his heels.

And the worst part about what had just occurred in the carriage was this: he had invoked his father. The instant those vile, backward thoughts about women had passed his lips, Perry had recognized the voice. His father's.

The realization had been sickening.

Was this how Richard had felt when he once asked, in an anxious tone, if he was turning into their father?

Perry shuddered, staring resolutely ahead as he guided his gelding along the winding road.

He might be a worthless spare, with no other purpose than to exist in the unlikely event something befell his elder brother, but he hoped he was more of a gentleman—more of a man—than the creature who had sired him.

In the distance, he could already make out the blackish-brown haze that hung over the rooftops of London, stark against the soft, green countryside.

They were drawing near.

The stench would rise soon, worsened by the heat of late June. The new King sat uneasily upon the throne, and rumors swirled that Queen Caroline might face public trial for adultery. As a result, much of the peerage was forced to remain in London.

No man should be made to suffer London in the height of summer—when the air turned to soup and the river reeked of decay.

Perry would return to the carriage before they reached the city limits. He would offer a proper apology for his uncouth behavior.

The low opinion of women he had so casually voiced ... it made his stomach turn.

It had not even been deliberate. That, somehow, made it worse.

He needed to make it clear—to both Miss Davis sisters—that he did not truly think in such degrading terms. Hearing those words emerge from his own mouth had been mortifying.

More mortifying still was the knowledge that their late father would have been pleased.

Perry closed his eyes for a moment, inhaling deeply as the countryside rolled beneath his horse's hooves.

First, he would clear his thoughts.

Then he would repair the damage.

THE CARRIAGE CAME to a gentle halt. A moment later, Mr. Balfour reappeared, opened the door, and lowered the steps before climbing in to rejoin them. A footman adjusted the traces, then disappeared once more.

The gentleman looked across the aisle at Emma, clearly preparing to speak.

But before he could begin, she jumped in.

"Mr. Balfour, I wish to apologize."

His mouth closed in surprise, a faint frown forming between his brows. After a few moments of silence, he said, "I do not understand."

"I have been belligerent since the moment you arrived at Rose Ash Manor," Emma said in a rush. "I have had time to reflect, and I wish to apologize for my behavior. What the earl is doing for my sister"—she winced at the ungrateful words—"and for me as well, is exceedingly generous. And you have been most kind to deliver his message and escort us to London."

She pressed on, her voice gaining strength. "Your travel arrangements have been very considerate. The inns you chose have served excellent meals, and our room last night was far more comfortable than one has a right to expect at a public house. I regret my rudeness and failure to acknowledge the trouble you have taken to make our journey a pleasant one."

Mr. Balfour stared at her, visibly taken aback. In fact, her words seemed to unsettle rather than please him. At last, he gave a deep sigh.

"It is I who should apologize," he said. "I manipulated matters to secure your cooperation. And my words earlier were inexcusable. For them, I again beg your forgiveness. You are both fine young ladies of quality and intelligence, and I am ashamed to have suggested otherwise."

Emma bit her lip. She had no idea what to say next. The moment teetered into awkward silence.

Jane, as ever, rescued them.

She leaned forward, a warm smile on her face. "Mr. Balfour, we are practically family through Ethan, and we shall all be residing at Balfour Terrace. Could we not do away with formalities? Please call me Jane. Emma?" she added, glancing over.

Emma gave a reluctant nod. "Yes. Please. It will be easier to know one another if we relax such things. You may call me Emma."

He considered their request with surprising seriousness. "My close family call me Perry."

"Well then, Perry," Jane said brightly, "we shall forget your earlier remarks. No harm done. The conversation simply became rather excited. People often say things they do not mean in the heat of emotion. My sister regrets becoming so reactive. It is not her usual manner."

Emma blinked in confusion at that unexpected defense. Her sister truly was growing into a most accomplished peacemaker.

Perry smiled and leaned forward, taking Jane's hand to drop a brief, courtly kiss upon her fingers before sitting back.

"Then a truce has been called?" Emma asked cautiously.

He turned to her, a devilish glint sparking in his eye. Her breath caught. *He really is unbearably handsome.*

"I would not say that," he murmured. "We have nearly two hours yet to London. And since we are now family, I must inform you how deplorable that shade of mud is upon your person, Emma."

She groaned. "Not this again."

Jane gave a little hum and waited until Emma glanced over. "Perry is correct, I am afraid. That color is most unbecoming on a lady with your complexion. When we reach Balfour Terrace, you must change before you disembark. The day dress, at least, is fractionally more flattering than the carriage dress."

"Not you, too!"

Jane clapped her hands. "What fun we shall have at the modiste! I am so grateful to you, Emma. Without your care for Ethan, none of this would have happened. I owe you everything."

Perry chuckled. "Three cheers for Emma!"

Emma sank into the plush squabs and folded her arms in protest. Worse than condescending Mr. Arrogant was so-called-family-member Perry joining forces with her sister to tease her about her attire.

Zounds. This is going to be a very long summer.

Emma cowered in the corner of the carriage, peering out the window in horrified dismay.

London was so... enormous.

Buildings stretched endlessly in every direction, lining streets that branched and twisted like tangled ribbon. People swarmed the thoroughfares—on horseback, in wagons, on foot. Liveried servants perched atop elegant town carriages, while scruffy drivers lashed dilapidated hackneys with frightening speed.

And then there was the smell.

It defied proper description. A heady mixture of coal smoke, river rot, body odor, and what was unmistakably human waste. The air itself felt thick, as if the city exhaled a foul, greasy fog.

But worse than the scent was the noise.

Hawkers bellowed. Hooves clattered. Wheels shrieked against cobblestone. Whistles pierced the din. The entire city seemed to tremble with its own deafening cacophony.

Emma wanted to leap from the carriage and run all the way back to the quiet lanes of Somerset.

Her fingers crept into her pocket to seek comfort in the cool, familiar shape of the tin monkey. It reminded her why she had made this journey: *Ethan*.

At the end of all this madness, she would see him again. She would ensure with her own eyes that he was safe and cared for, not neglected and forgotten by Lord Arrogant—as was so often the way among the nobility, from what little she knew.

"Look at all those shops!" Jane's delighted voice rang out.

Emma flinched as a hackney careened far too close for comfort.

"Are we viewing the same city?" she muttered, clutching her skirts. Her sister was utterly enchanted, while Emma had never been more petrified in her life. "Zooks! Can we go back home?"

Perry cleared his throat. She glanced over to find him watching her.

"You will get used to it, Emma," he said, his tone surprisingly gentle.

She stared back at him, wide-eyed. "Never!"

He contemplated her for a moment. "We shall always be in a carriage when out, and the coat of arms gilded on the side makes others wary of interfering with us. Most of the time, you will be in residence at Balfour Terrace, which is a large townhouse in a clean and respectable neighborhood. In fact, you will scarcely leave Mayfair. It shall be much improved once we pass through to where we are headed."

Emma tilted her head. "Are you comforting me?"

"I am."

"But I thought teasing me was your preferred entertainment."

He grinned, flashing an unnervingly perfect smile. "We are nearly home. Not much need for entertainment at present."

He looked positively boyish in that moment—light-hearted, dashing, younger somehow. Something about the curve of his lips, the warmth in his eyes ... it stirred a most inconvenient longing.

She wanted to leap into his arms and press her lips to his, then bury her face in his silky hair and discover whether he smelled of clean linen, polished leather, and fresh country air. That was her guess.

Emma gave herself a firm mental shake. *Think of him as family, you silly chit!*

Without thinking, she reacted exactly as she would to one of her younger brothers when they had needled her too much. She stuck out her tongue.

Perry froze.

His gaze locked on her mouth. Slowly, unmistakably, he turned a deep shade of red. Even his breathing changed.

Emma's eyes widened in horror, and she hastily pulled her tongue back in, clamping her lips shut as she blushed to the roots of her hair.

Perry continued to stare—until, with obvious effort, he reached up to fidget with his perfectly tied cravat.

He must think I am a lunatic.

Without a word, he turned sharply to look out the window. "See? We are entering Mayfair."

Emma swallowed, then followed his gaze. As promised, the buildings had become grander, the streets cleaner, and the quality of vehicles noticeably improved. There was even a touch of greenery, a welcome sight amid the endless stone.

Soon, the carriage turned into a quiet, elegant street before rolling to a gentle halt in front of a massive townhouse, several bays wide and rising in graceful tiers of pale stone.

Jane, seated closest to the grand residence, gave a breathless giggle behind her hands as she craned her neck to take it all in. "My word, it is magnificent. Is this Balfour Terrace?"

"It is," Perry replied, though his tone had gone a touch too clipped.

Emma flicked a glance in his direction. His posture was stiff, his expression unreadable. He looked entirely unlike the boyish man who had teased her just moments before.

Have I gone too far? she wondered. *Likely no other lady of his acquaintance has ever stuck out her tongue at him.*

He must think her the very worst sort of uncouth, ungovernable woman.

Emma discovered, to her dismay, that she was genuinely upset.

A heavy weight settled on her chest when she noted how carefully Perry avoided looking in her direction. As the footman opened the carriage door and lowered the steps, he did not so much as glance her way.

Perry disembarked first and offered his hand to Jane. Emma watched, motionless, as her sister took his arm with an easy laugh.

He did not turn back.

Instead, he escorted Jane toward the townhouse steps, his posture stiff and impassive.

A waiting footman held out a hand to assist Emma, but she scarcely noticed.

He left me behind.

The realization pricked at her eyes. She had not imagined how much she had come to enjoy his teasing—his attention. She had believed, foolishly, that something had begun to grow between them, awkward and barbed though it was.

But she had misjudged. Clearly.

He was appalled.

Emma swallowed the bitter taste of regret and forced her shoulders back. She removed the mud-colored carriage dress with stiff fingers and folded it over her arm. Shaking out the skirt of her day gown, she stepped down onto the paving and followed the pair up the steps, her limbs stiff and uncooperative.

The great doors of the townhouse opened. Her anxiety redoubled.

I am about to meet Lord Arrogant himself, and I look a fright. And Perry... Perry had poked fun at her clothing and then left her behind without so much as a glance.

And now—he was ashamed of her.

She adjusted her bonnet, the one she had donned before entering the city. Her hands were trembling so violently she barely managed to tie the ribbons.

Inside, the hall was dim after the brightness of the street. Emma blinked rapidly, trying to adjust.

She saw him at once—a tall, striking gentleman who looked very much like Perry, though with a sharper jaw and an air of command that marked him instantly as the elder brother.

He offered Jane a warm smile and bowed over her hand. "Miss Emma Davis, what a privilege!"

Jane gave a delighted giggle as she dipped into a curtsy. "I am not Emma, my lord. I am her sister, Jane Davis. Emma is just behind me."

The earl straightened, his expression turning serious as he looked past her.

His eyes found Emma.

And hesitated.

He seemed ... perplexed. Not cruel, not cold. But certainly not impressed.

He is disappointed.

Emma's heart sank. She had been right to fear this moment. Perry had found her childish, and now his brother found her lacking altogether.

She closed her eyes for the briefest instant and swallowed hard.

Her hands were shaking.

Do not cry. Do not cry, Emma Davis. You must not cry.

She stepped forward, curtsied as best she could despite her shaking knees, and murmured, "My lord."

It was all she could manage.

You have only just arrived, and you are already a failure.

AFTER THE INTRODUCTIONS CONCLUDED, with Emma uncharacteristically quiet, Richard turned a questioning look toward his younger brother. Perry tilted his head, silently promising they would discuss the matter shortly. First, he needed to ensure the young ladies were shown to their rooms to refresh themselves and change into suitable attire.

He spoke to the family butler, issuing instructions with his eyes firmly averted from Emma. He did not dare look at her. Not unless he wished to behave like a savage and throw himself at her—to steal a kiss, to taste her mouth, to discover the softness of her sweet face beneath his hands.

Ever since she had stuck out her tongue at him—a gesture so ludicrous and sweet it unmoored him completely—his composure had been in tatters. Obsession, unfamiliar and searing, had surged through him like an invading force, laying waste to his carefully cultivated defenses. Then she had appeared without that blasted mud-colored gown and his restraint had hung by the thinnest of threads.

She was the very worst temptation.

Gravitating toward Jane had been a pathetic attempt to ground himself. To seem rational, light-hearted, whole. But the truth was, Emma had shattered something inside him, and he was now staggering through to pick up the pieces.

He had never felt such a maddening compulsion in all his five and twenty years.

Once the Davis sisters were shown to their rooms, Perry made his way to Richard's study, where he poured himself a generous measure of brandy before dropping into one of the armchairs upholstered in cheerful ivory fabric embroidered with red, gold, and green florals—wholly unsuitable for the gloom that had settled over him.

Look at me. Cataloguing upholstery to avoid my own thoughts. My unmanning is complete.

Richard entered, closing the door behind him. He crossed to his desk and lowered himself into the chair behind it. "Why are there two Davis girls?"

Perry took a long sip of his drink. "Emma did not want to come. I had to ... manipulate her agreement. I said you had invited both of them."

Richard groaned and sank his head into his hands. "Let me guess. Two wardrobes. Two dowries."

"You make it sound as though you are bound for debtor's prison."

"Of course not. But one of the secrets to increasing one's wealth is not to set it ablaze."

"Stuff and nonsense. You can afford it."

"I have made a great many amends lately, if you recall. Each one comes with its own expense."

Perry's lips twitched. "Yes, well, now that you are enamored of only one woman, you are practically saving money."

Richard chuckled. "Indeed. No more bills from milliners and jewelers. Sophia may be the greatest financial strategy I have ever enacted."

"True love as a sound investment. Very you."

Richard shot him a look. "Why did you not send a message ahead to inform me? Radcliffe is scrambling to prepare a second room. He is quite put out."

"You cannot tell when Radcliffe is put out. He is the most unflappable butler in Mayfair."

"You are such an bounder, Perry."

Perry did not argue. He looked down into his drink, swirling the amber liquid slowly. Thoughts of Emma swirled with it—her fierce spirit, her maddening tongue, her bold eyes that saw too much. He wanted to kiss her until they both forgot how to breathe.

What had she done to him?

He could hardly remember what it was like to draw air without thinking of her mouth.

Should he confide in Richard? Tell him he was losing his mind? No. He could not. He was not accustomed to sharing. And this—this craving for an innocent—was too shameful.

"I suppose," Richard said, "we ought to see what the young ladies require. Tutors, wardrobe fittings, deportment training. I shall have Johnson see to it. The sooner, the better."

Perry hesitated. He would not see her for days now—not properly. And the thought of her flitting around his brother's townhouse while he haunted his clubs left him inexplicably glum.

Why did the idea of being apart from her feel so dismal?

"I can save you the expense," he heard himself say. "I shall tutor them."

The words were out before he could claw them back.

He stared into his glass in horror.

What the devil am I doing?

Richard blinked. "I am sorry. Did you just offer to tutor two young ladies in dancing and deportment?"

Perry frowned. "No. That is—I meant to say—"

"Perry, this is wonderful!" Richard's face lit with something dangerously close to pride. "You are finally taking Sophia's advice. A project! And you are the most socially adept man I know. Who better?"

Perry shot to his feet. "No. No, I did not think it through. I am far too busy. Tell Johnson to hire someone."

But Richard was already advancing on him with a grin. "Do not be absurd. You are perfect. You read every etiquette manual cover to cover at Oxford."

"To perfect the art of seduction, not to transform country lasses into debutantes."

Richard waved a hand. "You have no designs on innocent young misses. You have said as much. No danger there."

Oh, brother, if only you knew.

He was a danger. To one innocent miss in particular. And if he spent another moment alone with her—unbuttoning her gloves, adjusting her waltz hold, watching her eyes lift to his in admiration—he could not be trusted.

He needed to retreat. Now.

But he had just volunteered to stay.

Heaven help me. I am undone.

CHAPTER FIVE

"You are a mere spare! Why would I waste coin on Eton for you?"

July 1805, the late Earl of Saunton to his son, Peregrine, on his tenth birthday after he requested to join his older brother away at school.

Emma had composed herself by the time the hawkish butler ushered them into a grand bedchamber. Servants were moving briskly about the space, carrying steaming pitchers and setting out fresh towels. The air held the fragrant scent of lavender soap and beeswax polish.

"This is your room, Miss Davis," the butler informed her with an efficient nod. "We are preparing the one next door for your sister, but we thought you might wish to refresh after your long journey, so I trust you are amenable to sharing for an hour or two?"

She inclined her head politely. "Of course. Thank you, Mr. Radcliffe."

The butler gave a smile so faint it might have passed unnoticed if she had not been watching him closely. His eyes crinkled with subtle amusement. "You are welcome, Miss Davis. I do not wish to be presumptuous, but Lord Saunton asked that I assist you in becoming acquainted with the customs of high society. It is customary to address a butler by his surname only."

"Oh! Is that not what I did?"

"Just Radcliffe, no Mister."

Emma blinked. "Truly? Why?"

He offered a slight shrug. "I could not say. Tradition, I suppose."

"I see. Thank you ... Radcliffe."

"My pleasure, Miss Davis. We are all very pleased to host you. Master Ethan will be most excited when he learns you are here."

Her heart lifted. "Is he expecting me?"

"No, my lady. His lordship wished to surprise him. Once you and Miss Jane are ready, I shall show you to his lordship's study, where Master Ethan will be brought down."

Emma's face lit with a genuine smile at the thought. She longed to see the boy again, to hold him close and hear his clever chatter.

"If that is all, I shall leave you to it. We have set out tea and light refreshment on the table there." He gestured toward a delicate round table near the hearth, set with a polished silver tea service that gleamed in the afternoon light. A small vase of white roses added a touch of elegance.

The silver teapot rested beside a matching cream jug and sugar bowl, flanked by fine porcelain cups edged in gold. On a separate dish, there were lemon slices, dainty currant scones, finger sandwiches with cucumber and watercress, and a selection of small, iced cakes, each one more delicate than the last.

"My apologies again for the temporary inconvenience of sharing," Radcliffe added with a courteous bow.

He then stationed himself at the door, waiting with the gravity of a palace guard until the last of the servants had quietly exited. Once all was in order, he departed the room, leaving the sisters in privacy with a maid ready to assist them in changing and tidying themselves.

Emma walked farther into the bedroom, which was as large as the drawing room of Rose Ash Manor. The ceilings soared overhead, adorned with ornate plasterwork and a central medallion from which hung an elegant crystal chandelier. The pale green walls were accented with gold filigree, and two tall windows framed in ivory damask drapes overlooked a leafy courtyard below.

She ran her hand along a polished walnut dressing table with a beveled mirror, where delicate glass perfume bottles and silver-backed brushes gleamed in orderly rows. Across from it, a canopied bed dominated the room, dressed in layers of ivory and pale green silk, its carved headboard an elaborate masterpiece of acanthus leaves and laurel branches. A pair of high-backed chairs flanked the hearth, which was empty beneath the marble mantel.

"This is rather stately, is it not, Jane?" Emma said, blinking around her in awe.

But Jane was speechless, her attention fixed on a large armoire carved with birds and trailing vines. "This is as large as our gardening shed!" she exclaimed. "His lordship must have given you one of his most luxurious guest rooms!"

A discreet cough drew their attention. The maid who

had accompanied them offered a modest correction. "It is a family room, miss."

Jane turned wide eyes to her sister. "A family room! We are in the family wing in the townhouse of the Earl of Saunton. He has practically declared us to be his relations, Emma! What an honor!"

"Miss, may I assist you to undress while the water is still warm?" the maid offered with gentle urgency, gesturing toward the two gleaming copper bathtubs that had been placed in front of the fireplace, each steaming gently and surrounded by towels and scented soaps.

Within thirty minutes, both sisters stood freshly bathed, hair still damp and dressed in clean chemises, admiring the crackling fire that warmed the enormous room.

A firm knock came at the door, and before Emma could call out, it opened to reveal a graceful woman with red-blonde hair pinned in a crown of curls, her carriage elegant yet warm. Behind her stood the lady's maid who had accompanied them on their journey.

"Emma, Jane—I am so pleased to finally meet you. I am Sophia, the earl's wife."

Both young women sank into curtsies, though Emma felt a touch absurd to be bowing in little more than her shift. "My lady," they chorused, polite but hesitant.

"Nonsense!" Sophia said with a light laugh, her sapphire eyes gleaming. "You are to call me Sophia. We are practically family. I am ever so grateful that you are here to help with Ethan, and there shall be no ceremony within the walls of our home."

Emma hesitated, struck by how young and vibrant the countess appeared—perhaps only a few years older than herself. She had a glowing complexion and a natural grace that made Emma feel all the more self-conscious. But there was something genuine about her smile, and the warmth in her voice seemed to cast away formality like sunlight chasing shadows.

Emma dipped her chin in a nod. "We appreciate the offer of sponsorship ... Sophia."

The countess beamed. "Wonderful. I have brought Miss Adèle Toussaint to assist you to dress, so that we may go downstairs and meet the earl properly." She turned and gestured to the elegant brunette lady's maid behind her, who curtsied in greeting. "Miss Toussaint is the most skilled lady's maid in all of London. We shall be providing you each with your own abigail for the rest of the Season, but I asked Miss Toussaint to lend her expert eye today."

Emma's breath caught at the notion of being dressed by such a consummate professional in matters of fashion.

"Now," the countess continued with a grin, "which one of you is Emma?"

EMMA AND JANE followed the countess down the grand staircase and into the entry hall, both attired in their best gowns. Emma marveled at how Miss Toussaint had managed to tame her unruly curls with some sort of miraculous French hair tonic. Her hair now framed her face in perfectly shaped ringlets—light and bouncy and utterly transformed. The effect gave her a much-needed boost in confidence after the nerve-racking arrival earlier, when she had misstepped before both the earl and Perry. The latter had avoided her entirely, which she could not help but take to heart.

She had only just arrived in London and already felt herself failing at this visit to high society.

Still, her spirits lifted with each step as her curls bounced about her shoulders. Her gown, though plain in comparison to the countess's wardrobe, had never looked so well. Feeling just the smallest bit proud, she paused in the hall, her gaze rising in wonder.

It was a revelation.

The black-and-white checkered marble floor gleamed beneath the light of two immense chandeliers. Italian frescoes adorned the high ceiling—depictions of Greek gods cavorting on Mount Olympus, their limbs graceful and animated with a sense of divine mischief. The walls were lined with dark walnut paneling, rich and lustrous, and set with carved chairs and antique console tables adorned with porcelain and ormolu clocks. The air smelled faintly of lemon oil and lavender.

Emma bit her lip, awe curling into doubt. This was a world far above anything she had ever known. The entry hall alone was worth more than the entirety of Rose Ash Manor and its surrounding lands. How could she possibly belong in such a place?

Jane, with her graceful bearing and natural beauty, looked entirely at home. But she—Emma—was simply herself. Loyal. Bookish. A touch clumsy. And, now, far too aware that she had likely offended the only gentleman in this city who had looked at her with something other than indifference.

She quickened her step, trying to catch up as Sophia and Jane passed into a corridor beyond the hall. Her shorter stride made it difficult, and she arrived behind them slightly out of breath.

The countess paused at a door and rapped her knuckles against it. Emma inhaled deeply, willing her pulse to slow and her expression to remain serene. From within, the earl's voice called for them to enter.

Sophia swept into the room first, followed by Jane. Emma stepped in last—and halted in her tracks.

Perry sat by the hearth, one leg crossed over the other, his expression unreadable. The moment he noticed her, he averted his gaze and rose from his seat as though to take his leave. The movement pierced her with a sensation not unlike a blade to the chest.

He is still offended. He cannot even bear to look at me.

Her eyes stung with the prickle of unshed tears. A hot flush rose over her cheeks, leaving her feeling foolish and out of place all over again.

"Perry, wait a moment, please," the earl's voice rang with quiet authority.

Perry stilled at the door, his shoulders stiff.

"Miss Jane, would you accompany my brother to the drawing room? Ethan will join us there shortly. I should like a word with Miss Davis."

Jane inclined her head with graceful ease. "With pleasure, my lord."

"My wife has suggested we set aside formalities," the earl added with a kind smile. "Ethan is my son, and you are Ethan's kin. For all intents and purposes, we are extended family. Please—call me Richard."

Jane curtsied with a delighted smile. "Then I ask you do me the same honor. Jane is far simpler, I think."

His eyes warmed at her ease. "It will be my honor, Jane." He offered her a brief bow, and Emma could not help but notice the gentle affection in his manner.

She watched, heart in her throat, as Jane and Perry departed the room together, his arm offered politely. Perry did not look back.

Richard gestured toward the armchairs arranged before the fire, and Emma followed him numbly. Sophia settled with effortless grace onto the edge of a plump ivory chair embroidered in red, gold, and green, her indigo day gown immaculate. Her posture was elegance itself, and she looked lovely, framed by the bottle-green silk of the study walls.

Emma, aware of her every movement, fidgeted awkwardly as she perched beside her, adjusting her skirts and folding her hands tightly into her lap in an effort to emulate the countess's poise.

She could not recall the last time she had felt so entirely out of place.

"I am ever so grateful that you have come, Emma."

The earl's voice was warm, his tone sincere. Emma blinked, realizing he was addressing her directly. She turned to face him and did her best to set aside the gnawing ache in her chest. Perry's sudden disaffection was inconsequential, she told herself sternly. She had come here for Ethan. That was what mattered.

"It is my pleasure to assist ... Richard," she said, managing a polite smile.

"Not Lord Arrogant, then?"

Emma choked, her breath catching mid-sentence. Her eyes widened in alarm. Had she truly said that aloud?

Sophia's hand flew to her mouth to cover a laugh that she valiantly tried to suppress.

Richard, for his part, grinned with unconcealed amusement. "My brother has informed me that you did not wish to visit," he said, eyes sparkling. "He also mentioned your sobriquet for me, which I rather expect my wife will now use for the remainder of our marriage. I suppose I have earned it."

Emma stared at him in horror. Her cheeks flamed, her thoughts a chaotic tangle of humiliation. Lord Arrogant. She had only ever used the name in jest—and only to Perry. That he had repeated it to his brother felt like a betrayal of something private, something shared.

She had grown to rather treasure their verbal sparring, their challenging conversations. But to hear that he had passed her words along so casually—so humorously—tore at her composure.

The earl continued, seemingly unaware of her distress. "Still, I hope we shall cooperate to help Ethan settle in better here in our home. I know we may not have much time, of course, as such lovely ladies as yourself and your sister will be snapped up by the discerning gentlemen of London in no time."

Lovely ladies. Snapped up. Was he mocking her?

Emma blinked rapidly. Her vision blurred, and the lump in her throat grew to the size of a fist. She could not speak. Could not breathe. Had Perry laughed about her with his brother? Was Richard now treating her like some country dullard to be humored and gently teased?

She tried to swallow her feelings, but they had built too high, too fast. Before she could stop herself, tears spilled over her cheeks. A soft, gasping sob escaped her lips, and she lifted a trembling hand to cover her mouth, horrified that her carefully constructed composure had shattered so swiftly.

∼

Perry strode back down the hallway to find Richard leaning against the closed door of his study, arms folded, his gaze fixed on the floor with a scowl of bemused frustration.

"What is this?" Perry asked, slowing to a halt. "I thought you were speaking with Emma about how to handle Ethan's transition, so we could tell him she is here?"

Richard glanced up, his expression equal parts bewildered and guilty. "I made her cry."

Perry stiffened. "What did you do?"

The sharpness of his tone made Richard blink. Perry never barked. But if his brother had upset Emma—hurt her in some way—he would set the matter straight, even if it meant using his fists.

Richard looked genuinely taken aback. "I honestly do not know. One moment I was welcoming her, thanking her for coming. The next—tears. Sophia took charge and shooed me out. I have been exiled from my own study, loitering like a useless footman. Just more proof that I have no skill in managing family matters."

Perry exhaled, rolling his neck to ease the tension that had gripped him since hearing Emma was upset. "You did just fine by me when I needed you," he said, quieter now. "It has been a long journey, and Emma never wanted to come to London in the first place. Now tell me—exactly—what you said."

Richard frowned in concentration. "I thanked her for coming to help with Ethan, told her how grateful we are ... then I mentioned we would work together to help him settle in."

"And?"

"And then ... I think I said she likely would not be with us long. That such a lovely young lady would surely be married off quickly."

Perry closed his eyes and leaned back against the opposite wall with a groan. "She believes herself plain. Unattractive. Between that, the journey, and my relentless teasing, she likely thought you were mocking her."

Richard looked stunned. He opened his mouth to respond, hesitated, and then closed it again, clearly sorting through several thoughts. At last, he said, "I have so many questions."

"As do I," Perry muttered. "But for now, I expect you to fix this. Make her feel welcome. Make her feel safe."

Richard nodded slowly. "She does not look plain to me. That ebony hair, those eyes. Her skin is ..." He trailed off.

"Flawless," Perry finished quietly. "And those fierce black eyes—they could stop a man mid-breath."

At that, Richard turned his head sharply to study his brother. Perry looked away.

He had not fully recovered from the earlier madness of wanting to kiss her when she had stuck out her tongue like a mischievous child. Her playful defiance had nearly undone him. And then, when she entered the study—without that dreadful carriage dress, her curls artfully tamed, her eyes searching—he had fled. Left her alone.

He had promised she would be cared for, and then he had abandoned her on the threshold of Balfour Terrace like a footman shirking his duty. Perry straightened. "I left Jane alone. I should go check on her."

Richard gave him a long look. "Perry?"

He paused at the door. "She is not difficult to understand. She is direct. Honest. Intelligent. But ... unguarded." He stopped, not knowing how to describe what made Emma so utterly unlike anyone he had ever met. Emma was ... Emma.

And heaven help anyone—family or not—who made her feel small.

Still, Perry could admit one thing without shame.

"The clothing must go," he muttered.

Sophia was seated on the low table between the armchairs, her elegant hand covering Emma's as she struggled to regain her equanimity.

"I assure you, the earl was not mocking your appearance, Emma. You are utterly lovely. The matters you mentioned are easily solved—with the right modiste and a skilled abigail to tame your curls. You cannot possibly think my appearance is effortless? Without Adèle to dress my hair, I am quite helpless. Truly, while she was away, I barely left the townhouse! I do not know how to style my hair in the latest fashions. I simply point at a fashion plate, and she performs her magic."

Emma gave a watery laugh. "I would not even know which fashion plate to point at. Jane is artful with such things. But I ... I have no knack for this."

"Emma, it is simply a matter of practice. I suspect Jane has spent time studying publications, trying styles, observing what suits her. While you, my dear, were busy teaching our little Ethan to read and play chess. That takes patience and devotion. Now that you have the chance to focus on yourself, I promise you will gain the skill you seek."

"You really think so?"

"I do."

Emma gave a hiccup as the last of her tears dried. "I

thought ... I was certain the earl was mocking me. Just as Perry used to do."

Sophia tilted her head slightly, one arched brow lifting in question. "Used to?"

Emma nodded, lips pressing together in dismay. "Until I upset him. Now he will no longer even look at me."

Sophia was silent for a moment, thoughtful. "This has been a sudden and rather dramatic change of circumstance, has it not?"

"It has. I am quite out of sorts," Emma admitted. "I do not belong here. The idea of a Season is laughable. Jane is beauty and elegance. I came for her sake. But there will be no eligible gentlemen for me."

"Why would you say that?"

"I have not been courted in Derby, as a tenant farmer's daughter, nor in Somerset, after we became landowners thanks to the earl's generous gift. If I did not succeed in those modest circles, why would I turn heads in London? My lack of polish will be glaring in the company of true society."

Sophia looked down and idly smoothed the folds of her gown, a delicate blush creeping into her cheeks. "Emma, I shall confide something to you. I partook in three full Seasons without being courted. I had begun my fourth when the earl staked his claim and swept me away two months ago."

Emma blinked in astonishment. "Your fourth?"

Sophia nodded with a soft smile.

"And the earl was the first gentleman to show you genuine interest?"

"He was."

Emma stared down at her clasped hands. "And you truly believe he is the right gentleman for you?"

"Without question. He is perfection. But only for me. You see, it is not about turning heads or dazzling drawing rooms. It is about discovering the right partner—the one who complements your spirit and meets you where you are. My advice? Do not worry about what society thinks. Search instead for the gentleman who understands you—and whom you can trust with your heart."

Emma was quiet, digesting that. At last, she raised her eyes to meet Sophia's. "I would like to find someone like that."

Sophia gave her hand a tender squeeze. "And so you shall."

A tremulous smile spread across Emma's lips. She still felt like a right ninny for her emotional outburst, but she was grateful for the countess's kindness. Sophia was not at all what she had expected—and Emma liked her very much.

"I am quite embarrassed," she admitted.

Sophia waved a hand with gentle dismissal. "Pish. We are family here. And we bear some blame for your disorientation. We dropped you into this strange new life far too suddenly."

Emma let out a sigh of relief. The countess squeezed her hand once more, and the two sat in companionable silence while Emma's shoulders eased and her heart calmed.

"Emma, if I may ask a question?" Sophia waited for her nod of agreement. "You said Perry used to mock you. What did you mean?"

Blushing, Emma dropped her gaze, her fingers twisting in her lap.

"We had been sparring these last couple of days, and we had just agreed that, for all intents and purposes, we are all family, so we should relax the proprieties. Then he teased me about something and I ... It was deplorable behavior on my part."

Sophia cleared her throat delicately. "I beg your pardon, but I do not understand the issue?"

Emma lifted her hand to rub her face in distress. "Well, he must have been offended by my conduct, because he has grown quite unfriendly since."

"Emma?

She looked up, tentatively, into the countess's kind blue eyes.

"Perry may possess the glib manners of the *ton*, but I assure you, he dons them like armor. From what I have seen, he plays the role to serve his own ends, but it is just that—a role. True etiquette is not deeply important to him. He is playful with family. I cannot imagine a moment of teasing, even spirited horseplay, causing him offense. Will you tell me what happened? Exactly?"

"I stuck my tongue out at him," Emma murmured. "He stared at me most oddly, turned quite red, and seemed to have a mild apoplexy, in that he could not breathe properly. Since then, he has avoided looking at me in the most obvious way." Her voice faltered, thickening with emotion. "I thought we had a rapport of sorts. But now he knows I am the most uncouth of women."

Sophia pressed her lips together, clearly fighting a smile. The corners of her mouth twitched before she drew a steadying breath and said gently, "My dear Emma, I do not believe for one moment that Perry was offended. Quite the opposite. I suspect you caught him unawares—and left him thoroughly flustered. I am quite certain that he shall return to your side before long, and that the teasing will resume without delay."

With that, Sophia stood in a graceful swoosh of skirts

and made her way to the door. She appeared to be mumbling to herself as she went, but Emma caught the faint words: "And if he does not do so of his own determinism, I will meddle—because Perry has finally found himself an interest, it would seem."

The door opened, and the earl stumbled slightly as he entered, recovering his dignity before glancing between them.

"Are we all right, then? Everything sorted? Why does Emma still appear to be upset?"

"It is nothing that a few moments of orientation will not mend," Sophia said smoothly. "Come and finish saying your piece to Emma, so we might bring Ethan down."

The earl returned to his seat beside his wife and gave Emma a somewhat sheepish look.

"I apologize for any insensitivity on my part, Emma." He tugged at his cravat, visibly uncomfortable. "Perry explained my blunder, and I think I understand now. Please rest assured, I truly meant my words. I find you to be a lovely young woman, and we already have several fine gentlemen in mind to introduce to you—once you feel sufficiently prepared."

Sophia smiled warmly. "There is no rush. Take all the time you need to settle in. In fact, I insist that Perry himself assist the young ladies, Richard."

The earl shot her a look of mild perplexity, his green eyes so like Perry's and Ethan's. Yet only Perry's gaze left Emma wanting to press her hands to his chest and breathe deeply to discover if he truly smelled of leather, clean linen, and country air.

"That is what he said," Richard remarked. "Before he tried to retract the offer. Perry seems quite invested in what happens to Emma, for reasons I cannot quite decipher."

Sophia turned her gaze back to Emma. "There. You see? Perry is content—more than content—to spend time in your company. All will be as it was before long, dear."

Emma could not deny the flicker of hope that warmed her chest. As maddening as Perry's teasing could be, she had grown to treasure their back-and-forth. How humbling it was to realize that she missed his attention. His absence had left her feeling oddly adrift.

CHAPTER SIX

"Stewards exist to take care of the estates. Bankers exist to provide an estate owner with concerns. Drink exists to make us forget our concerns. But none of this signifies to you because you are my spare, so you exist to entertain me. Drink up."

July 1806, the late Earl of Saunton to his son, Peregrine, on his eleventh birthday after he posed a question about the tenants of Saunton Park.

The entire family, Emma and Jane included, had gathered in a large, tasteful drawing room decorated in hues of burgundy and navy. An intricate Persian rug graced the gleaming floorboards, bordered by an eclectic mix of armchairs and low tables. The gentle hiss of gas lights, evidence of the earl's great wealth, echoed faintly in the background, casting a warm glow into the corners of the cozy space. Through the paned glass of the tall sash windows, Emma glimpsed the lush greens and soft florals of a summer garden. She made a mental note to explore it when the opportunity arose.

As Sophia had predicted, Perry had been particularly attentive since her arrival. His face had softened with concern as she took her seat, and he had leaned toward her to murmur in a low, solicitous voice.

"Have you been taken care of, Emma? Do you need anything?"

Though his tone lacked its customary sardonic edge, the familiar twinkle lingered in his green eyes. At the very least, he was no longer avoiding her gaze, and he had thrown her several glances since their entrance—each one a small but precious balm that mended the frayed edges of her earlier distress.

Feeling more her usual self, Emma looked about the room with curiosity. Her gaze caught on a fine chess table placed near the fireplace, its elegant carved pieces arranged in anticipation of play. She straightened in delight. Perry followed her gaze.

"It is for Ethan," he explained, his voice amused. "He will be down shortly, and he will expect to play with each of us in turn. Hopefully, the surprise of your visit will exempt me from my match this evening."

Emma's eyes sparkled. "You truly play with him?"

"Did you think I was jesting? The little tyrant releases none of us without a daily match. I take it you are the one who taught him to love the game?"

Emma nodded with pride. "I adore chess. I have read several treatises on the subject, but Ethan's skills were still rudimentary when he left us in Derby."

Perry leaned one elbow on the armrest, his expression softening. "His skills are advancing rapidly now that he insists on playing at least once a day. You will be impressed. He will have you at the board before nightfall."

Emma smiled with growing satisfaction. "I am so pleased. Truly. I must admit, I feared he would be neglected in a noble household. But from what I have seen and heard, he is thriving. It is a great relief."

Perry snorted softly, the sound oddly affectionate. "The entire household revolves around Master Ethan. Even with a second child on the way, I suspect he shall forever hold center stage."

Both Emma and Jane gasped and clapped their hands over their mouths in unison. "The countess is with child?" Jane whispered, eyes wide.

Perry smirked. "Good heavens! Ladies and their endless fascination with babies. Yes, there is a babe on the way. Sophia and Ethan debate baby names in the evenings after they play. He is quite excited to have a younger brother or sister. I hear all about it during our own match, of course."

Emma let her hands drop back into her lap, her smile softening. "You are a good uncle, Perry."

He shifted in his chair as if startled by the unexpected compliment, his gaze cutting back to her in wary curiosity. "Why do you say that?"

"You spend time with him. You listen to him. That is what a good uncle does."

He arched a brow. "And what if I am a terrible influence? Have you considered that?"

Emma tilted her head. "That seems unlikely. You are intelligent, well-versed in etiquette, and I would wager you are patient and playful with him. A child would be fortunate to have an uncle like that."

For a moment, Perry simply looked at her, something unreadable passing through his expression before he settled back against the upholstery with a faint, self-deprecating smile. There was color in his cheeks, and though he said nothing more, she had the impression her words had pleased him more than he wished to admit.

Emma looked toward the door in anticipation, her thoughts drifting to Ethan, her beloved boy. In only moments, they would be reunited.

And perhaps, too, she and Perry had taken a small but important step toward repairing the strange bond that had so quickly formed between them.

At that moment, the door opened, and all heads turned as a young nursemaid entered, holding the hand of a small boy dressed in short breeches and a miniature coat of fine blue wool. The sight of him so grown, so dapper, startled Emma. The sable waves that framed his face gleamed under the light, and his green eyes widened when he beheld so many gathered. Yet it was the shadows under those bright eyes that tugged at her heart—evidence he had not been sleeping well.

Ethan took a moment to survey the room, taking stock of the unfamiliar faces, before his gaze found Emma seated near the window. His entire face lit with joy.

"Emma!" he cried, wrenching his hand free of the nursemaid's and darting across the room. Emma dropped to her knees to receive him, catching him in a tight embrace, her eyes stinging with unshed tears at seeing him.

"Ethan, you look so handsome!" she whispered, pressing her cheek to his.

"What are you doing here?" He pulled back, gazing at her in wonder.

"Your papa said you needed me, so I came to visit," she said softly, brushing a kiss to his forehead.

Ethan flung his arms around her neck once more and

buried his face into her shoulder. "I am so happy you are here! I missed you so much."

"I missed you, too." Emma gave him another squeeze before lifting him onto her knee as she resettled herself on the chair. "Now tell me, why have you been so desperate to see me? You have all these new relations to play chess with, a nursemaid to look after you, and a governess to teach you your lessons. It does not sound like you have any time to miss me."

Ethan leaned close, glancing around at the others before whispering into her ear, "They all get up so late. It is not like the country. I miss feeding the animals with you in the mornings."

Emma's heart clenched. She gave him a quiet hug and whispered back, "Do your governess and nanny not rise with you?"

"Yes, Daisy does, but we do not feed the animals. There are too many people here. And I miss the horses and dogs. It is different in *Lun-den*."

She smiled gently. "Who is Daisy?"

Ethan pointed to the nursemaid who had accompanied him in. The young woman offered Emma a warm, if slightly concerned, smile, and Emma returned it with a nod of appreciation before turning back to the little boy in her lap.

"Morning chores with you were my favorite part of the day," she said. "But now that I live in Somerset, I no longer feed the horses either. Shall we go visit the stables and see what they are like here?"

Ethan's eyes gleamed. "They are very nice. I did not want to *com-puh-lain*."

Emma shook her head. "Silly goose. They are your family now, and your papa wants what is best for you. Come. Let us go explore the stables, shall we?"

"I knew you could fix it," Ethan said, beaming.

Emma glanced up and caught the earl watching them, a faint crease of concern marring his brow. Raising her voice so all could hear, she addressed him directly.

"I think a visit to the stables would be an excellent adventure. Will that be acceptable, Richard?"

The earl gave her a thoughtful look, then stood. "I would love to visit the stables. Would everyone like to join us?"

Sophia rose, her smile warm. "I think we can all enjoy a stroll through the gardens and a visit to the mews."

She moved to open the garden door, and the group began filing out, the nursemaid bringing up the rear as Emma took Ethan by the hand and followed. The earl waited at the threshold for the pair to reach him before falling in step beside them.

As they walked across the lush lawn toward the mews, Richard glanced down at his son. "Do you like the stables, Ethan?"

"I do, Papa. Emma promised I could start riding just before I left the farm."

"Would you like me to teach you?"

Ethan turned to him, his chest puffing up with pride. "You want to teach me?"

"It sounds like great fun," the earl replied. He threw Emma a wink before continuing. "The only trouble is, I prefer to ride at dawn."

Ethan's face lit up. "At *sun-na-rise*? I would love that! I promise to stay in bed. Can we go tomorrow morning?"

"If you sleep tonight, then yes—we shall ride together in the park. And then we will see about teaching you to ride properly."

Ethan squealed in delight, tugging on Emma's hand as

they hurried to catch up to the others who had disappeared into the entrance of the mews. Inside, the air was rich with the scent of oats and clean straw. Soon they had gathered a small bucket of feed, and Emma lifted Ethan onto her hip so he could offer a handful to the first horse in the row. When he was done, the earl stepped forward to refill his small palm, and together they made their way down the line, Ethan chatting excitedly about how enormous the horses were and how he could not wait to ride at his papa's side.

PERRY WATCHED as Emma and his brother walked to each occupied stall, helping Ethan feed each of the mounts. Observing the joy on her face as she chattered softly to the boy pulled at old, forgotten memories he had long since buried.

Memories of soft embraces. The fragrance of gardenias. His mother's calm presence as she held him the way Emma now held Ethan. He remembered how she used to talk to him about the flowers in the garden, how he would pluck one in bloom and she would tuck it into her golden hair, bestowing him with a radiant smile of gratitude.

He had been a few months older than Ethan when those embraces ended, and his mother abruptly vanished from his life. Many weeks later, his father had told him coldly, with no more sentiment than if discussing the loss of a horse, that his mother was dead.

That devastated little boy still lingered within him. Those hours in the garden had been the last moments he had known joy, the last time he had believed life held any promise.

As always, the memory pulled the shadows of his

fifteenth year with it—when he had stumbled upon his vile father with the girl from the village, and the last vestiges of innocence had been destroyed. Perry pushed the thought away. The pain was still so fresh it might have happened yesterday.

Eventually, the party returned to the drawing room, where Richard sat down at the table for his daily chess game with Ethan. Emma and Perry were once again seated together across the room, observing from afar.

"You are so patient with him," Perry murmured.

Emma watched the little boy with warm appreciation lighting her features. "I could be nothing other than patient with the dear boy."

"Have you always spent so much time with him?"

She shrugged. After a quiet moment, she spoke, her gaze drifting toward the fireplace as though seeing ghosts in its swept hearth.

"When Ethan was a babe, he did not speak. Not a word. My parents despaired that he might be mute, or somehow ... impaired. But I knew better. He was watching. Learning. Ethan likes to do things properly. I believed that when he was ready, he would speak. So I spent time with him—played with him whenever I could. And I talked to him like he was already a person. We had so many one-sided conversations ... and one day, not long after his second birthday, he answered me."

She gave a wistful smile. "It was a full sentence. He asked me if he could have an apple. He had a little trouble pronouncing the words, but he said them all. Yes, he is brilliant—but you must be patient, or you miss it. All of his uniqueness."

Perry let out a long breath, almost a sigh. "I have not been very patient with you, have I, Emma?"

"No. You have not."

"Will you allow me to start afresh?"

She turned to him, her smile gentle. "I believe I can be tolerant of your past behavior, if you show a concerted effort to improve our relations. The countess informs me you are to tutor us. I hope you know what a challenge you have taken on with me. I am not skilled in social graces."

"It is not as difficult as all that," he replied. "I would appreciate a fresh start so I apologize for being sarcastic with you while you are trying to navigate this new world. I shall endeavor to assist you rather than judge you."

"That is all I can ask of you, Perry."

He smiled at her, something warm and soft rising in his chest. For a moment, he let himself imagine it—waking each morning to this woman beside him. Her bright intelligence, her strong heart, her maddening, captivating honesty. He could picture a life of laughter and simple joys.

But the moment passed. He—the worthless spare, with nothing but time and an allowance dependent upon his brother's goodwill—had nothing to offer her. Emma deserved far better than a man like him, one who wore masks and fled from intimacy, afraid of the secrets that might be revealed.

He sat forward, forcing out the words before he gave in to the temptation of staying—of imagining he had a place in this strange, warm world where people like Emma smiled at him with hope.

"Well, I must be off. I am meeting my friends. I shall leave you to your time with Ethan."

He rose and withdrew from the room, wondering if he had imagined the brief flicker of disappointment that crossed her face. In truth, he would have much preferred to spend the evening with Emma. But he needed to step aside

—to give her room to find an eligible young man, someone who could offer her everything she deserved.

If only I had anything to offer her.

It would be too easy to lose himself in her—too easy to imagine a lifetime of waking to her smile, of hearing her forthright laugh, of kissing her until he could taste her joy. But he could not allow himself that fantasy. Not when reality offered nothing but shadows.

EMMA WATCHED Perry leave with a touch of regret. For the first time since they had met, they had fallen into true companionable discussion—an exchange she had enjoyed more than she cared to admit. Her fondness for him was growing, despite her firm decision to avoid any attachment. The relief that the countess had been correct—that he had gravitated back to her side—was a pleasant surprise.

How had Sophia so accurately predicted what would happen?

Emma turned to observe the countess, who was seated beside the chess table, her attention on the ongoing game between her husband and their adopted son. Sensing Emma's gaze, she looked up and gave a quick wink before turning back to the board. Emma smiled and lifted her teacup for a sip of the warm brew that had been handed to her upon their return to the drawing room. For the first time in two days, she allowed herself to relax.

Jane, seated beside her, was in full spirits, chattering about how exciting it was to visit London. The countess seemed to believe that Emma could navigate this daunting change in circumstances, and Perry had reassured her— quite sincerely—that she would have the full support of the family. Emma was still astonished by what the earl had revealed earlier: Perry had offered to tutor them. The fact that he had later retracted the offer did not signify in her mind. He had offered, and that was what mattered.

The evening progressed at a gentle pace. They had enjoyed a fine dinner, just the four of them—Emma and Jane, the earl and the countess—followed by a few rounds of cards. Conversation had flowed easily, and the young ladies had begun to feel more at home. When they finally retired, much later than they were accustomed to, both were yawning from exhaustion.

Emma had tumbled into bed the moment her maid had helped her out of her gown and into a night rail. For once, she had fallen instantly into sleep—until she woke with a start. Somewhere in the distance, a clock was striking midnight. She turned over, attempting to reclaim the deep sleep she had been enjoying moments before.

By the time the clock announced the half-hour, she had given up entirely.

She considered tapping on Jane's adjoining door to see if her sister was also awake before scoffing softly to herself. Everyone in the Davis family knew that once Jane laid her head on a pillow, she slept as long as she wished and awoke bright-eyed and full of cheer, no matter the hour or circumstance.

Slipping from the bed, Emma padded across the carpet and lit an oil lamp using the low light of the banked fire. The night had turned chill with gusting rain, and the maid had insisted on lighting the fire before leaving. Now, Emma was grateful for both the warmth and the illumination.

She pulled her thick wrapper around her and stepped into a pair of slippers, setting off in search of the lower level, where the library was located.

It took nearly fifteen minutes to find her way. She tried several doors before a footman appeared, presumably returning to resume his duties in the entry hall. The earl had mentioned they were maintaining increased security after a recent incident, and Emma noted the footman's burly build and slightly disheveled appearance. He seemed less a servant by trade and more a soldier in livery. Nevertheless, he was polite and efficient, guiding her to the library with a short bow before disappearing once more.

Heaven. That was the only word that came to Emma's mind as she stepped inside.

The room was long and narrow, its walls lined with shelves crammed with books of every subject imaginable. Tables and chairs had been thoughtfully placed between the shelves, while flickering wall sconces, not yet extinguished for the night, cast a welcoming glow.

Emma wandered the room, orienting herself to its organization. When she discovered a shelf filled with recent political speeches, her heart leapt with excitement. Quickly scanning the spines, she selected a volume and moved to the velvet sofa before the fireplace.

She kicked off her slippers and tucked her feet beneath her wrapper, opening the book to the desired page. The rustling of the pages, the flicker of candlelight, the warmth of the fire—it all made for the perfect retreat from the confusion of the day.

Emma exhaled slowly. The weight that had pressed on her since they left Rose Ash seemed to lift, if only slightly.

She was in London. She had a book in her hands. And for the moment, that was enough.

A sound startled her awake.

Emma's eyes flew open, her heart thudding as she tried to determine where she was. It took a few dazed moments to recognize the surroundings. She had fallen asleep in the library. The book she had been reading was now closed and resting on her stomach. Sitting up, she rubbed her eyes and took in the flickering light of the sconces, the fire banked low in the grate.

Then she heard the noise again—a muffled laugh and the unmistakable thump of a shoulder against a door.

Quickly standing, she tightened the sash of her wrapper and moved instinctively toward the shadowed corner of the room just as three men stumbled in, shutting the door behind them with a clumsy bang that echoed through the silence.

Perry was in the center.

He looked thoroughly dishevelled, and, if she was not mistaken, entirely the worse for drink.

"Have you been drinking?" she demanded, arms folded.

Perry blinked. His gaze was unfocused when it found her across the room. "Emma."

"Indeed," she replied, dryly. "A better question would be—have you been over drinking?"

"Jus' a tipple or two," he slurred, swaying slightly where he stood.

Emma raised an eyebrow. "Your friend appears to have had far more than two tipples."

She nodded toward the tall gentleman clinging to the nearest bookshelf like a lifeline. His chestnut hair was tousled, and he looked as though he feared the floor might betray him.

Perry grinned foolishly. "Brendan Ridley. Friend of the earl's from our Eton days. Son of a baron from Somerset—you are practically neighboursss!"

Emma scowled, dipping into a terse curtsy. "Pleased to meet you, Mr. Ridley."

"Whazat? Who's talking to me?" Ridley mumbled, peering into the shadows like a man seeking a ghost.

Perry ignored the exchange and gestured toward the other gentleman. "And thisss is Lord Julius Trafford, eldest son of the Earl of Stirling."

Emma turned her attention to Lord Trafford. He was tall and wiry, with a striking contrast of wheat-blond curls atop his head and close-cropped brown hair at the sides. Of the three, he seemed the least unsteady—but the most unrepentant. His gaze dropped to her chest and lingered.

Emma instinctively lifted her chin and placed her hand on the knot of her sash, confirming that her wrapper was securely tied. Her night rail was high-necked and modest, and the wrapper thick. He could see nothing more than she might wear to breakfast, and yet ... the boldness in his stare was unmistakable.

She refused to curtsy. Nor did she acknowledge him with speech. Let him take the hint.

From the corner of her eye, she saw Perry weaving toward the drinks cabinet.

She had half a mind to sweep out of the room altogether, but she wanted her book—and her dignity. Reaching for the lamp on the end table, she extended her hand—

And froze.

Trafford was suddenly beside her, having crossed the room without sound. He loomed, a silent shadow at her elbow. Startled, she flinched, taking a step back, only to watch in disbelief as he reached past her and plucked up her book from the sofa.

∼

TRAFFORD WANDERED over to the sofa, holding Emma's book aloft and squinting at the title by the glow of the fire. Perry blinked blearily from across the room, resisting the urge to groan.

The fool could simply turn to the left and read it by the lamp!

Instead, Trafford barked a loud, jarring laugh. Perry flinched belatedly, feeling the echoes in his skull.

"Would you look at this! *A Selection of Speeches Delivered at Several County Meetings in the Years 1818 & 1819!* What is this little bluestocking about, then? Interested in politics, are you, mouse?"

Emma's chin lifted. "That is Miss Mouse to you," she retorted. "And no, I am interested in agricultural reform and the manner in which future Parliamentary actions may affect rural landholders and estate management ... you insolent oaf!"

Trafford's brows rose. "That is Lord Insolent Oaf, if you please. And what do you care about land management? Should you not be having your hair styled or ordering fripperies from Bond Street?"

He reached out a hand and caught a single curl between his fingers. Perry, watching from across the room, sobered instantly. Trafford's fingers. On Emma.

No!

He launched himself forward with the intention of removing those fingers—and possibly his friend's entire hand—when Emma got there first.

She thrust a finger in Trafford's face, her voice ringing with righteous fury.

"Land ownership is changing! You may pretend it does not matter, but those who do not evolve will become irrelevant. The future does not care about your title, my lord—it cares about your ability to manage your estates wisely. Those who do not adapt will be left behind—extinct!"

Perry froze mid-step, utterly transfixed.

She was glorious.

Black eyes alight with fire, her cheeks flushed with righteous indignation, her petite form radiating strength—it was like watching Joan of Arc take the field against the most ridiculous army of dandies. The firelight glinted in her dark curls, casting a halo about her.

And he—idiot that he was—had mocked her for that brilliant mind.

He also could not deny a stab of jealousy. *Arguing is our thing.*

Did Trafford stoke her flames as he did? No ... no, this was not flirtation. This was true anger, and Perry felt both relief and awe in equal measure.

Trafford squinted down at her. "Why should a sweet young thing like you care about such things?"

Emma's voice did not waver. "You should care, Lord Oaf, because one day you shall inherit lands from your father. If you remain ignorant of the changes ahead, you shall find yourself selling off your family holdings for pennies on the pound to fund your overindulgent ways. The world is shifting, and if you will not keep up, you shall be swept aside, you ... you oversized twit!"

Trafford gaped at her.

Perry decided he had allowed this farce to go on long enough. Weaving slightly, he seized Trafford by the arm and steered him toward the door with more force than finesse.

"My apologiesss, Emma, for inflicting my friendsss upon you. If I had known you were in here ..." he trailed off. "I would never have brought them inssside."

Her black gaze was impenetrable as she watched him tug Trafford away. It struck him then that she was not simply angry—she was disappointed.

That hurt more than the indignation.

"Ridley!" he barked, startling the lolling figure still half-propped against the door. "Time to go!"

Brendan Ridley blinked like an owl, bobbing his head vaguely before lurching into motion and staggering out the door.

Perry shoved Trafford after him, muttering, "You complete donkey."

Trafford grumbled, "What was she on about? Agricultural speeches? Pennies on the pound ..."

His mumbling faded behind them.

Perry felt the weight of shame descend upon his shoulders. He had sought to forget the haunting memories of his father by returning to old habits. And in doing so, he had made a spectacle of himself before the one woman who made him feel something other than hollow.

He would pay for this come morning.

Not just with a headache, but with the certain knowledge that Emma Davis now thought him no better than Lord Oaf himself.

CHAPTER SEVEN

"I arranged for her to visit you for your birthday. After that fiasco with your brother, I thought it best to ensure your first experience was with only one woman—no confusion this time."

July 1807, the late Earl of Saunton to his son, Peregrine, on his twelfth birthday to explain the presence of the lightskirt in his bed.

∽

"Well, well. If it is not Sir Drinksalot!"

Perry groaned, clutching his head as Emma's voice struck him like a church bell to the skull. "Let me get some coffee in me first, and then you may proceed to mock me."

Jane perked up with interest, putting down her fork. "Coffee? I have seen advertisements for it, but I confess I am not familiar with it. We never drank it at home. I suppose we could now that we are landowners, but as tenant farmers, we never encountered any, owing to the price."

Perry dropped heavily into one of the delicate chairs at the breakfast table. The piece gave a creak of protest, which echoed in his skull like a death knell. "You will encounter it shortly, I assure you. Marcus? A pot, if you please. A large one."

The footman nodded and moved swiftly to the sideboard, where a silver coffeepot already awaited him. Evidently, word of Perry's late-night adventures had reached the staff. From the sympathetic arrangement of strong coffee and headache-friendly fare, they had clearly anticipated his condition.

The tall, slender pot was placed before him, Marcus laying out a cup and saucer with practiced efficiency.

"It is darker than tea!" Jane squeaked, wide-eyed. Perry winced. Was she always this enthusiastic, or was he merely afflicted?

"Yes," he bit out.

"It smells heavenly!"

"Yes."

He raised the cup to his lips and drank, only wincing slightly as the heat seared his tongue. Even so, the bitter brew was salvation in liquid form.

"May I try a cup?"

Perry stilled, frowning into the steam. "It is more of a gentleman's drink."

"Why? Does it contain spirits or some such thing?"

Emma snorted softly. "No, Jane. It is simply one of those things men like to keep for themselves, to exclude women."

"Perry will let me try it. He is practically our family."

Perry scowled but lacked the will to argue. If it would quiet her exuberance, she could sip brandy straight from the decanter for all he cared. "Marcus, another cup, if you would."

A second cup was placed on the table, followed by a rounder, smaller pot of coffee. Marcus poured carefully, ensuring not a single drop escaped the elegant spout.

Jane inhaled deeply. "Goodness, it smells divine." She took a cautious sip, then made a face. "Oh! It is quite bitter."

She returned the cup to its saucer with theatrical delicacy.

Perry drained his and poured another, the world sharpening with each sip. Perhaps he would survive the day after all.

"I wonder if it would taste better with cream and sugar?" Jane mused, mostly to herself. "I shall try it as I take my tea, I think."

Marcus, ever attentive, placed a delicate silver cream jug and sugar bowl in front of her.

"Thank you, Marcus."

Perry, his vision clearer now, arched a brow. "One does not thank the servants, Jane. One does not even notice them."

Jane blinked in confusion, her mouth parting slightly.

From the corner of his eye, Perry observed Emma's eyebrows draw together.

"Why not?" asked his little hoyden.

Not mine, he reminded himself, fighting the inconvenient urge to grab her and erase that frown with a wholly inappropriate kiss on her pink lips.

"You will move amongst the *ton*. That is simply how things are done."

"Sir Drinksalot is giving us etiquette lessons over breakfast while he can barely hold himself upright?"

His lips quirked into a half-smile. "Indeed. As your tutor, it is my solemn duty to correct your every mistake."

"And what of yours, Mister Carousing-After-Midnight?" Emma fired back.

"A lady does not remark upon the activities of the gentlemen around her."

She sat back in her chair, her posture radiating belligerence. "Well, that is convenient. For the gentlemen."

"It is," he agreed with a maddeningly sanguine expression.

Emma huffed. Retrieving her fork, she stabbed at her eggs, no doubt imagining they were his ribs. Jane, mercifully unfazed, stirred her coffee with care, added sugar, and lifted the cup again with reverent anticipation.

"Zooks! That is delicious," Jane cried, staring down into her cup with awe. She took a long, appreciative sip and dabbed delicately at her mouth with a napkin.

Emma leaned toward her. "Just be sure not to drink it in company. Heaven forfend a lady be caught sipping a gentleman's beverage."

Perry grinned. "See? Already you are learning, Emma. Before long, you will be a perfectly polished lady of the *beau monde*."

She growled softly and turned her attention back to her breakfast, deliberately ignoring his bait.

"I would like to point out," she said loftily, "that family, integrity, and upholding one's honor are far more important than which beverage one drinks and whether one is so crass as to thank the servants for their service."

"You would think that was the case."

"Are you saying it is not?"

"I would say," he replied slowly, "that etiquette is the grease of social interaction. Each level of society has rules of conduct to facilitate their affairs. Ignoring those rules marks you as someone who does not belong."

"And why should I care whether spoiled lords like your friend Trafford believe I belong?"

"If you are to live within this world, you will need the cooperation of others. These are peers. They hold the power of the realm in their hands. Flouting the rules will place you at a disadvantage. You must learn to play the game—then you may begin to win it. That said, Trafford was unforgivably rude, and you were fully within your rights to defend yourself. Vigorously."

Emma looked thoughtful. "What about integrity and doing what is right?"

"What of it?"

She gave a vexed sigh. "How does one's honor fit into this world of rigid rules?"

Perry sipped his coffee and sighed. It was far too early, and he was too far into his convalescence from the night before to engage in philosophy.

"I suppose it might be possible to do both," he allowed. "Surely great statesmen must navigate etiquette and ideals in equal measure. They must envision a better future and use grace and persuasion to bring it about."

"You mean like you persuaded me to leave Somerset? By manipulating the invitation to include Jane?"

"Precisely."

Jane's cup clattered onto its saucer. "I was not included in the invitation?"

Perry closed his eyes in pain. "Of course you were! Emma was merely posing a hypothetical situation. Were you not, Emma?"

Emma set her jaw and glared at him over the pristine linen tablecloth. "Yes."

Jane looked between them, her brow furrowed. "I do not understand. Was I invited or not?"

Emma's lips pressed together as Perry gave her a long, warning look. At last, she relented.

"Of course you were invited, Jane. I was only—" she exhaled through her nose "—posing a hypothetical situation."

Relief softened Jane's features. She turned back to her coffee, added more sugar and cream, and took another sip. Perry grimaced. She was utterly spoiling the brew, but he had not the strength to object. His sparring with Emma had exhausted what little fortitude remained in him.

Then he remembered the previous evening—how she had stood, fierce and resolute, holding her ground before Lord Oaf. She had been incandescent.

He sat straighter, admitting the truth: he had dragged his aching body down to breakfast solely to see her. To bask in her nearness. She invigorated him.

You have nothing to offer her, you worthless bounder.

The reminder did nothing to dampen his awareness of her. He dropped his gaze to his plate and focused on forcing down enough food to restore himself.

Emma knew her brow was furrowed, but try as she might, she could not relax the muscles in her face.

"But what if I do not want the soup?"

Perry rubbed his hands over his face, clearly still recovering from the night before. "You must accept the soup."

"What if I do not like the soup that is served?"

"It does not signify. One always accepts the soup."

Jane interjected, still babbling incessantly, as she had

been since breakfast. "I like soup. I like all kinds of soup. In fact, there are few soups that I would ever think to reject. I like brown soup. And white soup, especially with ground almonds, though I am not so fond of it when anchovies are added. It quite spoils the taste, in my opinion. Do you think soup will be served tonight for supper? What am I saying? Of course there will be soup ..."

Emma shook her head in dismay. What had gotten into her? Jane was frequently exuberant, but this was an entirely new level of enthusiasm.

"As I was saying"—she glared at her sister, who belatedly realized she was chattering and slapped a hand over her mouth as if to hold the words inside—"why must I eat soup if I do not want it?"

Perry growled, then lifted his head to glare at her. "Emma, one must accept the soup. I do not know why this is the case—it simply is. If you dislike the soup, or if it is soup in general that you so eloquently despise, then toy with your spoon and pretend to consume it until the fish course arrives."

"I do not understand why it is poor manners to reject soup!" Emma brought her fist down on the table, causing the porcelain and silver to clink and jump.

Perry groaned at the cacophony, clutching his head in agonized frustration. "Jane, could you leave us for a moment? I would like to converse with your sister."

Jane unclamped her hand from her mouth and stood. "I think I shall locate some tea. I am quite parched, for some reason."

With that, she made her exit. Once they were alone, Perry turned to Emma.

"I feel I owe you an apology for what transpired in the library. I did not know you were in there."

"Your friend, Trafford, was a complete boor. He raked his eyes over me as if I were a street harlot!"

Perry frowned. "What do you mean?"

"His eyes ..." Emma waved at her bodice. Perry's gaze dropped to where she indicated, lingering several seconds longer than was appropriate, before snapping back to her face. He looked dazed.

"I am sorry. I quite forgot what you said," he admitted.

Emma clenched her fists. "Trafford was most unseemly in his gaze! Not to mention insufferably rude about my reading."

Perry's face hardened, his features set into grim lines. *Is he angry with me... or with Trafford?*

"Trafford can be an arse—" He caught himself. "I mean, he can be a ..."

"I grew up with rambunctious brothers. Arse is not the worst I have overheard."

"Then Trafford calling you a bluestocking was not that devastating?"

"No, I suppose not. I find it an honor to be associated with such intellectuals. Both Sarah Fielding and Samuel Johnson were members of The Blue Stockings Society. I do not care if it is now considered a derogatory term for educated women—I would have proudly taken a seat at one of their meetings."

"Then why are you still angry with me? I swept them out the moment I realized it was ill-advised to inflict them on you. I am apologizing again. What more do you need from me?"

Emma dropped her eyes, toying with the linen tablecloth. "I disliked seeing you in that state," she mumbled.

"Miss Mouse," he said softly, "are you concerned about my welfare?"

Her cheeks warmed. "I am. You should not spend time with someone like Trafford. He is an ... arse."

Perry was silent for a long moment. "I think ... you might be saying ... that I am not?"

"No ... you are ... you. Not like Trafford."

Emma glanced up, testing the waters. Perry appeared bemused—but undeniably pleased.

"That might be the nicest compliment anyone has ever paid me."

"I barely said anything," she muttered, mortified.

"Nevertheless ... thank you, Emma."

Hesitantly, she raised her eyes to his. "You are welcome, Mr. Arrogant."

Perry chuckled. "May we continue this lesson, then?"

Emma rolled her eyes. "As you wish. Let the arbitrary rules of dinner time commence."

"We shall have to find Jane, then."

Within ten minutes, they had all resumed their places at the dining table.

"As I was saying, one always accepts the soup course ..." Perry cast Emma a look of mock severity.

"And if one does not wish to eat it," Emma recited with a sigh, "one toys with it until the fish course."

Perry grinned. "Precisely. Then one quietly sips from the side of the spoon—never the tip. And one must avoid vulgar slurping noises—"

"Zounds, Perry! We have eaten soup before!" Emma protested.

"I felt I should be thorough. But I am pleased to hear it. I shall be watching this evening to ensure you both conduct yourselves with the utmost decorum, so I expect you to be on your very best behavior."

"We shall see," Emma replied pertly, though a secret smile tugged at her lips.

He was staying home tonight.

And that, she could not help but admit, made her exceedingly glad.

As their dinner lesson continued into the afternoon, Perry suggested various dishes, prompting Jane and Emma to select the appropriate utensil for each. It turned out they were relatively well-versed—aside from one minor misstep when both sisters chose a fork in response to his query about tarts, rather than the correct spoon.

By the time the lesson on table manners had concluded, Emma felt relatively confident she could dine within high society without appearing a complete ninny. Even the rules of precedence when entering a dining room did not seem overly complicated—so long as they accepted that they were likely always to be the lowest ranking members at any such event. Emma, by virtue of being the elder, would outrank Jane by a hair.

Now, if only she did not look like an unfashionable relic from a far-flung estate, she might consider being seen in public to discover whether all gentlemen of the *ton* were as rude as that Trafford fellow—or whether there might be some worthwhile personages of character to meet.

As she climbed the steps to return to their rooms, Emma glanced down at her gown, and all her newfound confidence evaporated, leaving a tight knot of anxiety in the region of her stomach. Raising her eyes to look at Jane, who walked beside her on the stairs, did nothing to restore it. Her sister looked utterly delightful in a day gown of deep blue-green—a creation she had sewn herself. The color perfectly complemented her silky ebony locks, golden skin, and bright blue eyes.

Emma exhaled a long breath. Nothing about this trip was turning out to be simple—not her role, not her appearance, and certainly not her conflicting feelings regarding the handsome Mr. Arrogant, whom they had just left behind to change for dinner.

For some unfathomable reason, she was drawn to the charming, indolent gentleman—a fact that was both illogical and deeply problematic. She would be fortunate to catch his attention for more than a moment, let alone sustain it for a lifetime. Which, of course, was academic. They had absolutely nothing in common.

Nevertheless, as her slippered feet ascended the grand staircase, Emma could not deny the truth that pressed on her heart like a physical weight: she was no longer guarding her emotions with the careful discipline she had so recently resolved to uphold.

THE NEXT MORNING, Emma paced up and down the corridor outside their bedchambers, her stomach growling in protest. She paused to glare at Jane's door. What on earth was keeping her?

Several more minutes passed without any sign of her sister. At last, Emma crossed the hall and knocked firmly. No response. That was most peculiar. Jane was invariably the first one awake, eager for breakfast and conversation. Had she already gone downstairs without her?

Frowning in bewilderment, Emma opened the door and stepped inside. The room was still dark, the heavy curtains drawn against the daylight. She peered around, surprised to see the bed still occupied.

Jane is still sleeping?

Padding closer, Emma called gently, "Jane?"

There was no reply. Anxiety stirred. Her sister never overslept. Drawing back the covers, Emma revealed the familiar tumble of dark curls on the pillow. Still no movement. Panic flared. Reaching down, she shook Jane's shoulder.

"Jane!"

Her sister's eyes flew open. Both girls jumped in shock before letting out relieved gasps.

"Emma?"

"You are still asleep?"

Jane blinked blearily. "What time is it?"

"Well, there is just enough time left for a quick breakfast before Perry accompanies us to the dress shop."

Jane groaned. "That late?"

"What happened? You always sleep like the dead!"

"I do not know. I simply could not fall asleep. I was awake until sunrise."

Emma's jaw dropped. "But you never have trouble sleeping. You are the envy of the entire household!"

"I was restless. Look—" Jane gestured to the side table where her embroidery frame displayed the finished rose-and-ash motif she had begun in Somerset. "I must have passed out just after dawn."

Emma shook her head in wonder. "Well, you've had a few hours at least. But we must keep the appointment Perry made. Get dressed. Quickly. You can eat downstairs."

Jane stretched with a loud yawn. "This is an outrage. I was so looking forward to meeting a London modiste, and now I must prop myself against the counter like a rag doll."

Emma smirked. "Perfect. It will mean I can speak to her without you monopolizing the conversation. I have far more need than you do. You already look genteel."

"I have tried to advise you on colors, but you never listen to me!"

"I am quite sure I shall not look half as elegant in those rich shades you wear."

"Hmph. Wait until the modiste confirms everything I have ever told you. Then you shall owe me an apology for months of stubborn resistance."

"Jane, stop quarreling and get dressed. I need something that will not make me feel like a poor relation."

Jane shot her a sideways glance, suspicion gleaming. "Why? Do you wish to impress someone? A certain Mr. Arrogant, perhaps?"

Emma dropped her gaze. "I have no idea of what you speak, you silly creature. Just hurry."

Soon they were racing downstairs to eat their eggs and ham in unseemly haste, fortunately without any witnesses to their indecorous display. Emma dabbed her mouth with a napkin, her thoughts already leaping ahead to their meeting with the dressmaker. Meanwhile, Jane sighed blissfully as she lifted her freshly poured coffee.

"Oh my, the whole day seems brighter now!" she declared, sipping with dreamy reverence.

Emma shook her head, amused despite herself, and rose from her chair.

She needed that modiste like a parched woman needs water.

CHAPTER EIGHT

"Steer clear of intelligent women. They are dull company and see through a gentleman's attempts to charm."

July 1808, the late Earl of Saunton to his son, Peregrine, on his thirteenth birthday.

It was with some trepidation that Emma ascended into the Saunton carriage after Jane. She was anticipating their arrival at the modiste while simultaneously dreading it. Emma was certain that nothing could be done about her appearance, while hoping that a magical transformation might occur to make her look as fine as her beautiful sister.

Distracted by her thoughts, she sat down rather too firmly—only to miscalculate and land with a thump on the carpeting in the aisle between the seats. Her buttocks smarted, while a fiery blush spread across her cheeks.

Perry coughed behind her from the open carriage door,

completing her humiliation when she realized he had observed her graceless landing. He held out a gloved hand to assist her, which she reluctantly accepted, raising herself onto her knees before fumbling to her feet. She nearly flinched at the tingle his touch produced, even through the gloves they both wore.

Once she was seated, he let her hand go and climbed in to sprawl across the opposite bench.

"Signora Ricci is very talented. She shall make up a full wardrobe befitting a young lady of the gentry." Perry was clearly attempting to settle her nerves after the embarrassing spill, which Emma both appreciated and resented. Why could she not be a charming young lady who might attract the attentions of a gentleman such as he? It was laughable to think she would ever entice a worldly man of such high standards with her gauche lack of polish.

"Oh, yes! A visit to the modiste shall work wonders!" Jane's attempt to smooth over the mishap was transparent. Emma felt her blush threaten a second appearance. Desperate to change the subject, she searched for a topic that would not lead back to her unfortunate tumble. She could feel Perry's gaze upon her as she stared down at her clenched fists. This was mortifying.

"I am very pleased with the progress we made yesterday. Once your wardrobe is ready, we shall invite our cousin and his wife to dinner, so you may practice with the peerage."

Jane perked up. "Your cousin?"

"I forgot to inform you. The Duke of Halmesbury is our cousin. The duchess shall sponsor you once you are ready to enter society."

"Oh! Her Grace is the duchess you mentioned at Rose Ash?"

Emma was grateful that Jane and Perry had entered into a discussion of family connections while she took a few moments to recover her composure. She might miss some of what was said, but Jane could recount it to her later.

"Yes, Halmesbury is very influential, and the duchess is an amiable young lady. I believe you shall find much in common, as she, too, grew up in the country and has only recently come to London for the first time."

Emma drew calming breaths and gazed out the window as the carriage rattled through several blocks before slowing in traffic. Soon it drew to a stop in front of a narrow shop. The gold lettering above the entry proclaimed they had arrived at *Signora Ricci*, much to Emma's relief.

She was long past due to tame her wild hair and to wear something that complemented her figure, rather than simply covered it. Privately, she admitted that had always been the general purpose of the clothes she selected for herself.

It was time to make a change—something a little more daring and contemporary than her collection of muted, dowdy gowns. Her eyes flicked to the source of her newfound interest in fashion. Despite herself, she wished to attract a glance of admiration from the handsome gentleman who glanced back at her, a question written in his emerald gaze. If she could see his face suffused with admiration for her womanly form, even once, she might then follow through with her pragmatic decision to steer her thoughts away from such unattainable desires.

The fierce yearning that pierced her heart—to be the object of his desire for even a fleeting moment—was bittersweet. The countess had assured her she might attain a level of competence in her appearance. Emma remained unconvinced, but it gave her hope that she might someday elicit Perry's fleeting esteem.

Though she knew she could never hold the attentions of such a sophisticated rogue, she would be forever grateful if she might experience his regard and know what it was to be beautiful and desirable, such as her younger sister, who never lacked admirers in Derby, nor at Rose Ash.

She was determined to obtain at least one gown that elevated her appearance, before she inevitably ruined it with an awkward stumble or ill-advised comment on a topic that would send any well-bred gentleman into panicked retreat.

Lost in her thoughts, she failed to notice that she was the only one remaining in the carriage. Perry stood, holding out his hand to assist her, a quizzical expression across his features. Emma drew a shuddering breath, still mortified from her earlier mishap, then grasped his hand to disembark. She nearly wept at the untimely heat that surged through her at the contact.

Collect yourself, Emma! Perry is not—and never shall be—your young gentleman!

"Are you all right, Emma?"

She pressed her lips together, unable to voice complaint over his solicitousness, though she was ashamed to be receiving it due to her lack of poise. That he was so attuned to her embarrassment only worsened it.

"I shall never be ready to enter society."

Perry appeared genuinely concerned. "I do not believe that is the case. I would never have manipulated the situation if I thought it would do you a disservice to be here. I swear it."

"We are both witness to the fact that I do not belong. I

am not cultivated. Jane shall do splendidly, while I shall make a disgrace of myself."

Unlike Perry. He was perfection itself—immaculately attired, his broad shoulders filling his forest-green coat, cutting a dashing figure with strong thighs, slim hips, and a flat abdomen. He possessed the languid grace of a cat and the predatory gleam of a wolf.

Perry lifted a hand to tuck an unruly lock behind her ear, the carriage door shielding the intimate gesture from the street beyond.

"I believe you belong wherever you choose to be. You are a determined young woman with strong opinions, and in certain circles, that shall be welcome. I would change nothing about you."

Emma's heart melted. She stared into his captivating eyes—flecked with emerald and gold—knowing she must mask the adoration surely written across her face.

"Except, of course," he added, his gaze dropping, "for this unholy mess of a dress. This, I would gladly burn on your behalf."

Emma's feet landed back on the ground with a firm mental thump. She was almost grateful for the rude awakening. Swatting his hand away, she pushed past him and marched through the shop door, which Jane was holding open with a questioning eyebrow at the unseemly delay.

Staring down into Emma's coal-black eyes, Perry could see the warm affection his words had inspired. It had thoroughly dismayed him to find himself swaying toward her, a heartbeat away from leaning down to claim her pink lips.

But she was not one of his wayward widows, and he

had no right to her sweet fire. Desperately, he had sought for something—anything—to put distance between them.

Unfortunately, his gaze had once again fallen upon her bodice, with the impressive curves it concealed beneath that ghastly mud-colored gown. The vile garment had provided the perfect inspiration to push their interaction into the abrasive once more.

Truly, that dress belonged in a fireplace. It was indescribably awful.

With their bristling animosity restored, Perry followed her into the shop to introduce her to Signora Ricci.

SIGNORA RICCI WAS an attractive Italian woman in her late thirties who spoke almost as much with her hands as with her voice. Emma was gratified to note that the modiste did not appear to be the least judgmental about her appearance —although her reaction to the much-maligned carriage dress had been barely concealed horror. With a sharp order in Italian, she had the gown whisked away by an attendant and promptly called for a pelisse from the back.

"We have a young woman who no longer needs *il pelisse*, and I think *il colore* is perfect for *la donna!*" she exclaimed, clapping her hands. "This color, it is *non va bene*. Miss Davis, you need color!"

Soon, Emma was enveloped in a deep blue pelisse— slightly too long, but cut so well it enhanced her figure in a way she had never before experienced. She stared at her reflection, astonished by how the rich hue made her hair gleam and her complexion glow. Perhaps Jane had been correct all along about Emma wearing the wrong tones?

The garment was whisked away again, this time for

alterations, with Signora Ricci adamant that Emma must leave the shop wearing it. Emma did not dare ask after the fate of the mud-brown carriage dress. She suspected it no longer existed.

The modiste presented fashion plates suited to Emma's contours, then turned them toward Perry, who studied them thoughtfully and nodded his agreement. Once they had selected several styles, Signora Ricci began draping bolts of rich fabrics—silks and velvets—in vivid colors across Emma's bodice to study the effects. Her eyes widened in wonder as the mirrors reflected back a version of herself she had never imagined: softened, luminous, lovely.

Once, she caught Perry's reflection as he smiled faintly at her repeated gasps of amazement. A rush of warmth bloomed in her chest at his quiet attention.

After several hours of discussion and selection, Perry placed the order for both sisters—expedited, no less—and scheduled the first fittings. As they waited for the altered pelisse to return, the three of them wandered over to admire a display of gloves near the front windows. Perry advised they purchase a variety of colors to match their new wardrobe.

Just then, the bell above the door chimed as it opened, and two women—both in their late twenties—swept into the shop. Emma's eyes widened at the vision of an attractive redhead dressed in a gown cut so low and tight that it could scarcely be decent. From the corner of her eye, she saw Perry stiffen.

The women spotted him immediately and approached in a swish of silk and a cloud of sweet perfume.

"Mr. Balfour! It has been too long!"

Emma noted how Perry flicked a glance in her direction

before bowing politely over the woman's hand. "Lady Slight. What a pleasure."

"Have you taken up with someone new, Perry?" Lady Slight purred, turning her frosted blue eyes on Emma and Jane with naked disdain.

"These are Miss Davis and Miss Jane," Perry replied smoothly. "They are houseguests of the earl—distantly related to the Balfour family."

Emma wondered if he and the earl had discussed precisely how their introductions were to be handled. She and Jane curtsied with impeccable decorum.

"Relations?" Lady Slight's voice was sugar-sweet and laced with venom. She inhaled delicately, before the two women tittered into their gloves.

Emma narrowed her eyes. She knew derision when she heard it, and this was not Perry's style of teasing. This was something else entirely—mean-spirited, bordering on cruel.

Without thinking, Emma stepped in front of Jane in a defensive stance. If these harpies dared insult her sister, she would not hesitate to retaliate. She only wished she were wearing that blue pelisse rather than the hideous gown that now seemed even more mortifying under Lady Slight's icy gaze.

"Surely, you jest!" Lady Slight crooned. "I cannot believe these girls are related to the preeminent Balfours. This young woman—her hair is as artless as the Scottish Highlands, and—heavens, a double-dimity petticoat! Do they still make such things? Confess, Perry—these are rural strumpets you're dressing for amusement."

Emma's fury rose, but her tongue stilled as Perry stepped forward and lifted a hand to stay her. She obeyed his silent instruction, curious to see how he would handle such insolence—and whether he would defend her.

"Now, now, Harriet," Perry said with cool amusement. "There is no need to be jealous. The earl has developed a deep and abiding interest in familial matters. You would not want word to reach him that you were unkind to his houseguests. Saunton is an affable man, but when it comes to defending his family ..." He trailed off with an elegant shrug.

Lady Slight's expression flickered. Her smile faltered. "Perry, you must know I was only teasing. Miss Davis, of course you knew I was jesting?"

Emma inclined her head. "But of course. Any friend of Perry's is a friend of ours." Her voice was light, her smile serene.

Inside, she was awash with admiration. Perry had neutralized the encounter with finesse, all without a single word of overt rebuke. He had protected them both and preserved the illusion of civility—a lesson in etiquette and strategy that Emma could not ignore.

At that moment, the altered pelisse was returned. As the two ladies wandered off in search of other prey, Emma slipped it on with Jane's assistance. The soft fabric enveloped her in renewed confidence.

They exited the shop moments later, the memory of Lady Slight already dissolving into the bustle of the London street behind them.

∼

When Perry stepped out into the street, still unsettled by the social skirmish he had only just averted, his attention was immediately drawn to a scene unfolding down the block. An older gentleman, accompanied by a footman, had just taken delivery of several bunches of moss roses from two young flower girls.

The girls' expressions were pinched with fury, while the overweight fop, overdressed in a plum-coloured coat and silver-buckled shoes wholly unsuitable for the street, smiled down at them with appalling condescension. He threw back his head in laughter, then turned and ambled away. His footman, clearly uneasy, hesitated before following, his arms filled with the stolen flowers.

Perry's mouth tightened. No coin had changed hands.

His suspicion was confirmed when the older flower girl wrapped her arm around the younger. The smaller child's shoulders shook with silent sobs.

Familiar rage rose in Perry's chest. It was just the sort of cruelty his father would have found amusing during his own wretched reign as Earl. He strode across the street without hesitation.

"Good afternoon, ladies. Do you require assistance?"

The older girl looked up, one hand gripping a basket of blooms, the other still embracing her sister. They were barefoot, clad in well-worn, repeatedly mended frocks—dark calico, clean, and threadbare. Her ruddy face was set with a belligerence that reminded Perry of Emma. "Tha' skinflint refused to pay us and walked off with our profits for the day! We be orphans, we be, and we need tha' coin!"

His jaw clenched. "Did he offer a reason?"

"Said we should feel privileged to serve a gentleman like him." Her voice wobbled despite her anger. She could not have been more than fourteen. The younger child, perhaps nine, peered up with tear-streaked cheeks.

"And 'ee called us hussies!" the elder girl burst out.

"Said we could make up our profits on our backs. But oi'm a good girl, oi am! Oi never go among boys!"

Fresh tears welled in her brown eyes. Perry looked up and down the street, but the man had vanished.

These girls were clinging to the margins, and this loss might well tip the balance. He pasted on a mild smile.

"I shall pay for his flowers."

The girl immediately stiffened, then raised her chin with a pride worthy of a duchess. "Oi do no' want no charity."

Perry withheld a wince. He should have anticipated her reaction based on her indignant protests. "Then allow me to make a purchase."

He glanced back to where Emma and Jane were approaching, drawn by the commotion.

"These ladies are visiting from Somerset," he said smoothly, gesturing to the sisters. "Miss Davis has spoken most fondly of her garden. I had promised her flowers. Might you have anything of fine quality?"

The older girl's expression transformed as instinct took over. "Oi sell only the finest, sir. Got primrose, wallflowers, and green lavender. No roses, though ..." She looked regretful but held up her basket.

"Miss Davis, would you care to inspect the wares and give your opinion?"

Emma stepped forward solemnly and examined the bunches. "These are flowers of excellent quality, Mr. Balfour."

"How much for all of them?" he asked.

The younger child perked up, sniffling, as the elder calculated.

"That'd be one shilling, sir."

Perry hesitated with exaggerated incredulity. From the

corner of his eye, he saw Emma tuck a stray curl under her bonnet—discreetly flashing three fingers in the process.

He straightened. "One shilling? For such beauty? I cannot in good conscience pay less than ... three."

The younger girl's mouth dropped open while her sister beamed. "Cor, sir, tha' be right kind of you!"

Perry drew out his purse and, careful to conceal the transaction from the street, passed her the coins. She smartly scanned the crowd before concealing the shillings somewhere on her person. He then took several bunches of primrose and lavender, which he handed to Jane, and passed more blooms to Emma before gathering the last of the wallflowers himself.

Bowing slightly, he said, "Thank you, ladies. As you can see, Miss Davis is delighted."

Emma smiled down at her bouquet as if it were a priceless treasure.

"Ye be welcome, mister!" The girls spun on their heels and disappeared down the lane, their basket bobbing behind them.

Perry exhaled in relief, following Emma and Jane back to the carriage. The footman opened the door, and the sisters climbed in with their spoils, still holding the flowers. Perry followed, settling back with the scent of lavender and primrose wrapping round him like a perfumed cloak.

"It smells like a perfumery in here," Jane declared, delighted, her face buried in a bunch of lavender.

Emma raised her head, eyes dancing. "You are a good man, Peregrine Balfour, to help those girls while allowing them their dignity."

He flushed, glancing out the window. "I despise it when the privileged abuse their status. Nobility ought to mean something more than coin and title."

Her mouth curved into a crooked smile. "Well said, sir."

He shrugged. "They deserved our support."

Emma watched him a moment longer, her expression soft with admiration, before returning to fiddle with the blooms in her lap.

After dinner, Perry sat alone in the study, a glass of wine in hand, still unsure what to make of the day. The scent of green lavender lingered faintly in the air, having been placed in vases about the room. The flower girl had not lied—her blooms were indeed sweet.

Richard entered and dropped into the opposite armchair, lifting a steaming cup of tea. He stared at it with a look of suspicion, then scowled before taking a sip.

"Will I ever grow accustomed to drinking tea?"

"There are other unspirited beverages available to you," Perry offered dryly.

"Unspirited," Richard repeated with a chuckle. "Perfectly put. It describes the beverage and myself of late. But I must admit, I feel sharper since I switched to it. Clearheaded. Sophia says it improves my disposition."

He paused, swirling the tea in its cup. "I want to expand the estate's output—secure something lasting for Ethan. He will need every advantage I can provide. An inheritance of his own, perhaps. And I must consider the possibility of future daughters. All of it requires foresight."

Perry regarded his older brother with quiet reflection. Richard had always been the charming one, good-humored, well-liked. But he had not endured their father. He had been sent off to Eton at nine and returned only for brief visits, largely absent during the earl's most vicious years.

Perry, by contrast, had never escaped.

He often thought himself too serious, too shadowed. He could summon charm when needed—most often in the company of rakish friends or worldly women—but it was a masquerade. He rarely smiled with genuine feeling.

Not until the last few days.

Emma had coaxed real smiles from him. She made him laugh. He had even felt … lighter. But that, too, was dangerous. He had nothing to offer her. He was no suitor. He was a spare, living on his brother's grace.

Richard's voice pulled him back. "What of you, Perry?"

He frowned. "What about me?"

"Do you have any thoughts for your future?"

Ah. Here it was. Big brother's obligatory appeal to purpose and self-worth. Ever since Sophia had come into his life, Richard had become insufferably introspective. There had been discussions of legacy, of meaning, of family.

But Richard had not endured their father's gaze in the dead of night.

Perry deflected. "Are you cutting off my allowance?"

"Of course not," Richard said, straightening in his chair. "It is your right to benefit from the family fortune. It is only fate that made me the heir."

Perry gave a glib smile. "Then I shall continue frittering my coin on worthless pursuits. It is my obligation as a man of leisure."

Richard leaned forward, undeterred. "I have been reflecting on something. Did I ever tell you—on my twelfth birthday, our father arranged for two street women to visit my bedchamber?"

Perry went very still.

"I ran," Richard continued. "Locked myself in a guest room for days. A maid smuggled me food." He gave a hollow laugh. "It was ... grotesque. Did he ever—? I mean, with you—?"

Perry's heart thudded painfully in his chest. The walls of the room pressed inward. He could not speak.

Change the subject.

"Our father lived for pleasure and died of the pox," he said lightly. "What more is there to say?"

But his tone was too smooth. He could feel it.

He rose to his feet. "If you will excuse me, Trafford is expecting me."

That was a lie, but he needed air. Space. Anything but this.

Richard's voice stopped him at the door. "Perry."

He froze.

"If you ever need to speak of it—truly—I am here. I wish I could have done more to protect you."

Perry forced a scoff, masking the roiling mess beneath. "How sentimental you have become since you married, Saunton."

But he could not quite pull off the sneer. Not when he remembered what Richard had given him in those early days of grief—freedom. Options. The first kindness he had known in years.

He wanted to say thank you. But his throat tightened. The words would not come.

"Goodnight, Richard."

His hand trembled on the handle. And then he was gone.

CHAPTER NINE

"It is despicable how you treat the boy. Allow me to take him to my home and educate him properly."

July 1809, Peregrine's maternal grandfather to the late Earl of Saunton, on the boy's fourteenth birthday.

∾

When Perry awoke, he found that the weather had turned gloomy overnight. A torrent of deafening rain roared against the roof and windows so that one could barely hear one's own thoughts. Perfectly fitting for his dark mood.

His valet cheerfully dressed him, chattering on about the heavy downfall and how it had prevented Cook from going to market, despite Perry's best attempts to glower him into silence.

Eventually, he made his way downstairs to the breakfast room, feeling far worse for wear. He had drunk wine until the early hours with Trafford, who had waxed poetic about a widow he was currently pursuing—and even read aloud some rather pitiful verse he had composed for the inane woman.

It had all been intolerable, hence the wine. He had even contemplated seeking out Lady Slight. Just a fortnight earlier, he had enthusiastically visited the woman at her townhouse in Grosvenor Square, but now the thought of returning to her was singularly unappealing—for reasons he preferred not to examine. The widow, it seemed, had lost her allure.

So he had drunk and debated and smoked cigars until he was sure everyone at Balfour Terrace had long since retired, returning home at last to stumble into his room in the family wing.

Now, near midday, he squinted against the glare in the breakfast room, where every available lamp and candle had been lit to ward off the dismal gloom. He was dismayed to find the entire family present—including the Davis sisters. His brother and Jane sipped coffee, while the countess tackled a hearty portion of eggs and ham with obvious enthusiasm, no doubt due to her current condition. Emma sat quietly, sipping her tea, while Ethan babbled ceaselessly, each syllable another hammer-blow to Perry's aching head.

He had hoped to avoid them all by coming down late, but they must have either risen late themselves—or, worse, waited for him to eat.

He passed the chattering assembly without a word of greeting, nearly tripping over the chair piled with cushions so that Ethan could reach the table. Clenching his jaw in repressed irritation, he skirted around his nephew and made his way to the sideboard, dishing up a generous portion of eggs and ham and adding a thick slice of toast.

Returning to his usual seat, he scowled in confusion at the wrapped package resting on the table before him.

"What is this?" His tone was hostile—he heard it himself—but a sinking feeling gripped him, warning that something deeply unwanted was about to occur.

Emma, seated directly across from him, leaned forward slightly to examine the package he indicated with his fork. "It is a birthday present—from Jane and me. Sophia mentioned the occasion after dinner. Our family always makes a bit of a fuss, so we thought ..." She gave a small shrug.

His chest tightened. His jaw slackened.

It had been ten years since anyone had acknowledged his birthday.

Ten years since he had walked in on his father with the village girl. The last birthday that had meant anything at all —before his father's descent into madness.

Panic rose, swift and choking.

There was no fifteenth birthday. That day does not exist.

He repeated it in his mind like a litany until the ache in his chest eased and the memory retreated.

"I do not want it," he snapped.

The room fell silent. All chatter ceased. The clink of cutlery halted. Everyone stared.

His brother's brow furrowed with concern that Perry neither wanted nor deserved. He only needed to be left alone. To forget. Not to pretend he was someone worthy of kindness. Of love. He was a dark soul, and there was no redemption in store for him.

Emma calmly reached across the table and picked up

the package. "We did not mean to offend you. We thought it would be a kind gesture."

"Feeling guilty for your ingratitude, more likely," he sneered.

The words were cruel. He nearly winced at himself. He was being a belligerent bounder. But he needed these overtures to stop.

Emma lifted a hand to her brow and looked down at the linen-wrapped gift with an air of disappointment. He hated himself for the expression on her face.

Richard spoke, trying to ease the moment. "Brother, this is my fault. I told them you would appreciate it. Please, sit and have breakfast in peace."

But Perry could not. He shoved back his chair, nearly knocking it over, and stalked out of the room without another word. His face burned. His thoughts were a tangle of shame and fury. He needed—desperately—to find a drink.

PERRY SAT ALONE in the narrow library, staring at the brandy he had poured. At present, he was merely a man who had poured a drink before midday.

But if he drank it ...

If he drank it ...

If I drink it, I become my father.

His brother's recent crisis over the same matter, just a few months prior, suddenly made a sickening sort of sense. Perry would pay any price not to become the man who had sired them.

Light footsteps echoed on the parquet flooring, soft and certain. He knew who it was without turning.

"Did I do something wrong?"

He dropped his head into his hands. "No, Emma."

"Oh."

He exhaled slowly. "My birthdays have never been joyful occasions. I do my best to forget them. You took me by surprise, and ... too many unwanted memories surfaced at once."

Her skirts rustled as she came nearer, then she slipped quietly into the chair beside him. He breathed in the subtle scent of chamomile and wildflowers. The darkness within him eased, just slightly. His shoulders relaxed.

Still staring blankly at the rows of book-laden shelves, he clenched his jaw and preempted the words forming on her lips. "I apologize for my ingratitude. It was thoughtful of you."

"Thank you. I am sorry your birthdays have been so horrid."

He curved his mouth into a humorless smile. The books across from him stared back with stoic indifference, unmoved by the moment, just as they had been unmoved by all the years before.

"Will you give us lessons today?"

"I shall."

"If you would prefer to take the day ... although it is raining, and—"

"I would rather remain busy."

"Oh."

Perry stilled. Emma acquiescing so easily unsettled him. Next, she would offer comfort, perhaps friendship. And from there, it would be but a short, fatal step toward ... more.

And that must not happen.

He turned his eyes to her. "It is pronounced rain, by the way."

"What is?"

"You said rah-ahning. It is raining. Rhymes with Spain."

To his annoyance, Emma took no offense.

"Truly? I never noticed! Rah-ahn ... Spain ... ray-ahn ... Spain ... raaayn ... Spain ... rain ... Spain." Her face lit up. "Did I say it correctly?"

"You did." He arched a brow. "Why is your hair still untamed?"

He watched her stiffen at the jab. "The earl does not currently employ a lady's maid, so his man of business will be hiring one for us."

"Ah, yes. My brother did very little entertaining before he married. Except, of course, for single female visitors of a particular persuasion."

Emma scowled, as he had expected. At his indelicate innuendo, she stood abruptly.

"I shall be in the breakfast room with Jane when you are ready."

She stomped from the room, her steps heavy with irritation.

Perry grinned, suddenly buoyant. It was so very easy to bait her.

Taking hold of Perry's hand, Emma stepped into his embrace. He led her through several steps before sweeping her into a twirl—only for Emma to land squarely on his foot. Perry yelped, squeezing his eyes shut as his square jaw tensed.

"I apologize."

"You did that on purpose."

"Why would I do that?" she asked, all wide-eyed innocence.

"Because you are angry with me, and instead of expressing it, you have chosen to passively attack me every chance you get."

"That sounds far too complicated. A simpler explanation might be that I am clumsy and not very good at dancing."

He glared down at her, resentment stiffening every line of his six-foot-something frame. Emma sucked in a breath as she stared into those startling eyes—emerald green flecked with gold—even in the midst of mutual vexation.

The music from the pianoforte came to an abrupt halt.

"I am so tired!" Jane's lament interrupted their eye combat.

In unison, they turned to find her slumped over the bench, fatigue writ large on her features.

"Are you still having trouble sleeping?" Emma's brow furrowed. Jane rarely struggled to sleep. She could relax in the middle of a thunderstorm, or a family debate about crop rotations.

"Ever since arriving in London, I cannot sleep until the sun rises. Perhaps it is all the excitement. I fear I cannot play another note!"

Perry's deep voice sent a traitorous shiver across Emma's skin. "I need to practise the steps with Emma. You may rest, Jane. Until she masters the basic movements, there will be no further advancement, so I will simply count out the beat."

Jane nodded and stood, smoothing her skirts. Even in exhaustion, she looked elegant. She drifted across the room and curled up on a nearby chaise.

Turning back to Emma, Perry drew a breath, visibly composing himself. "Can you make a sincere effort to learn the steps?"

"I am such a lummox. I shall never learn this," she muttered.

He sighed. "Emma, the inability to dance is not a character flaw. It is a matter of persistence and practice. This might be more difficult for you than for some, but you can do it."

Emma inclined her head. Perhaps she could try harder.

Perry began to count in a low, steady voice. "One, two, three—confound it!"

He broke away, limping several steps as he tried to conceal his agony. Emma winced.

"I am sorry."

"We have been at this for an hour, and I swear you grow heavier with each step. For such a little thing, you are astonishingly solid. Where do you pack all that weigh—"

His gaze dipped. A strange expression flickered over his face, and he abruptly bit off the rest of the sentence.

Emma looked down. Had she spilled tea on herself at breakfast? She craned her neck to peer down her bodice, then raised a single brow at him.

Perry was now staring at his boots, muttering to himself.

"Perhaps it is cumulative?"

He blinked, confused. "Pardon?"

"Perhaps each time I step on your foot, the pain accumulates?"

"Perhaps," he snapped. "Or perhaps you are deliberately stomping harder every time."

"Do not be ridiculous. I would never hurt you on purpose. Tell him, Ja—"

A nasal snore interrupted her. They turned to the chaise to find Jane fast asleep, her mouth open in unflattering repose.

Perry stared. "Does your sister require a physician?"

"I do not know. She seems fine except for failing to sleep at night. Perhaps a little more excitable than usual, but mostly herself. I think the anticipation of the ball must be keeping her up." Just the previous morning, the earl had announced his intention to host a ball, the first to be held at Balfour Terrace—or any Saunton holding—since Richard had inherited the title. It was to be attended by friendly peers and allow her and Jane to practice their entrance to society among familiar faces. Familiar to the earl and Sophia, that was, not Emma and Jane. Jane had clapped her hands in gleeful pleasure at the news, while Emma had prevented a groan from escaping her lips. She had not wanted to sound ungrateful.

"I suppose she will fit right in with the usual Season schedule, then."

"Late to bed, late to rise?"

"Of course. No person of good breeding is familiar with early morning," Perry quipped.

"Well, that settles it. I do not belong here. I still rise early every morning!"

Perry frowned in disagreement. "It was a jest. Richard himself goes riding at sunrise since you arrived and Ethan is sleeping through the night."

Emma quelled her own irritation. Irritation that Perry still teased her. Irritation that she could not master the simple steps of the waltz. Irritation that she was so utterly distracted by the pleasure of being encircled in his powerful embrace that she simply could not calculate where her feet were supposed to land each time he attempted to tutor her.

Not to mention irritation that she still wore her frumpy gowns, while he was so perfectly attired every time she saw him.

He looked especially fine, despite his sour mood, in his buckskins, snowy linen, and navy wool coat, while she still wore her worn-out muslin. Pursing her lips in displeasure, she breathed in deeply through her nose to settle her nerves.

"If you will be patient with me, we can try again."

Perry walked back and placed his hand on her waist. Once again, her heart fluttered at the feel of his warmth seeping into her skin. Blowing a fortifying breath, she willed herself to concentrate as he took up her hand in his.

"One, two, three; one, two, three; one, two, three; one, two, three ..."

Somehow, this time, perhaps in the absence of music to distract her, Emma stepped in time and they completed several repetitions without incident. As they drew to a halt, she laughed joyfully, looking up at him. "We did it!"

Perry bent his head to look down at her, a strange expression crossing his face as his eyes dipped to her chin. Emma froze in anticipatory silence, barely daring to draw breath as the moment stretched into eternity. As slowly as the movement of the sun across the sky, he lowered his head. In dizzying delight, she realized ... "Are you going to kiss m*mphh*—"

All further words were cut off as his warm, firm lips found hers and Emma received her very first kiss.

Quivering delight spread from her lips. In raptures, she raised herself onto her toes to press closer to him, his spicy scent entrancing her senses. Dropping her hand, his arms gathered her closer, bands of steel and muscle as he encircled her and lifted her off her feet to press his lips to hers.

Emma was dizzy with sensation, reminding herself to breathe, taking in air before losing herself further into the maelstrom as her hands stole over his broad shoulders.

She murmured in surprise when their kiss deepened. He tasted of coffee and fruit as he gave a low growl of approval, intensifying her own response.

"I have dreamed of this ..." he whispered in her feverish skin as he nuzzled her cheek.

A loud snore caught Emma's attention. In a daze, she remembered her sister—her innocent, younger sister—was just fifteen feet away and could awaken at any moment. Perry sluggishly raised his head. His eyes slowly regained focus.

A look of rousing horror crossed his visage while she continued to gaze up at him and he down at her. Slowly, he stepped back and, for several moments, they just stared at each other.

"I ... shall ... see you tomorrow ... at breakfast." With that, he sank into a tense bow before bolting out the door. Emma watched his exit with dazed delight, lifting her fingers to stroke her lips in bemusement.

She had fervently wished to be the object of his interest if even for a few moments, and it would seem that she had received far more than she had bargained for when she made her plea to the universe.

Perry definitely was interested in her. Now that she possessed such knowledge, she would need to ensure she did not act on it. He was a rogue, and he would never pursue an honorable courtship with her. If he were ever to marry, it certainly would not be to a country mouse with tangled hair and atrocious style. It would appear she had wished for fire, and now ... now it threatened to envelop her entirely.

CHAPTER TEN

"A real man does not concern himself with the feelings or emotions of women or other inferiors. It makes him appear weak. Fear not, son, I will teach you to be a true gentleman."

July 1810, the late Earl of Saunton to his son, Peregrine, on his fifteenth birthday.

~

"I am warning you, Emma! If you snap at me one more time, I shall plant you a facer, and you will have to explain to the Balfours why your eye is blackened!"

Emma sighed heavily and slumped back in her chair. "I am truly sorry."

"I must confess it flabbergasted me when you insisted we sit in the drawing room and embroider. You hate to embroider. Is that why you are such poor company today, or is there another reason?"

Emma stared down at the tangle of threads stretched

over her embroidery frame and chose to obfuscate. "It is so frustrating that I never improve at this."

"You never improve because you attack it in the same ill-advised manner each time. If this were any other subject, you would take a moment to reflect, perhaps approach it differently, with patience—but we both know you have no true interest in needlework."

Emma had hoped it would distract her from the embrace with Perry, after reading had failed to settle her thoughts. Jane was right. She had attacked the embroidery in a frenzy, all while stinging her blameless sister with sharp words. Carefully, she picked at a poorly placed thread to remove it.

Jane lowered her head and resumed her needlework, which looked faultless. "So ... the embroidery is the reason for your foul mood?"

Emma licked her lips. "Of course."

"So, it has nothing to do with the fact that Perry left during our dancing lesson?"

She hesitated. "Of course not."

"Or that he kissed you?"

Emma stabbed her thumb with the needle, dropping her embroidery frame as she flushed in humiliation. Her eyes remained lowered as she mumbled, "How do you know that?"

"I was only pretending to sleep for the final few moments. I pretended to snore as a discreet way to interrupt, once it became clear the two of you needed to be interrupted."

"Thank you."

"My pleasure. I knew there was something between the two of you. But what does it all signify? Will he court you?"

Emma groaned and dropped her head into her hands. "That seems rather far-fetched. He is a rogue, after all."

"Not that far-fetched. The earl had a terrible reputation, but it is clear he is reformed. He spends all his time with Sophia and Ethan when he is not engaged in business. Who is to say that Perry is not prepared to follow his brother's example?"

Emma raised her head and contemplated the Monnoyer still life above the fireplace. It was exquisite in its detail—a vase overflowing with trailing blooms. The riot of colors—from blossom pink to turkey red and deep burgundies—felt more lifelike than any painting ought. She imagined, for a moment, what she might look like in a gown of such richness, while she tried to untangle the knot of feelings in her chest.

"I dare not hope for such a thing," she said at last. "I cannot allow myself to fall in love with a man I cannot rely on. It would break my heart."

Jane tilted her head, her eyes thoughtful. "That is a possibility, then? That you could see yourself falling in love with Peregrine Balfour?"

"I admire him, despite his excesses. He is intelligent and … he possesses so much potential, if he could only apply himself."

"Oh, my goodness," Jane breathed. "I would never have thought of such a man for you, but now that I have seen you together … it is clear there is a connection. A deep one. Perhaps—"

Emma waited, but Jane left the thought trembling in the air like the rain clouds pressing against the windows.

"Perhaps?" she prompted gently.

"Well, you love lively debate, and he is an enigma—a

challenge, if you will. As for his interest in you—you are steadfast, loyal, the very essence of reliability. Perhaps the orphan in him seeks your attention."

"Orphan? You are so fanciful, Jane."

"The man was barely five when his mother passed away, and his father died while he was still a lad. Perhaps he was one of those boys kept in the nursery, entirely neglected by a cold father. Is it truly inconceivable that Perry is starved for love and affection? And we both know there is something dark in his past—just look at his temper this morning at breakfast. Who has their day ruined by receiving a gift? There is a story there. A compelling one."

Emma squinted at her sister in surprise. "When did you grow so insightful?"

"I am a woman now. You just never noticed because you still think of me as your little sister. But I have grown up, surrounded by love, and I can see that not everyone has been as fortunate. One day, I hope to have a large family of my own. The Davises have much to bring to the world, Emma—in how we love, in how we live."

"Yes, you do have much to bring," Emma replied softly. "And I apologize if I have condescended to you in the past."

Jane waved her embroidery frame in the air with a dramatic flick. "Forget about it. It is the natural order of things for big sisters to mother their siblings. But do not think I missed your deflection. I stand by what I said: you have much to offer that gentleman. It would not surprise me if something develops—despite your best intentions to protect your pride."

"*Pride!*"

"Sister, it is no secret in our family that you are so terrified of embarrassing yourself that you avoid socializing entirely. You are intelligent and enterprising, but you could be more adventurous—willing to pursue your own path outside of Papa's interests."

Emma's jaw dropped. "What the blazes, Jane?"

Jane shook her head in gentle reproach before setting aside her frame and needle. She picked up her cup of coffee and sipped deeply, then returned it to the saucer with calm precision.

"It is not ladylike to curse," she murmured primly. "Mama made me promise I would encourage you to meet gentlemen and try new things."

"What? She made *me* promise to protect you!"

"Then we both have our orders, do we not?" Jane said sweetly. "And I believe you should take a chance on love."

Emma's gaze turned wary. "Jane, I appreciate that you are an optimist. But I cannot give my heart to a man who cannot love me back."

"Nothing ventured, nothing gained," her sister replied, unabashed.

Emma let out a long, regretful breath. Jane's advice was terrible—well-meaning, yes, but hopelessly misguided. They both liked Perry, that much was true. But Jane believed in a future that could never be. His behavior that very morning had proven it: fleeing their embrace like a frightened rabbit. That was not the act of a man intent on courtship.

No. Emma would stick to her original plan. She had come to London to help Jane meet a suitable young man, and once that was done, she would return to the comfort and safety of Rose Ash Manor. There, she would assist Papa with the new estate, just as she always had.

And if foolish, romantic fantasies of a life with the enigmatic Mr. Balfour teased her thoughts—well, she would sweep them into the farthest corners of her mind.

They were nothing more than dreams.

Trafford wavered unsteadily on his feet as he concluded his rambling recital, flinging out one arm with drunken flourish and inadvertently flinging droplets of claret onto Perry's head. A few men seated around the glossy walnut table offered a lackluster clap. Trafford bowed dramatically, then collapsed into his creaking chair with the smugness of a man who fancied himself Byron reborn.

Perry stared into his own burgundy-hued wine, feeling as though it were staring back—mocking him. He felt hollow. Again. Always.

He wondered what Emma was doing at that very moment.

The other men launched into an amicable quarrel over whose verse was the most inspired—Perry stifled a groan. The evening was devolving into absurdity. If he could trust himself in her company, he would be at Balfour Terrace, perhaps seated across from her in the drawing room, engaged in the kind of sparkling debate he had come to crave.

But no. He could not risk her. Everything he touched eventually wilted or burned. His very presence seemed to stain the good in others. His brother was the only soul who had survived him unscathed—and even that had been a close call.

The flickering sconces on the dark panelled walls did little to illuminate the corners of the room, where tobacco smoke curled lazily above velvet armchairs and lacquered card tables. The hum of male voices mixed with the clink of cut crystal, muffled by thick Turkish rugs. White's was exclusive, prestigious, and filled with men who fancied themselves philosophers—but Perry saw only masks. He was tired of masks.

He could not allow Emma to be dragged into the shadowy pit that was his past. To desire her was perilous. To act on that desire would be unforgivable.

Confound it! Stop thinking about it. Stop thinking about her.

Brendan Ridley leaned closer across the table, lowering his voice beneath the din. "Is it just me, or have these evenings grown particularly asinine of late?"

Perry huffed out a breath. "Perhaps. Or perhaps it is our own state of mind that is shifting."

Ridley frowned. "Hmmm. I do not know. After our little carouse the other night, I felt positively wretched. I cannot even remember what prompted us to drink that much."

"That might have been my fault," Perry admitted, rubbing the bridge of his nose. "I was in a foul mood and encouraged a handful of idiotic drinking games. I sought to forget my thoughts by drowning them."

Ridley's brow furrowed, eyes glassy under the flicker of lamplight. His chestnut hair fell in loose waves over his collar as he tilted his head, trying to recollect. A long-time friend of Richard's from their Eton days, Ridley had married into the extended family when his sister wed their cousin, the Duke of Halmesbury. A good man, despite his frequent flirtations with mischief.

"Did we go to Balfour Terrace that night?" he asked cautiously.

"We did."

"Blazes." Ridley looked alarmed. "I cannot recollect a single moment."

"We were only there briefly. You said very little."

Another drunken clubman rose unsteadily to perform a loud, horrendous ode to a barmaid in Kensington. Perry winced at the rhymes, then turned back to Ridley—who had not yet dropped the thread of their conversation.

"Why are you so maudlin, friend?" Ridley asked, studying him.

"I am thinking about a woman."

Ridley grinned. "Ah, well then! That I can help with. I happened to encounter Lady Slight, and she mentioned you—glowingly. Apparently, you spent a memorable night together last month?"

Perry gave a noncommittal shrug. "It was ... pleasant." But not memorable. Certainly not in comparison to—

"Well, it is not how the widow remembers it. She would be delighted to receive another visit. I could not even charm my way through her door in your stead. She remains rather taken with you."

"I did not mean I am thinking of women." Perry drew a long breath. "I meant one woman. Singular."

Ridley's grin faded as comprehension dawned. "Ah. A particular young lady has caught your attention?"

"Yes. But there is nothing to be done about it." The confession left Perry's mouth before he could second-guess himself. It was a strange relief to speak the truth aloud, if only once. He could not tell Richard, of course. His brother would immediately intervene to end the acquaintance. And perhaps he should. But Perry was not ready. Not yet.

"She is unavailable?" Ridley asked. "Do I know her?"

"You met her the other night. At Balfour Terrace."

Ridley blinked, confused. "I do not remember meeting

anyone. I thought Saunton no longer permitted loose women near the family wing?"

Perry's gaze sharpened. "She is not a loose woman. She is a houseguest. Saunton and the countess are sponsoring her for the Season."

Ridley sat back slowly in his chair, the color draining from his face. "Good Lord, Perry. Tell me you are not taken with a young lady?"

Perry cleared his throat, stiffening his spine. "It will pass."

"Blazes, I hope so," Ridley muttered. "You are younger than I am! Please do not tell me you are considering the parson's noose. What would I do with myself? Left alone in the company of these buffoons?" He gestured toward the other club members—one of whom had begun weeping in earnest over his own ode to a lost mistress.

Perry summoned a mirthless chuckle. "Never fear. It will pass. No young lady deserves the likes of me."

A flicker of genuine concern passed across Ridley's features, but Perry raised his glass quickly in a toast to forestall further inquiry. He could not afford sympathy tonight.

Not when his heart already lay in pieces on the drawing room floor of Balfour Terrace.

"One, two, three; one, two, three; one, two, three." As the music came to a close, Perry drew them to a halt.

When they stopped fully, Emma's face lit up, her coal-black eyes shining as he stepped back and released her hand. "I did it! I completed the entire set!"

"You did. You were remarkable."

"Thank you so much, Perry. You have been a wonderful instructor."

"I concur," Jane called from the pianoforte. "I have tried to teach Emma many times, to no avail. You have performed a miracle."

Perry suppressed the swell of pride her words stirred. "Emma deserves the praise. She has worked very hard at this."

"I could not have done it without you. You are ... an excellent dancer." Emma dropped her gaze, a becoming flush blooming on her cheeks.

Perry's pulse kicked. Was she thinking about the kiss, as he was? He had labored to keep it from his thoughts, avoiding any time alone with her, terrified he would yield to the temptation to kiss her again—worse, to seduce her. She responded with such fiery innocence, and he had no right to kindle that flame.

She was meant for a gentleman. A true gentleman. One with honor and a future, who would marry her and give her a home and children. Perry had nothing to offer but charm, regrets, and a family name he barely deserved.

"If we are finished for today, I would dearly love to take a nap." Jane's interruption was pointed.

Emma frowned. "You did not sleep again?"

"I did not. Who can sleep when our first ball is nearly upon us?"

"You do not want to attend with dark circles under your eyes."

"Precisely. That is why I wish to lie down." Jane's eyes sparkled with mischief. "In fact, you finish discussing any further preparation for the dances, and I will leave you to it."

Perry narrowed his eyes, suspicion rising. Jane was matchmaking. That had been no casual exit.

I am alone with Emma.

His breath shortened. Every fiber of his being was straining with awareness. Days of waltzing instruction, hands on her waist, her perfume in his lungs, the way her eyes danced when she caught on to a step. He longed to devour her again. The taste of her lips haunted him.

He must leave. Now.

He turned toward the door.

"Are we ever going to speak about it?" Her voice was low, tremulous—but it stopped him as effectively as a shout.

"Speak about what?" He kept his face averted. He dare not look at her—his wild, glorious creature with storm-dark curls and eyes that unpicked every knot of his soul. One glimpse and he might forget every vow he had made to protect her from himself.

"The kiss. Our kiss." The words were scarcely above a whisper.

He swallowed hard. They were not meant to be alone. He had no plan for this moment.

"Jane thinks you could be honorable. That you might court me, if you were encouraged."

His chest ached. How he wanted to deserve her. But he could not. He must not.

"You think I am dishonorable?" he asked, hoarse.

"I do not know. I think you are invested with much potential, but you bury it so deep only the most astute observers can see it."

He flinched. *Potential?* No, she was wrong. She might be brilliant, but she did not know him. Not truly.

Spinning, he stalked toward her and leaned over her

chair, his voice harsh. "I am acting with honor, Emma. I have stayed away from you, have I not? There are no hidden depths to plumb. What you see—" he threw out his arms, presenting himself like a rogue on a stage—"is all there is. So no. We shall not discuss what happened. And we certainly shall not spend time alone."

He turned on his heel and strode into the corridor, slamming the door behind him.

The flash of pain in her eyes would haunt him. But it was better this way. He would rather bruise her heart now than destroy her completely later.

CHAPTER
ELEVEN

"He died. Did I forget to mention it? My memory is not what it used to be."

July 1811, the late—and frail—Earl of Saunton, to his son, Peregrine, on his sixteenth birthday, in response to a query about his maternal grandfather.

∽

After the dancing lesson, Emma had little time to dwell on her interaction with Perry or his remark about lacking depth. The first delivery of their gowns had arrived, much to her relief. The Duke and Duchess of Halmesbury were expected for dinner, and she had been terrified that she might be forced to wear one of her frumpy frocks, despite Signora Ricci's confident assurances of timely delivery.

The countess had arranged for her lady's maid to assist Emma and Jane in dressing for dinner—a complicated feat for one abigail to prepare three ladies. Sophia had adjourned to her chambers early to ensure there would be ample time for everyone.

Emma lifted her hand to toy with an errant curl, her nerves fluttering. She could only hope that Miss Toussaint could repeat the prior miracle with the hair tonic, despite the limited time at hand.

Ethan moved a chess piece on the board between them, his small brow furrowed in fierce concentration. After a careful moment, he released the knight to complete his move. "And then," he continued, his voice dropping in pitch as he checked for eavesdroppers, "Papa galloped in Hyde Park!"

Emma gasped. "What? That was terribly naughty!"

"Papa said it was sunrise and the park was mostly empty, so we could risk it for a few minutes."

Across the room, the earl raised his head from the book he was writing in. "Ethan! That was meant to be a secret," he said in an admonishing tone that held more amusement than reproof. "Now Emma will think we are ne'er-do-wells who flout the rules of Hyde Park."

Ethan's brows knit. "What is a *nair-air-dwell*?"

"It is a little boy who makes his papa look like a scoundrel in front of the ladies," Richard replied with a theatrical sigh.

"What is a *scown-drill*?"

Chuckling, the earl rose and crossed the room. Leaning down, he scooped Ethan up into his arms. The boy squirmed and giggled in protest. "Papa! I am in the middle of a game!"

"Chess is for little lads who keep their secrets. Come along. I shall teach you the meanings of your new vocabulary."

"Are we really nair-air ... dwells?"

"How about I explain it first and you may decide for yourself?"

Emma watched their affectionate exchange with a sharp pang of longing. Would Perry one day have a son? Would the boy have dark curls and piercing green eyes like Ethan? A lump formed in her throat. Would she ever have a son of her own? She pressed her lips together, the sudden wash of emotion threatening to rise.

Desperate for a distraction, she stood abruptly and summoned Jane to join her in their chambers to await their turn with Miss Toussaint.

Two hours later, she tilted her head from side to side in front of the mirror, taking in the unfamiliar figure reflected back at her.

"You look so beautiful, Emma!" Jane's voice was thick with emotion.

Emma turned, startled. "Are you crying?"

"It is just ... I have never seen you like this. Sophia!"

Her sister's voice trembled as she called for the countess, who came to stand behind Emma. Her reflection appeared in the mirror beside them as Emma stared, hardly believing her own eyes.

"Signora Ricci is an artiste," Sophia murmured. "The cut of the dress perfectly suits your figure, and that color—Mazarine blue silk—" she bit her lip.

Emma turned her head. "Are you going to cry, too?"

"You just look so beautiful," Sophia whispered, her eyes glistening.

Miss Toussaint had tamed Emma's hair into a cascade of glossy curls, artfully mounted into an elegant coiffure. Along with the deep blue silk of the gracefully draped gown, Emma was forced to admit that she had never looked so comely—despite her mild discomfort at the low-cut bodice, which revealed the upper slope of her bosom. She was, quite possibly, fit to meet a duke—a peer second only to royalty.

"If you are concerned about meeting the duke, do not be. He is the kindest gentleman of my acquaintance," Sophia assured her gently. "He and the duchess are fully aware that this is a practice dinner for you both, and they will do everything they can to set you at ease."

Emma smiled at Sophia's reflection in the mirror. The Balfours had turned out to be as generous and warm as her own family, and despite her earlier misgivings, she was profoundly grateful for all they had done.

"Thank you," she murmured. "For everything."

Sophia looked close to tears again. She cleared her throat and touched her middle in that same protective gesture Emma had noticed more and more of late. "It has been our great pleasure, Emma. What you did for Ethan can never be repaid. The earl is ... so relieved that his unintentional neglect has caused no lasting harm. A family like yours, cherishing our boy until we knew he existed ... it is more than we could have hoped for. You nurtured his character—and his genius."

Emma gave a tremulous smile, blinking back the tears that stung her own eyes.

"Goodness! Look at us." Sophia reached for a handkerchief and gave a little laugh. "We are turning into watering pots. Come. We must go down and prepare for the arrival of the duke and duchess."

She ushered them from Emma's room, and Emma took a moment to smooth her skirts. She could not help hoping that Perry would be at dinner, despite her very best intentions to keep her distance from the rogue. If he had found her desirable before, what would he think of her now—

elegantly attired and coiffed like any other lady of fashion?

The evening began without incident. The Duke of Halmesbury was warm and composed, with the imposing appearance of a Viking god, towering over the earl and even Perry. The duchess was a genial young woman with unusual brandy-colored eyes that glinted beneath the gaslights. But Emma barely noticed the impressive couple after Perry entered the drawing room.

His emerald gaze had found her instantly—and to her great, irrepressible gratification, it had remained fixed on her for the rest of the evening.

They were seated beside one another at dinner, and he kept her engaged in animated conversation while the footmen served the first course. Despite her earlier resolve, Emma could not help but bloom beneath the glow of his attention. For the first time in her life, she felt beautiful.

"Thank you, Timothy, but I shall not have the soup tonight."

Perry's confident voice rang out, cutting through the hum of conversation. The footman froze in confusion, halfway to placing the bowl before him. The table quieted. Perry's smirk was unmistakable as he met Emma's startled gaze.

"It was a jest, Timothy. You may leave the soup."

The servant exhaled in visible relief and lowered the bowl gently before retreating. The other guests resumed their conversation as though nothing had occurred.

Emma thumped him lightly on the thigh beneath the table with the back of her fist. "You did that to make fun of me!" she whispered.

Perry grinned, boyishly pleased with himself. The soft lighting made his features appear younger, less guarded.

"I merely demonstrated what would happen if you ever dared disdain the soup."

She pressed her lips together to smother the giggle building in her throat. "In that case, Sir Galahad, I thank you for sparing me from the gravest of social crimes."

"Heaven forfend you commit social suicide over a bowl of broth."

The giggle escaped. She laughed aloud, and the sound was a delight—light, silvery, and so unforced that it seemed to catch even the duchess's notice across the table, who smiled faintly at her.

Emma flushed, dipping her head to sip her soup from the side of her silver spoon like the well-coached lady she was trying so very hard to be.

Perry was enjoying dinner with Emma at his side in the lavish Saunton dining room. Not in the practiced, feigned manner he had cultivated over the years to conceal his thoughts—but genuinely, viscerally enjoying her company.

From the moment he had entered the drawing room earlier, he had seen the difference in her. His wildflower had found her confidence. She stood with poise, her chin lifted, her gaze bright. The transformation was not only in the graceful fall of her Mazarine-blue gown or the artful sweep of her dark curls. No, it was something internal—a glow from within that rendered her incandescent.

He had made certain to arrange a seat beside her for dinner. How could he not? She had pulled him into her orbit, and there was no use pretending he wished to resist it.

After his jest with the soup, she had thumped his thigh

beneath the table, and it had taken every scrap of his control not to seize her hand in his own and trace the elegant curve of her fingers. Bare fingers. She had removed her gloves for dinner, and the sight of her unadorned skin was enough to distract him with the notion of how soft her skin would feel against his.

He clenched his jaw, suppressing the surge of whimsy. It was no longer mere fascination. He was, he feared, falling into infatuation. Despite his best intentions to stay away—to protect her from his darker inclinations—he had failed miserably. He was a moth to her flame, and the worst part was that he no longer wished to pull back.

Emma leaned in with a mischievous gleam in her eye. "Did you notice that Jane and I both sipped the soup from the side of our spoons? Without instruction or supervision? I believe we might be ready to dine without your constant oversight, Mr. Balfour."

Perry chuckled, the sound low and warm, but his focus remained on the graceful slope of her neck. The candlelight danced across her skin, golden and tempting. He dragged his gaze higher with effort, avoiding the view afforded by the bodice of her gown.

He leaned back slightly, attempting composure—and caught the duke observing him from the head of the table. Halmesbury gave him a knowing smile before returning his attention to the earl. Perry blinked, then realized he had failed to respond to Emma's teasing.

"So," he said smoothly, "you claim to be prepared for an evening without my guidance, Miss Bluestocking?"

"I am quite certain I could manage," she replied pertly, tilting her head just enough for another curl to tumble against her cheek.

"But would you want to?"

The question left his mouth more softly than intended. There was humor in it, yes—but beneath the jest lay something that felt perilously close to hope.

Emma stilled, the jest fading from her expression. She glanced at him, her gaze unwavering. "No. It is better when you are present."

His heart stopped. The words were simple, but her sincerity hollowed out his chest.

He drew in a deliberate breath, inhaling the delicate chamomile fragrance that had been teasing him all evening, and let it sink into him—this moment, this closeness, her sweetness. He would remember it, cling to it, when the time came to step aside and let her go.

EMMA SAT ON HER BED, her gaze unfocused as her thoughts drifted back to her earlier exchange with Perry. It pained her that he thought so little of himself. Over the past days, he had been a marvelous tutor, guiding her with patience and cleverness. Thanks to him, she believed she could now survive the upcoming ball without incurring any great disaster.

There could be no doubt—Peregrine Balfour possessed untapped potential. The problem was not capability, but intent. He had no desire to mature, no interest in embracing the responsibility that lingered just beyond his reach. That, she reminded herself sternly, was why she must avoid him. She had no wish to suffer the heartbreak that would surely follow if she allowed her foolish heart to wander too far.

Her fingertips lifted unconsciously to her lower lip, tracing the place where his mouth had pressed in a kiss of such fire, she had trembled for hours after. She had not known such intensity could exist—an embrace so consuming, it stole breath and reason alike.

Shaking her head, she dropped her hand and exhaled deeply. No good could come from dwelling on impossible dreams like some heroine in a gothic novel. Her sister had been wrong to encourage her, and she had been wrong to listen—just because she wished it were possible that Perry might come up to scratch.

Soon, Jane would meet an eligible gentleman, and then it would be time to go home. She had a life to return to. A *real* life. This world of elegance and moonlit kisses belonged in books, not in her practical future. *This is Elizabeth and Darcy's fault,* she thought irritably. *They planted these ideas in my head with their everlasting love and glorious misunderstandings!*

She allowed herself one final moment of reflection—one last bask in the memory of his regard—before rising from the bed and tightening the sash of her wrapper. She needed a distraction. A new book, perhaps, to see her through what would otherwise be a restless, tormented night.

She padded to the door and turned the handle, easing it open.

And stopped dead.

"What the living blazes—" she gasped, clapping her hand over her mouth in alarm, praying her outburst had not woken anyone in the family wing.

Perry stood in the hallway, framed in the doorway, staring down at his Hessians as though he had been in the middle of a fierce debate with them.

"I could not stay away any longer," he said, still speaking to his boots.

Emma's breath hitched.

He was disheveled—his jacket missing, shirt unbuttoned at the collar to reveal the strong line of his throat. His sleeves had been rolled up, exposing the lean muscles of his forearms and the dark sable hair that dusted his golden skin. The lamplight from within her room fell over him like a benediction, and Emma had to clench her hands into fists to stop herself from reaching out and touching him.

Her heart surged with reckless joy even as her conscience screamed a thousand warnings.

He had come to her.

And now everything was in peril.

PERRY HAD STRUGGLED with his conscience since dinner. Emma had always been a temptation, but now—artfully attired, confidence blooming across her expressive face—she had become utterly devastating to his equilibrium. Her mere presence lifted his spirits. Her cleverness, her fire, the spark in her eyes when she laughed or challenged him—they undid him completely.

For weeks, the only shield he had possessed was the memory of her plain gowns and unfashionable hair. Now, even that fragile defense had crumbled.

He had tried to leave the house. Truly, he had. His boots had carried him down the corridor with every intention of seeking distraction among his friends, but somehow—without conscious thought—they had taken him here. To her door. And there he had stood, caught between longing and honor, until the door opened and she appeared like a vision conjured by the ache in his heart.

"I could not stay away any longer," he confessed, still staring at her slippers, ashamed and desperate all at once.

Emma said nothing at first, but she opened the door wider, allowing him in. Gently, she closed it behind him. Her fingers trembled ever so slightly on the handle.

"What is this?" she asked quietly. "Between us?"

"I do not know," he replied, lifting his gaze at last to meet hers. "It is powerful, is it not?"

"Not unlike the orbit of the moon around the earth." Her answer, so characteristically Emma, tugged a smile to his lips.

He could not remember the last time he had smiled this much. Since the day she had marched into the drawing room at Rose Ash Manor, she had brightened his world like starlight on black water.

Reaching out, he took a single dark curl between his fingers, letting it coil around his knuckle. "You looked beautiful this evening," he murmured. "A true lady of the ton. Except ... well ... you."

She tilted her head in bemusement. "Except me?"

"I meant ... you are better than any debutante or belle of the Season. They pale beside you."

Emma's dark eyes widened in wonder, and he saw it—hope blooming in their depths.

"My defenses are crumbling, Emma," he said softly, his voice hoarse. "I do not know how to protect you from myself anymore."

Her brows pulled together, gently furrowing her smooth brow. "Protect me? From what?"

But Perry could not answer. Not without unravelling the past he had spent a decade burying. Instead, he stepped closer. Slowly. Deliberately. His gaze dropped to her lips as he bent his head, giving her every chance to turn away.

She did not.

When his lips brushed hers, it was as though time paused.

Soft. Tentative. Reverent.

Emma made the smallest sound of wonder—a sigh, a breath, perhaps a whispered name—and Perry cupped her cheek, deepening the kiss with aching restraint. He kissed her slowly, reverently, as though he were memorizing her. Her arms lifted to twine gently around his neck, and he felt her lean into him, trusting, warm, entirely present.

He kissed her again—longer this time—until he had to pull back for breath, pressing his brow to hers.

"Emma," he whispered. "Sweet, feisty Emma."

She smiled up at him through lashes dark with emotion, and his heart fractured and healed all at once.

He drew her into his arms, holding her tightly but chastely, like something precious he could not bear to relinquish. Her cheek nestled against his chest, and he pressed a kiss to the crown of her head, memorizing the way she felt there. Perfect. Home.

I wish she could be mine. Forever.

But that was not his fate.

He had this moment. This kiss. This joy. And then he would let her go, so she might find a future worthy of her heart.

HE TASTED of wine and mint, Emma had discovered, while their lips molded together in a deep, spellbinding kiss. Her heart raced as she leaned into the strength of Perry's arms, safe in the circle of his embrace. There was a quiet desperation in the way he held her, as if he had yearned for this moment as long as she had.

They had not spoken of what this night might bring. He had made no promises, and she had not asked for any. But there, in the sanctuary of her softly lit room, with the hush of night around them, Emma could not bring herself to resist. She did not want to. Not now.

She had been fighting her attraction to the charming rogue since the day they met, and now—now that he had kissed her as if she were his very breath—she could no longer pretend it was anything less than love blooming in her heart. She trusted him, even when he claimed he could not trust himself. She believed in the goodness she saw in him, even if he could not yet see it in himself.

Perry's breathing was ragged as he drew her near, pressing his cheek to her temple, brushing a reverent kiss there before lifting her chin to seek her mouth once more. This time, the kiss was softer—slower—but no less intense. She felt his thumb brush the corner of her lips as he deepened it with gentle insistence, and her knees nearly gave way beneath the sweet pressure of his mouth moving against hers.

He pulled back slightly, his forehead resting on hers, both of them breathless.

"You are extraordinary, Emma," he whispered, his voice rough with emotion. "I have never met anyone like you."

She blushed at his words, caught off guard by the reverence in his tone. Her hand found his, their fingers entwining without thought.

"I have never felt this way before," she confessed, her voice just as soft. "You make me feel ... as though I matter."

"You do," he breathed, brushing his lips across her cheek. "More than I ever thought anyone could."

He kissed her again—this one lingering, his lips moving over hers with tender purpose, as if memorizing the shape and feel of her kiss. Her arms slid around his neck, drawing him closer, her fingertips trembling as they brushed the nape of his neck.

Perry's hands settled on her waist, then one slid up her back to cradle her head as he kissed her once more, deeper this time, yet still tender, still reverent. Emma sighed into him, her entire world narrowed to the feel of his lips and the aching sweetness that bloomed in her chest.

The moment was exquisite—achingly perfect. Not a single part of her wished to rush it. She wanted to remember every heartbeat, every breath, every soft sound he made against her skin. This was not a kiss of seduction. It was a kiss of longing. Of truth.

He pressed his lips to her forehead. "I should not have come," he whispered. "But I could not stay away."

Emma looked up at him, her eyes luminous. "I am glad you came," she replied, her voice steady. "Even if this is all we are allowed. This one moment."

They stood there, holding each other in the quiet hush of the night, their foreheads touching, breaths mingling, the unspoken words between them as powerful as the kiss they had just shared. Emma knew that something had changed. That this was not simply desire. It was something deeper. Something lasting.

No matter what the future held, she would carry this moment with her always.

CHAPTER
TWELVE

"Perry, it is most unusual that you have never left home to attend school like other boys—men—your age. As the new head of the household, I ... I wondered if you had any thoughts regarding your future?"

July 1812, Richard Balfour, the newly titled Earl of Saunton, to his brother Peregrine on his seventeenth birthday, two days after their father passed away.

∼

Emma woke midmorning and stretched with a luxurious sigh, the warmth of lingering memories bringing a faint smile to her lips. The night before shimmered in her mind like moonlight on water—Perry's arms around her, the tender weight of his body beside hers, his kisses like a benediction pressed along her temple and jaw until she had drifted to sleep.

Now, she was awake and alone, the sunlight slipping across the floor, and a bittersweet ache settled in her chest.

She had shared something extraordinary with him. Not merely a kiss—though there had been many, each one reverent and breathtaking—but a sense of trust and affection so deep it had made her feel cherished.

Love?

The thought struck her like a wave. She sat up, startled by the realization. Could she have fallen in love with a man as unrepentantly rakish as Perry Balfour?

Surely not. And yet ...

She pressed her palms to her cheeks, trying to cool the warmth there. Perhaps it had all been too heady, too enchanting. He had held her with such reverence, spoken to her as though she mattered—not as a passing amusement, but as something rare and treasured. And yet he had stopped short of any behavior that might ruin her.

He had protected her.

That thought alone offered a sliver of hope. But still, questions chased through her mind. Had he stepped away because he cared for her, or because he did not? Was he sparing her reputation ... or sparing himself responsibility?

Emma sighed deeply, drawing the counterpane tighter around her. Her joy waned under the weight of uncertainty. If Perry intended to pursue her honorably, he would court her openly. Perhaps he would. Perhaps the restraint he had shown was proof of his better nature—of an intention to woo her properly.

She prayed he would.

Rising from the bed, she tied her wrapper at the waist and tried to marshal her thoughts. She needed to be practical. To think. To steady herself. That was the sensible thing to do.

A small stack of torn cotton squares lay on the bed—an impulsive decision made to distract herself from overthinking. She had begun tearing an old night rail, her hands needing something to do, and before she knew it, the pile had grown. Not her best idea, perhaps, but in the moment, it had kept her from dissolving into a puddle of sentiment.

A knock at the door startled her. She jumped, one hand pressed over her heart.

"Come in!" she called.

The door swung open to reveal the countess, elegant as always in an blue and cream day gown that perfectly suited her golden hair. Behind her, Jane trailed in, rubbing her eyes and looking pale and weary.

"You failed to sleep again?" Emma asked with concern.

Jane groaned as she dropped into the nearest chair. "I do not understand it. I have never had trouble sleeping before. London is simply too exciting. My mind refuses to quiet until the sun rises."

"I offered to send for the physician," Sophia said with a trace of worry. "But your sister insists there is no time."

Emma blinked. "No time?"

Sophia's face brightened. "Signora Ricci has sent a new delivery, and the new lady's maid has arrived. I thought we could have you and Jane try everything on and see what adjustments may be needed."

At the mention of new gowns, Emma's spirits lifted. Fresh gowns meant possibilities. New beginnings. And perhaps, another opportunity to see Perry. She ought not to hope—but she could not help it.

"That sounds delightful," she replied, smoothing her wrapper. "I shall dress, and then we can go down."

As the other women stepped further into the room, Jane's gaze fell upon the pile of cotton squares on the bed.

"Emma ... what is that?"

Emma froze for a moment. "Oh. I tore an old night rail

that had grown too worn. I thought I might use the pieces to practice embroidery."

Sophia's brow lifted delicately. "We have spare fabric for that, my dear. I can have some sent up."

Jane, despite her sleep-deprived state, fixed her sister with a long, skeptical look. "Embroidery? This is the second time I have heard of you voluntarily taking up a needle."

Emma straightened her shoulders. "I mastered the waltz, did I not? I thought I should attempt to conquer another weakness."

"Well." Sophia offered a gentle smile, even if her eyes still held questions. "That is very industrious of you. The gentleman who marries you will be fortunate indeed."

Emma smiled faintly, uncertain whether her secret was safe—but knowing at least that her heart, for better or worse, was no longer entirely her own.

Perry ran a hand through his hair in mounting frustration. He had slipped from Emma's rooms before sunrise, careful not to be seen. There had been a moment—just a moment—when he was certain someone else stood in the corridor with him. He had paused, holding his breath, listening. But the silence remained unbroken, and he was left alone with his guilt.

Back in his chambers, he had dressed hastily and fled the townhouse before the household stirred. As the soft light of dawn bathed the quiet Mayfair street, he had wandered aimlessly until his feet took him to his club, where he picked halfheartedly at a solitary breakfast.

He could not stop replaying the night before in his mind. The way Emma had looked at him. The way she had touched his face. The way her kisses had unmade him. He had long suspected she would undo him entirely, and now he knew it with certainty.

He had held her. Kissed her. Lost himself in the heady wonder of her affection. But he had not gone further. Somehow, some part of him—some deep, hidden flicker of decency—had found the strength to stop.

Perry dragged in a sharp breath and clenched his fists to still their trembling. He could not—must not—touch her again. Her gentle affection had already branded him. And still, even now, he imagined her fragrance clinging to his coat. A memory he both savored and cursed.

But he would not ruin her. He could not. To steal her future, to tarnish her name for the brief indulgence of his own desire, would strip him of the final scrap of self-respect he had clawed back from the edge of ruin. He had already failed once in his youth—spectacularly—and he would not live through another fall.

Perry inhaled in a rush. *Do not think about that night!*

He ground the heels of his palms into his eyes. He must stay away. No matter the temptation. No matter the cost.

He would see to it that she was safely launched into society and matched with a man worthy of her intellect, her kindness, her fire. Not a wayward scoundrel like himself, born of rot and sin, who had spent too long pretending to be something other than the damaged man he was.

The next time he saw her, he would be cold. Curt. He would say whatever necessary to drive her away.

Even if it meant breaking his own heart.

"Are you listening?" Trafford snapped, startling him.

Perry blinked and looked down at the polished table. "Of course."

"Then why have I repeated myself three times to no effect?"

He sat up, forcing composure into his limbs. "Forgive me. I am not at my best today."

"I should say not. You have been intolerable ever since you returned from the country."

Perry forced a careless smile and lifted his wineglass. "I suspect your new conquest is proving disappointing, and now you seek to cast your vexation upon me."

He downed the contents in one go, the clink of the empty glass on the tabletop punctuating his resolve. "What shall we do tonight, gentlemen? The night is young, and so are we!"

Trafford stared at him, clearly taken aback by the sudden shift in tone. Across the table, Brendan Ridley narrowed his eyes, but said nothing.

Perry ignored both expressions.

Tonight, he would remember who he was: a disreputable scoundrel. And if he could not have the woman he wanted, he would lose himself in every diversion London had to offer.

Let them call him rake and reprobate. At least that was a role he understood.

On the third morning of taking breakfast without a single sign of Perry, Emma finally accepted the truth.

He was avoiding her.

The feckless rogue had become frightened by their connection, and now he resisted it in the only way he knew —by vanishing. She told herself she should be thankful they had only kissed. There was no scandal. No ruin. No risk of a babe. But the knowledge gave her little comfort as she listlessly picked at her breakfast.

"Where is my brother?" Richard growled, addressing his wife with a scowl. "I thought those days of vanishing without a word were behind us. Yet I have not seen hide nor hair of him in three blasted days! He promised to assist the young ladies with their dance instruction, and now the ball is nearly upon us."

"He is sleeping in his bed at night," Sophia said gently, her tone that of one soothing a volatile child. "I know he worries you, but he does come home. Albeit at unusual hours."

Richard's expression grew doubtful. "And how would you know that? I rise at dawn, and I have not laid eyes on him once."

"The servants have said that by the time they enter his rooms at sunrise, his bed is unmade," Sophia said, still in that careful, coaxing tone. "He is at least returning home. That is something."

"It is not enough." Richard's voice deepened with frustration. "There is something I must speak to him about—something of genuine importance—and he dodges me at every turn. This behavior is beyond the pale. I am quite out of patience."

"Richard," Sophia said in a warning tone, her eyes flicking toward Emma and Jane. "Do not frighten our guests."

Emma's stomach twisted at the mention of Perry. She was not frightened—she was furious. And heartsick. And increasingly concerned.

"Emma learned a great deal from Perry," Jane interjected, her voice firm despite the shadows under her eyes. "I can practice with her now and help polish the rest."

Emma caught the flicker of color in her sister's cheeks as she sipped the coffee she had grown so fond of. She was proud of Jane's poise and quick thinking.

"I agree," Emma added smoothly. "Jane and I have tried on our new gowns, and Betty has mastered the taming of my hair." She lifted a glossy curl between her fingers. The new lady's maid, Betty, had taken to her duties admirably after a little guidance from Miss Toussaint—and the mysterious hair tonic that now seemed to work miracles.

"Today we shall run the full set together. You need not worry about us," Emma said brightly.

But worry they must—about Perry.

Her heart throbbed with quiet alarm. Perry was not merely avoiding her. He was retreating from everyone. From life. That deep unease she had sensed in him since the first day in Rose Ash was not imagined. The last few days only confirmed her growing suspicion: he was a man tormented by shadows no one had seen clearly.

Emma's appetite was gone. Her chest ached with the dull pressure of guilt. She had missed the signs—too wrapped up in her own infatuation, her own pleasures. She had been selfish in her pursuit of stolen kisses, never stopping to ask why he so often looked like a man on the verge of unraveling.

She pressed her napkin to her mouth and stood.

"Shall we go practice now?"

Jane looked up in surprise but nodded. Emma needed movement—needed action—or she would go mad from the tumult of worry and resentment that now stirred beneath her skin.

She had a plan forming. And if Perry would not speak to his brother, she would find another way to reach him.

Whatever secrets haunted him, she would no longer stand by and allow them to consume him in silence.

THE TALL CASEMENT clock down the hall tolled twice as Perry entered Balfour Terrace, utterly exhausted. For days now, he had kept to a punishing schedule—riding, carousing, debating—anything to occupy his mind. Anything to keep himself from arriving, once again, at Emma's door.

Because the next time he crossed that threshold, there would be no stopping himself.

The memory of holding her, cradling her as she sighed his name in the solitude of their midnight embraces, still lingered. It mocked him with its sweetness. With what could be, if only he were someone else. Someone honorable. Someone who had not ruined a young woman's life. Someone who had not driven away every soul he had ever cared for.

He would lose Richard, too, if he made the same mistake with Emma. Of that he was certain. His brother would never forgive a betrayal so deep—not toward a young woman Richard now considered family.

Thank heavens he did not know about—

No. Stop. Do not think of her.

Perry ran a hand through his hair, as though he could dislodge the memories that had lodged there like thorns. For years, he had masked the wreckage of his conscience with smiles and glib lines. It was only now—after witnessing Richard's slow, stumbling redemption—that Perry had dared to hope there might be a path forward for him as well.

And then he had met Emma.

And he had remembered the truth. That he was the son of Satan. That no amount of longing could absolve a man of damnation.

Richard was a natural leader, a respected peer. Perry was nothing. Worse than nothing—a destroyer. And if he ever revealed the truth of that night, his brother would recoil. The last shreds of connection he held to anyone would shatter.

He still did not know why their grandfather had abandoned him. As a boy, Perry had pleaded with the old man to rescue him from Saunton Park. To take him to Shepton and save him. And his grandfather had promised he would. But instead, he had vanished from Perry's life altogether.

He had never returned. Never written. Never sent word.

The next thing Perry knew, the old man was dead—and Perry was left alone in hell with a madman for a father and no idea why the only person he had counted on had turned his back.

He had never dared to ask Richard. What if their grandfather had remained in contact with his elder brother all those years? What if Perry had simply been discarded as a hopeless case?

There were too many things he could not say. Not even to the one person who might have understood.

A sharp breath escaped him. These maudlin thoughts were dragging him under.

He missed the numbness. The easy, careless existence of a man who felt nothing and cared for no one. But ever since Emma had slipped into his life, he had begun to feel too much.

His feet slowed. He looked up and found himself outside her room. The door loomed, and without thinking, he raised a hand to press his palm flat against the wood.

Was she asleep beyond? Or lying awake, as he had done each night since?

He ached to return to that peace—to that warmth—to her.

But he must not. He must never again open that door. If he did, he would destroy her.

And this time, there would be no coming back.

He forced himself to move, turning down the corridor toward his own room. He would sleep for a few hours. Then flee the house again. The only reason he returned at all was to feel connected to something—to remind himself he still had family, even if the tie was fraying.

His obsession with Emma had proven what he had always feared: he was not capable of change.

But he could at least protect her. That, he would do. At the ball, he would ensure their connection was broken. Deliberately. Decisively. Something so unforgivable that she would never look at him again.

It was the only way to save her from himself.

Feeling grimly resolved, he reached his door and opened it—

Then froze.

His heart slammed into his ribs.

He was not alone.

A slender figure sat on his bed, lit softly by moonlight through the window. She turned.

"I have been waiting for you."

When the countess mentioned that Perry had been returning home in the early hours, Emma recognized an opportunity to make amends for her insensitivity. She had been so consumed by her own feelings, she had failed to see how deeply Perry struggled. Tonight, she would offer her support.

Long after the household had retired, Emma sat atop the tall bed, too restless to read. She rehearsed her words, fidgeting with her wrapper and twisting her hair into nervous knots.

The door opened without warning.

Emma gasped, her hand flying to her chest. She had not even heard his approach.

"I have been waiting for you," she whispered. So much for preparation.

Perry stood silhouetted in the darkened doorway, shoulders tense, his expression unreadable. He looked exhausted—wan and drawn—but her heart leapt at the sight of him.

He closed the door behind him with deliberate care.

Reminding herself that she had come for his sake—not to chase foolish dreams—Emma slid from the bed to stand at its foot.

"I see that," he said coolly.

The frost in his voice wilted what remained of her confidence. Her shoulders dropped.

So much for fire. So much for feistiness. She was completely unarmed.

"I wanted to ... verify that you were all right." The words sounded weak, even to her ears. She flinched inwardly.

They had shared something intimate—deeply intimate—yet still undefined. He had made her feel cherished even as he wrestled with his demons, and she had done nothing to help. She had failed him.

"All right?" Perry's voice was bitter. "You should return to your bed."

"I know I may not seem helpful to you, but I am not as fragile as you believe," Emma replied, forcing steel into her voice. "I assist my father with estate matters and I raised Ethan as though he were my own. I may be young—perhaps even naïve—but I am observant and practical, and I care for you."

Perry stepped forward. "Get out of my room."

Emma faltered. "Why? What have I done to upset you so?"

"Your presence upsets me."

The words landed like a slap. Sharp. Deliberate. Wounding.

She swallowed past the ache in her throat, her pride fraying. But she had come to offer comfort, not demand it.

"I see," she murmured, turning toward the door.

She reached for the handle—but Perry caught her wrist.

"Emma—" His voice broke on her name.

She turned slowly.

He tugged gently, drawing her into his arms. His lips descended, soft and searching, and she met him halfway, rising onto her toes to kiss him back with aching relief. His mouth lingered on hers before he turned his face into her hair, drawing a deep breath like a drowning man who had broken the surface at last.

"You always smell like freedom," he whispered against her ear. "My sweet, fiery Emma."

She closed her eyes, her hands resting against the warm breadth of his chest, her heart thudding against his as he held her tightly, as if letting go would cost him too dearly. For several quiet moments, he simply held her, his hands stroking the length of her back, grounding himself in her presence.

At last, he exhaled heavily and pulled away.

"Will you be at our ball?"

There were several moments of silence. Emma wished she could see his face, read his expression, understand what troubles he shouldered. "Of course I will be there."

His tone was odd, mounting Emma's misgivings that she had failed him in some manner.

"Will you dance with me?"

A long pause. "Perhaps. Goodnight, Emma."

Dismissed, she departed, casting one last glance to her beloved rogue before gently closing the door to stand in the hall and wring her hands in frustration. For a moment, she had made some progress with him, but then the moment had evaporated to leave her more worried than before.

CHAPTER
THIRTEEN

"You are an amusing fellow, Balfour. Care to join us for a drink?"

July 1813, Lord Julius Trafford to Peregrine, on his eighteenth birthday.

∽

Emma woke to the drumbeat of rain pounding on the windows, the heavy downpour blurring the glass as thunder rattled the panes in a bone-deep clatter. She blinked up at the ornate cornices of the ceiling, the patterns lost behind a sheen of unease. Was it an omen? A warning? Something wicked in the air?

She chewed her lower lip as she traced the source of her disquiet. Perry. His strange mood the night before haunted her. She missed him fiercely—but deeper still was the fear that he carried a weight she did not understand. If only men were as easy to comfort as four-year-old boys. If Ethan was troubled, she simply lifted him onto her lap and coaxed out the worry. But Perry was a grown man. He guarded his pain with silence, cloaked it behind rakish charm and veiled remarks.

Emma sighed. *I shall become a lie-abed, worrying over that enigmatic fool.* She was no help to anyone like this, not to Jane, not to Sophia—not even to herself.

Throwing the counterpane aside, she rose with new purpose just as a soft knock echoed on the door. Betty had arrived to assist her.

By midday, the rain had stopped. The sun emerged tentatively, streaking the tall windows of Balfour Terrace with light, as if nature herself wished to apologize for the gloomy start. The day passed in a dizzying flurry of motion. The countess oversaw a small army of servants and tradespeople. Flowers arrived in abundance, silver candlesticks were placed with precision, and beeswax candles thick as a man's wrist were arranged to soften the glow of the gaslights that already set the townhouse apart.

Every inch of the place gleamed. Windows sparkled, furniture shone, and a breeze of lavender and lemon oil wafted through the halls. Balfour Terrace was transformed into a golden dream of luxury.

Meanwhile, Emma and Jane practiced every motion and step of the evening ahead, determined to wear their new gowns and slippers with poise. Emma, especially, refused to trip or falter—*not tonight*. Not when she was being granted this extraordinary chance.

At midmorning, Sophia gathered them for tea in the music room, a tranquil sanctuary tucked away from the bustling preparations.

"Emma, I believe the evening will go well," the countess said, folding her hands in her lap, "but I must make a confession." Her fingers fidgeted. "It is rather a small ball, by society's standards. A hundred or so guests—those we like best. I admit, I become terribly anxious in large gatherings. I was willing to invite more, but Richard insisted we keep it manageable."

Emma's jaw dropped. "You get nervous? But you always seem so perfectly composed."

"I have years of practice." Sophia's smile was a touch rueful. "But yes, there are situations that make me uneasy."

"I feel dreadful. We would have forgone the ball altogether, Sophia. Truly, there was no need to put yourself through such a thing."

Sophia tilted her head, a warm reprimand in her eyes. "It is our great joy to introduce you and Jane to society, especially after all you have done for our family. I only wanted to apologize that it may not be as grand as you expected."

Jane leaned forward to clasp her hand. "Emma is quite relieved she need only contend with a hundred guests. Any more, and she would have swooned from fright. Our country assemblies are charming—but they do not boast footmen and chandeliers."

Emma smiled at her sister, pride softening the lines of her face. Jane had grown into herself, just as she had always known she would.

And Emma? She had drawn the eye of a gentleman—though not one who meant to pursue her. The moment dimmed again, her joy tinged with melancholy. She supposed that was her fate: to guide Jane through her debut, to fade into the background, to nurse silent heartache for a man who could not love her in return.

"Thank you, Sophia," she said quietly. "It was my greatest pleasure to care for Ethan. And I—we—are deeply grateful for the kindness you have shown us. It was difficult to lose him so abruptly, but now that I have seen how dearly you and the earl love him ... I am comforted beyond words."

Sophia's eyes glistened. A handkerchief appeared as if by magic. "When you are with child one day," she warned, dabbing delicately at her eyes, "the smallest thing can send you into tears."

Emma's heart twisted. The mention of future children should have filled her with light, but she could not imagine such dreams without Perry's smile beside her.

Sophia tucked the handkerchief away with practiced grace and rose. "I must see to the final arrangements. I suspect a footman is presently misplacing a candelabrum."

Once Sophia left them, Emma took charge of keeping herself—and Jane—occupied.

"Practice ball gowns? Truly?" Jane groaned as they marched up and down the music room in fine gowns not intended for that evening's festivities.

But Emma insisted. She was determined to ensure she could move gracefully in restrictive garments. There would be no stumbling or slipping—not tonight. She would not fall on her backside before half the *beau monde* the way she had tumbled before the carriage ride to Signora Ricci. That had been the first time Perry's touch had lingered. The first time his eyes had warmed with interest.

She pushed the memory away.

Tonight was not about her. Tonight was about Jane. Her sister must successfully launch and find herself a suitable gentleman. Emma had long suspected that London would prove a poor influence on her heart, and now she was certain. She had allowed herself to dream, to yearn—and now she must find a way to return to Rose Ash Manor with her dignity intact.

So she kept them busy, moving and turning, curtsying and pacing, until the early afternoon.

"It is time for a nap," Emma announced, at last satisfied that she could attend the ball without tripping over her own hem.

"Zooks, Emma! You are a virago!"

"You do not wish to nap?"

"Of course I wish to nap," Jane yawned delicately into her hand. "But need you be so imperious?"

"Determined," Emma corrected.

"What?"

"I am not imperious. I am determined. Tonight will be a success. You will meet dozens of young men who will wish to dance with you. You are as pretty as a princess, Jane."

Her sister's tired face softened. "Thank you. I do appreciate your efforts, I do. It is only ... I am so tired and you are so very demanding."

"I apologize if I have been curt. I am ... distracted, I suppose."

"You are thinking about Perry?"

Emma looked away, her gaze skittering to the window as a twinge of anxiety stirred low in her stomach. She could not speak of it. Not to Jane. Not when her behavior had been so reckless. Her beloved, annoying scoundrel had walked away from her without explanation, and she had no one to blame but herself for believing she might tempt a rogue into changing his ways.

How mortifying. How foolish.

Had she truly believed that Emma, a country mouse with ink on her fingers and unfashionable hair, could ensnare a gentleman like Perry Balfour into falling in love?

Her heart gave a painful squeeze.

If only he would talk to her. If only he would let her help.

"Why do you say that?" she asked carefully.

"Because he never left our side, and then after the dinner with the duke and duchess, he vanished," Jane said. "What do you think happened to send him fleeing?"

Emma's cheeks flushed as she remembered the kiss—the kisses—and the night that had followed. The heat, the tenderness, the whispered words. And then ... nothing. Distance. Silence.

"I do not know," she mumbled. "You would have to ask Perry himself."

Jane sighed. "I had hoped that you ..." She paused, her voice gentler. "I had hoped you would find your own gentleman, Emma. You were both so animated at dinner. I was sure ..."

Emma's throat tightened. Her eyes burned. She blinked quickly and pressed her lips together. It did no good to remember. That magical night only brought pain now.

Perhaps it was for the best. Perhaps it had only ever been a dream. Perry Balfour was a rogue with shadows in his eyes and secrets locked behind his rakish grin. And she had been foolish to imagine he might choose her.

Tonight must be about Jane. Her sister had grown into a graceful, beautiful young lady—one who would surely draw the admiration of eligible gentlemen. Emma would do her duty and shield her sister with pride, even as she guarded her own aching heart.

Still ... as they mounted the stairs to lie down, Emma could not keep her thoughts from straying. She could not help wondering whether Perry would make an appearance as he had promised he would while she led Jane up to their rooms for a lie-down. Her sister was exhausted, and Emma, too, had not slept well since Perry's abrupt departure from their daily routine. They would need their wits about them that evening when they met more than one hundred members of the *beau monde*, who the earl and countess had assured them would be a mix of suitable nobility and gentry.

SINCE THE BALL HAD BEGUN, Emma had kept watch for Perry's arrival.

Sophia had introduced her to a steady stream of distinguished personages, all of whom behaved with exemplary manners. Condescension had been minimal, and several guests proved to be genuinely pleasant. Emma supposed that since Richard had taken his by-blow into his household, he had swiftly learned which acquaintances were worth retaining—and which were best left behind.

"Emma, may I present Lord Lawson and his daughters?" The countess's voice called her back to the present. A swarthy gentleman with graying hair bowed deeply, flanked by two charming young ladies.

Sophia explained that the family was musically gifted—their musicales were the toast of the Season. Emma offered polite compliments and exchanged small talk with the daughters, all the while her thoughts drifting.

Perry had not come.

She kept smiling, kept dancing with the young men Richard introduced, all the while scanning the crowd for a familiar figure. Jane was radiant, dancing joyfully and laughing with charming suitors. Emma felt a flicker of pride—and a piercing ache.

He had said he would come.

As the night wore on and the candles burned lower, Emma began to suspect she would not recognize many of these guests again. Her memories of the evening would be fogged over by longing for someone who never arrived.

Then, sometime after eleven, she stood beside Sophia, listening to the countess's tiny and effervescent cousin Miss Abbott, whose laughter danced through the air like music. But Emma's mind was elsewhere—still scanning, still searching.

And then she saw him.

A familiar head of thick brown hair above the crowd. At first, she thought it must be the earl—she had made that mistake before—but then the crowd parted, and her heart leapt. It was Perry. And just behind him, Lord Trafford.

Her breath caught.

Then she saw the woman on Perry's arm.

Lady Slight. Clad in a gown so tight it appeared sewn directly to her flesh, her red hair perfectly coiffed, her flawless décolletage spilling over the neckline like cream from a dish. She clung to Perry's side as if painted there.

Emma's blood ran cold.

She stepped back from the conversation and slipped behind a nearby Corinthian column to gather her wits in the sheltering shadows. Her heart pounded in her ears.

He planned this. He must have.

To attend the ball—their ball—filled with friendly faces who had come to ease Jane and Emma into society, and to bring her ... it was a declaration. There was no them. No us. No special connection to speak of.

Now it made sense. His vague comment about the dance they once agreed to share. His unfulfilled promise to be present.

He had brought the lovely, wicked Lady Slight to deliver his message. *You are nothing to me.*

Emma placed her palm against the cold marble. She closed her eyes, willed herself to breathe.

Focus on Jane.

Her sister stood a real chance of making a match. Emma would ensure it. Jane was sweet, clever, beautiful. If she could help Jane find a suitable young man, then she could go home. Back to her father, back to her real life. Where she had control. Where she did not hand over her heart to city bucks with green eyes and reckless mouths.

Her resolve firmed, she stepped from behind the column and glanced around for Sophia and Miss Abbott, only to find them elsewhere in the crowd.

"Well, well, if it is not the country mouse."

Emma turned slowly and found herself nearly nose-to-bosom with Lady Slight.

Her last thread of composure snapped.

That obscene display of cleavage. That painted pout. That syrupy tone as the woman openly sneered.

Emma had not intended to confront Perry or his fashionable entourage. But if she were to be directly addressed by the strumpet, then she could hardly be held responsible for what followed.

She squared her shoulders and lifted her chin.

"Rather a country mouse than—than—than an adventuress."

The woman's eyes went wide. "You little upstart witch!"

"You bit of muslin," Emma snapped.

Perry appeared as if conjured, inserting himself with well-timed nonchalance. Emma suspected he had been watching.

"Ladies," he drawled. "Jealousy is such an ugly color."

Emma took a breath.

It felt so good to be near him, even as it hurt her.

Lady Slight smiled coyly. All evidence of hostility vanished from her beautiful, empty face. "I apologize, Perry. I know the young woman is important to your family. We merely quarreled for a moment. No disrespect intended."

Emma repressed a growl at the insincere performance.

Then Perry spoke.

"Lady Slight, come now. You are the widow of an esteemed viscount, while Miss Davis is merely the clumsy daughter of a tenant farmer—gifted some negligible land in an unimportant corner of Somerset. She barely possesses a dowry. You need not adopt any airs with her." His lips curved into a mocking smile as he turned his glittering eyes on Emma. "Does she, Emma?"

He lifted a brow, as if waiting for her to confirm her own insignificance.

Her heart shattered.

Shattered into a thousand sharp, aching shards. The bravado that had surged moments ago vanished like a snuffed flame. She could not even summon the strength to glare at him. She simply stood there—frozen—fighting the rush of tears as the blood drained from her face, her lips, her fingertips.

She had already understood. His arrival with Lady Slight had delivered his message loud and clear.

There is no us.

But this ... this was cruelty. Deliberate cruelty.

Emma had known it was a mistake to come to London. She had braced herself for snubs and mockery. But she had been willing to endure it all—for Jane. Her brilliant, beloved sister deserved a chance at happiness. Emma had hoped, too. Hoped to become a success. Hoped that Perry, the charming, complicated man who had once looked at her as if she were a marvel, might ... might come to care for her.

And now that man had torn her to pieces in public, wielding her deepest fears and insecurities like a dagger.

Even Lady Slight faltered, pity crossing her face at the viciousness of his remark.

The gentleman who had built her confidence ... who had once shielded her from this very woman's scorn ... now eviscerated her with calculated ease.

Emma could not speak. Her throat thickened, her breath caught. She had never, not once in her life, been so thoroughly betrayed by someone she trusted. Her father had protected her. Jane adored her. She had never needed a defense before—because those she held dear had never wielded words like weapons against her.

But Perry had.

And he had struck with precision.

He turned away without another word. "Come, Lady Slight," he said, offering his arm. "The country mouse has been struck speechless. We ought not waste our evening on her when there is much pleasure to be had."

Lady Slight hesitated. Then smiled. And took his arm.

Emma watched them go.

The pain in her chest surged, expanding until it drowned the room around her. The flicker of candlelight. The music. The press of fine gowns and gloved hands and glittering smiles. All of it disappeared.

All she saw was him.

Walking away.

With her.

Was that what she had been? Just a fleeting diversion? A foolish country girl dazzled by a rogue with a crooked grin?

They had shared kisses twice. One night of tenderness. A single night of aching closeness. Had that meant nothing to him?

Had she even qualified as a paramour? Or had she simply been a diversion?

Emma tried to think—to move—but her body would not obey. She stood rooted to the marble floor, breath shallow, eyes burning, mind blank.

She did not know how to recover from this.

"May I have this dance?"

It took several seconds for Emma to register that the Duke of Halmesbury—the blond Viking who had dined with them the week prior—was speaking to her. The earl had introduced him as a cousin, had he not?

The duke bowed and straightened, extending a large, gloved hand. "Please, Miss Davis. It will limit the gossip."

Only then did Emma realize that heads had turned. Members of the *ton*, elegant in silk gowns and crisp evening coats, were watching her. Watching the scene that had unfolded. And now, watching her—alone.

Somewhere distant, her hand lifted from her side and took his.

Still numb.

She was the most petite woman in the room, swept into the dignified embrace of a waltz with the tallest man she had ever seen. The duke topped six and a half feet easily.

Funny what the mind latches onto when one is in shock.

Emma dared not blink. If she did, the tears would come, and she would be undone.

As if sensing her fragility, the duke lowered his baritone voice to just above a whisper. "I have never seen Peregrine so lighthearted as he was at dinner. I was hopeful for him. But now ..." His eyes twinkled with rueful disapproval. "He is acting the arse."

Emma's eyes widened in surprise.

"Come now," he added mildly, "admit that is what you were thinking."

His dry humor pierced through her despair, and her lips twitched. *I live yet. I did not die moments ago.*

The duke watched her with thoughtful gravity as they twirled beneath the ballroom's glittering chandeliers. "Forgive my impudence, but have you considered that he might be afraid?"

"Afraid?"

"Of you. Of what you represent. Great joy is often accompanied by the risk of great pain."

She swallowed the lump forming in her throat. "I know it is fear. He could not truly prefer ... that woman."

"Brava, Miss Davis. No, he does not. Lady Slight is a decorative but empty package. This was a performance— for your benefit. A poor one, I must say."

It was a strange relief, to hear her suspicion voiced aloud. And stranger still, how comforting this duke was.

"What do I do?" she asked softly.

He considered her carefully. "My answer will not please you."

"Please."

"Do you know how Russia defeated Bonaparte in 1812?"

She furrowed her brow. "A tactical retreat?"

"Precisely. It is a strategy often employed in chess as well. I believe you play?"

"I do."

"Then you understand. I think you must leave."

"Leave?" Her breath caught. "Do you mean return home? To Somerset?"

"I do. If you stay, the wound will fester. But if you leave, he may begin to understand what he is losing. He is at a crossroads. Your absence might force his hand."

"How can you be so certain?"

He glanced to where his duchess stood beside Sophia, affection softening his features. "Because I was once that foolish. All men are, at some point. And absence ... has a way of clarifying what we truly value."

Emma turned the idea over. A retreat. Not defeat. A move to provoke reaction.

"Thank you," she murmured.

"No, thank you. I have spent years finding Peregrine to be cold, even charmless. But since the earl's marriage, and through conversations with Sophia, I now understand the depths of what those boys endured. If I had known, I would have done more. But I was too busy with my own complex affairs to notice." He shook his head. "It was uplifting to see him amused at dinner. To see him smile. And I believe you are the reason for it."

His words struck her heart. She had brought Perry joy. *Once.*

"You are practically family now," the duke continued. "And I have spent time with Ethan. I know what you have given this family. Peregrine needs someone strong to stand beside him. I hope he realizes that before it is too late."

Emma gave a small smile. "It is tempting to give up on him. But I am not easily dissuaded from my loyalties."

"And if he betrays you tonight? If he returns to the widow?"

"Then he is not the man I hoped he was."

The duke's smile was touched with sorrow. "Let us hope he is."

When the dance ended, he returned her to Sophia's side and bowed before moving to join his wife.

Emma laughed and smiled for the rest of the evening, floating through small talk, dances, and introductions. But her thoughts remained fixed on one singular plan: to go home. If Perry followed, it would be because he chose to. And if he did not ...

At supper, she conversed with a pleasant young man and said all the right things. If asked later what they discussed, she would have no idea. Her mind was elsewhere.

At last, with Jane chattering beside her, Emma returned to the family wing. Her sister, still flush with excitement, noticed nothing amiss.

But when Emma reached her room and dismissed Betty, she sank to the floor. Silent sobs racked her body as she curled in on herself.

She thought of the best night of her life. Followed by the worst.

She had flown too close to the sun, and her wings had melted. Now she was tumbling, and no one was there to catch her.

But she would not crash.

She would retreat.

And if Perry Balfour ever wished to find his way back to her ... he would have to follow.

CHAPTER
FOURTEEN

"Your turn to buy a round of drinks, Balfour."

July 1814, Lord Julius Trafford to Peregrine, aged nineteen.

Emma could not sleep. Not a wink. Close to sunrise, she rose and opened her door to the family hall so she might listen for the earl's early movements.

At the first light of dawn, she heard footsteps in the corridor. Darting out, she caught sight of Richard striding away in his riding attire.

"My lord, may I speak with you?"

Richard turned back. "My lord?"

"I apologize. I am anxious, Richard. It slipped out."

He compressed his lips, concern tightening his features—as if he already guessed what their conversation would entail.

"Shall we go to my study?"

"Betty has not come up yet. Will it be all right if ..." She gestured at her robe.

"Yes. Come downstairs. I shall send for tea and biscuits."

Emma joined him, descending the stairs together. They crossed the vestibule and entered the earl's study. She settled into one of the ivory armchairs, perching on the edge, wringing her hands in her lap while her mind spun with how to begin.

"Is this about Perry?"

Her lips quivered at the unexpected question. She kept her eyes downcast, dabbing at the corner of one eye with a fingertip. "I must return home this morning."

The earl sighed heavily. "May I speak candidly? I heard about the scene with Perry. I ... know the two of you were forming a bond. Halmesbury mentioned something. Did I do you a disservice by inviting you to London?"

Emma's shoulders eased. Clearly, the entire household had guessed the truth.

"You have been most generous, and I hold no complaint. I am grateful for the invitation—and for seeing Ethan so happy."

Richard exhaled in relief. "Perry is a good man. But our father ... well, he was not kind. Halmesbury believes I must speak to Perry about it—about the past. I should have done so long ago. I fear your departure might be the only thing to bring him to his senses."

Emma had nothing to offer to that. Her mind was already set. "I only wished to inform you and ask that you continue to take care of Jane. I do not wish to stand in her way."

"Of course. I owe you everything, Emma. I will protect

your sister with my life and ensure she meets only the best of men."

She nodded. "May I beg the use of a carriage?"

"You shall have two. There is that new wardrobe to return with, and I shall send footmen to ensure your safety. Naturally, Betty will accompany you to Somerset."

"That is unnecessary—"

Richard cut her off with the practiced authority of a man well accustomed to being obeyed. "You require a chaperon, and Betty is your maid. I shall hire someone else for Jane."

Emma snorted. "A lady's maid at Rose Ash Manor? You jest."

Richard's expression turned positively paternal. "I do not. I will pay her wages. Someone must care for your new gowns—and you. Betty was hired to serve you, and she shall continue in her post."

"But it seems far too extravagant."

"It is employment," he said flatly. "And I know you understand economics. Would you truly wish to deny another young woman the opportunity to serve Jane?"

Emma's mouth closed with a click. Her mother's words echoed in her memory—not all girls had the blessings they did. For someone like Betty, this was security. Independence. And for a new maid, a chance to build a future.

"I apologize. I had not thought of it in that light."

Richard smiled. "Good. I shall inform Betty and have your trunks prepared."

"Thank you, Richard. For everything. I did enjoy my visit, despite ... everything."

He hesitated. "I suspect I shall see you again soon. If I do not, my brother does not deserve you. In which case, you may return for another Season whenever you wish."

Emma rose.

"Emma?"

She turned.

"If there are any ... consequences ... you must inform me. I shall command Perry up to scratch, if necessary."

Emma blinked. "Consequences?"

Richard's gaze darted away. "Yes. You are to inform me immediately if there are any consequences to your stay in this house."

"I ... I suppose." She tilted her head, still puzzled.

"You promise?"

"I promise," she echoed, uncertain but sincere.

He gave a firm nod. Emma took it as the conclusion of their conversation and left.

Before she departed the household, she sought out Ethan in the nursery to say her farewells. To her relief, he took the news well. He was settled, secure. The troubles that had plagued him seemed distant now. They parted cheerfully, with Emma promising to show him around Rose Ash Manor during a future visit.

While Betty and the servants packed Emma's trunks, she and Jane lingered in a tearful farewell.

"I cannot believe Perry said such cruel things to you," Jane whispered. Emma had been forced to explain her decision to depart.

"He is reacting out of fear. Rather like when one of the barn cats is injured and lashes out when we try to help. But if he will not let me near, I cannot keep trying. I will not offer him my heart only to have it trampled. You can overpower a frightened kitten with a feed sack to give it care, but I have no bag large enough to trap Perry Balfour."

Jane tilted her head, processing the analogy. "He is still a wounded child at heart, is he not?"

Emma nodded gravely. "The duke and the earl both alluded to a troubled youth. It appears your intuition was correct, clever Jane."

"Are you sure about leaving? Perhaps if you gave him a little more time—he might come to his senses?"

Come to his senses. Emma's thoughts darkened. She had spent the entire sleepless night trying not to imagine Perry sharing a bed with the alluring widow. It tormented her—the thought of him kissing another woman. While Lady Slight cooed and clung and welcomed him with all the worldly experience Emma lacked.

She swallowed the bitter taste of jealousy.

"I am not equipped for this, Jane. I have no training in heartbreak. I need to go home. I need air and clarity. I need to get away from him."

Jane's voice dropped to a whisper. "Your heart? You are in love with him?"

Emma's voice broke. "I do not know. I think so. I was. Perhaps I still am. I just know I need space to breathe and mend."

Jane's lovely blue eyes brimmed with tears. She gripped Emma's hands. "This is not how it was supposed to be. He was supposed to recognize what he had. You were supposed to make the first match between us."

Emma pulled her into a tight embrace. Jane rested her cheek on her sister's hair, hugging her fiercely.

"You are such a romantic, little Jane."

"It is your fault. You read me *Pride and Prejudice*. And *Sense and Sensibility*. Elinor and Edward overcame everything—"

"They are fictional characters, you ninny."

"I know that. But the author was very persuasive. And when I saw you and Perry—"

"You saw me with my Wickham, I am afraid. Not my Darcy." Emma's throat tightened. It wounded her to say it aloud.

Jane wiped at her cheeks. "So, your Darcy might still be waiting somewhere out there?"

Emma attempted a smile. Given her luck, Perry had been both her Wickham and her Darcy in one infuriating package.

"Will you be all right without me, Jane?"

The question was practical, but it meant far more.

"Do not worry. Sophia and I get along splendidly. I met several excellent young men last night. One even owns land in Somerset. Sophia says we shall depart to the country soon—to Saunton Park—for a house party. I shall be near you again before long."

"I am so glad."

"Thank you for this opportunity, Emma. The men at home are mostly too old or not well read. Or both."

Emma cupped her sister's cheek. "Oh, Jane. It was my great joy to help you. I would let my heart break a thousand times if it meant your happiness."

They shared one last meal with Sophia, Richard, Ethan, and Jane. The morning sun shone soft and golden on the breakfast table as if trying to offer some blessing to Emma's departure. She made her goodbyes, hugged Ethan one last time, and stepped into the waiting carriage with Betty and her trunks—her heart heavy, but her will steady.

She prayed the road home might help her forget the rogue with the glinting green eyes.

And the pain of what might have been.

When Perry finally awoke, the afternoon sun slanted across the floor in long golden bars, and his temples throbbed with an unforgiving ache. He blinked against the brightness, wincing as the sensation of gravel behind his eyelids made him groan. Dragging a hand down his face, he shifted upright—only to realize the sheets smelled faintly of roses.

Roses?

His heart stumbled in his chest.

He sat abruptly, glancing around. Silk sheets. Delicate lace at the window. A tray of refreshments on a side table. The unmistakable scent of Harriet Slight's favored perfume. His stomach churned.

What had he done?

The weight in his chest settled like a stone. Had he truly drunk so much that he had fallen into bed with Lady Slight?

Shame, his old companion, slithered back into his gut with ruthless precision. But this—this was worse than shame. It was anguish. Deep, bone-cutting regret. Because even the idea of being with another woman now—any other woman—felt wrong. Unfathomable.

He had held Emma in his arms. He had tasted her laughter, her trust, her fire. He had vowed, in the private recesses of his heart, that he would protect her from men like him. Had he truly betrayed her so completely?

"Well, good afternoon, Mr. Balfour," a husky voice called across the room.

He turned.

Lady Slight stood by the tray, her golden wrapper tied loosely about her waist. She was elegance and sultriness, but her appeal, which had once stirred some weak semblance of interest, now did nothing for him.

"Would you care for some coffee?" she asked, picking up a delicate china cup.

Perry nodded mutely. Coffee might at least clear the fog of shame from his thoughts.

She handed it to him with a practiced smile, then seated herself lightly at the edge of the bed. Her presence felt suffocating. He sipped in silence, the hot liquid offering little comfort as his mind raced.

His voice rasped with uncertainty. "Harriet ... did we—?"

"Did we make mischief?" she said, one corner of her mouth lifting in amusement. The widow purred, her red hair swinging forward as she grasped the counterpane at his waist and pulled it back. "See?"

Perry looked down and saw what he had not noticed—or felt—in his groggy, wine-fogged state. He still wore his trousers.

Relief surged through him so sharply, he nearly collapsed back onto the pillows like a swooning debutante. Drawing a ragged breath, he clutched the sheet over his chest, his guilt retreating ever so slightly—just enough to breathe again.

"I ordered sustenance," Lady Slight perched like a lioness on the edge of the bed, caging him within her rose-scented sheets. "We might rediscover pleasure this evening, Mr. Peregrine Balfour."

But there would be no pleasure. Not here. Not with her.

Perry's heart—he could no longer deny it—was already occupied. Entirely. By one maddening, miraculous woman from Somerset.

My heart is occupied? The realization hit with the force of cannon fire. *What the devil does that mean?*

"I am afraid I must dress and return home, Lady Slight."

Harriet's expression shifted at once. She sat back abruptly, her wrapper falling open to reveal what many men would have found wildly tempting. But not Perry. Not anymore. The sight did nothing but solidify the regret knotting his gut. This had been a terrible mistake.

"Never say you are enamored with the country mouse?" Her voice dripped disdain.

"Enamored? No," he said, finally standing. "Hopelessly besotted. Wholly in love. Yes."

The words freed him. His gloom evaporated like morning mist, replaced by blinding certainty.

I love Emma.

And he needed to find her. Apologize. Beg her forgiveness. Then—then he would seek Halmesbury's counsel. The duke had guided Richard to redemption. Perhaps he could help Perry chart a course toward becoming the man Emma believed he could be.

"The little chit?" Harriet hissed, her eyes narrowing in rage. "Have you gone mad? What could you possibly see in such a dowdy, awkward creature?"

Perry met her wrath with calm resolve. "A world of possibilities. Hope. A future I never dared imagine until she came into my life."

He threw back the counterpane. Harriet shrieked in shock and leapt from the bed as he stalked toward his wrinkled garments, grimacing. They reeked of wine and roses.

I cannot appear before Emma in this state—she would never believe I had not touched the widow.

He must change first. And then, immediately, he would go to her. He had seen the torment in Emma's eyes after his cruel betrayal.

I need to erase that pain. Somehow.

The next two hours dragged like penance. He quarreled

with the widow, pieced together the hazy details of the previous night, and attempted to soothe her injured pride —not for her sake, but to prevent her from taking vengeance upon Emma. When he finally escaped the opulent townhouse, the sun was already low in the sky.

It was nearing eight o'clock when he burst into Balfour Terrace, heart pounding with purpose.

As he strode across the marbled entry hall, Richard's voice rang out like a whipcrack behind him.

"Peregrine Landry Balfour! I have been looking for you for days, you bounder!"

Perry halted, still facing the staircase in his haste. "I have no time, Richard. I must change, and then I must find Emma and beg her forgiveness—"

"That is regrettable," Richard said, his voice like stone. "Because Emma is gone."

CHAPTER
FIFTEEN

"We shall flip a coin to see which of us pursues the delectable widow, shall we?"

July 1815, Brendan Ridley to Peregrine, on his twentieth birthday.

Perry walked to the staircase and slumped down onto the third step, his knees refusing to function as he landed heavily.

"Gone?"

"She left midmorning"—Richard checked his pocket watch—"approximately nine and a half hours ago. I am afraid you have missed her."

"Gone where?"

"Home. To Rose Ash Manor."

Perry dropped his head into his hands as the last vestiges of his optimism shriveled and died. "She was meant to stay. To find another young man."

"Was that the plan? I venture that your understanding of the young woman is flawed."

Perry had known better. He had always known better. Had he truly believed that fierce, loyal Emma would quietly accept his calculated cruelty and then seek out another suitor? If he was honest, the notion had never rung true. He had not wanted her to find another man. He had wanted to be her man.

The truth was a bitter draft. His entire scheme had been a flawed computation of imagined reactions and warped logic meant to ease his own conscience. In truth, nothing he had done made any sense. He had acted like a man haunted—driven by demons—and in doing so, had destroyed the only good thing to happen to him in years.

If the goal had been to drive her into someone else's arms, why the devil had he humiliated her in public? At a ball held in her honor? What, precisely, had been the plan? To cut her so deeply that some gentleman in attendance—or worse, one who heard the tale secondhand—would inexplicably fall in love with her on the spot?

"Oh, my God. What have I done?"

"Plenty, by my count," Richard said darkly. "But this is not the venue for such a discussion. You will accompany me to my study. Now."

It was not a request. The tone was pure command. Perry had never heard his brother speak to him that way before. It sent a chill down his spine.

With a sickening sense of finality, Perry feared the moment he had always dreaded had finally arrived. His brother would sever ties with him—just as their grandfather once had. The weight of that possibility crushed the breath in his chest. The only faint hope he clung to now was that Halmesbury might help him untangle this wreckage. If it was not already too late.

Perry followed Richard down the corridor and sank into his customary armchair, left of the fireplace. He slumped, staring at the polished toes of his Hessians as if they held the answer to his undoing.

Emma was gone. And now, it seemed, he might lose Richard as well.

The silence in the study was thick. Stifling. As if time itself were suspended, waiting to see which way the sword would fall.

"I have been trying to speak with you for several days," Richard began, his tone clipped and low. "I saw you depart Emma's room the other morning. I prayed it signaled the beginning of something meaningful. But then I watched you, across the ballroom, give her what looked very much like the cut direct—while parading that merry ace of spades on your arm."

Perry flinched.

"She is an innocent girl. And I must admit to my deep disappointment—no, fury—at the idea that you might have ruined her and then broken her heart in such a public and deliberate fashion."

"I did not ruin her."

Richard's eyes narrowed in skepticism. One brow lifted, emerald eyes glinting with barely restrained ire.

"We kissed," Perry clarified, more forcefully. "But her virtue is intact. I swear it."

A tense silence followed. Richard studied him as if weighing the truth for cracks.

"Why?" he asked finally.

"I could not do it to her," Perry rasped, the truth

tumbling out. "I am a second son with no prospects. I have nothing of worth to offer her. But she ... she is a revelation. She deserves a man who can build a life for her. A husband who can give her everything. And I—" He broke off, swallowing hard. "I have only ruin in my wake."

Richard sat very still.

"I see," he said, but there was no judgment in his voice now—only something quiet. Something akin to sadness.

They sat in silence while Perry tried to gauge his brother's mood. Did the fact that Emma still possessed her virtue ease Richard's anger? Might he somehow emerge from this evening still welcome in this household? Still a brother who mattered?

The earl cleared his throat, and to Perry's immense relief, the thundercloud in his countenance began to lift.

"Then it is time we had a proper talk. Halmesbury took me to task for failing to speak with you—about our past. About your youth. He believes my negligence played some part in what happened between you and Emma."

Perry shook his head. "No, Richard. This is not your fault. I am responsible for my own mistakes."

"I do not deny that," Richard replied gently. "But I believe Philip meant something more nuanced. I have shared some of our experiences with him. About the Earl—"

"Of Satan," Perry murmured bitterly.

Richard's mouth twisted. "Yes. Quite. I told him about the women he placed in my bed when I was twelve. The revels. His illness. The madness. The mercury. I also told him about how he kept you shut away—no schooling, no family, no escape. Just spiteful tutors and his own warped attempts to mold you into his image."

Perry's head jerked up. "Wait—what do you mean, no family? What family?"

Richard paused, brows knitting. "You did not know?"

"Know what?"

"Our grandfather tried to take you from Saunton Park when you were fourteen. He was appalled by what he saw when he visited you. Said it should have been a celebration—a young man's passage into manhood—but instead he found you thin, quiet, and clearly in distress. He demanded Father release you to him, but as a peer, Father was untouchable. Grandfather tried for years to gain access to you."

Perry's heart thudded in his chest. "How do you know this?"

"He came to see me at Oxford. Just before he died. He explained everything and asked me to look after you. He made me promise, Perry. That once Father passed, I would ensure you had the safe home you deserved."

A trembling hand covered Perry's face. "He did not abandon me?"

Richard leaned forward, his expression gentle. "Abandon you?"

"I thought he had. That last time I saw him … I was desperate. Father was—pressing. Trying to turn me into some grotesque version of a gentleman. I begged Grandfather to take me with him. He said he would try. Then he vanished. When I was sixteen, I asked Father what had happened. He told me Grandfather had died."

Richard sat back with a pained look. "I am so sorry, Perry. I should have done more. I was so focused on escaping my own torment that I forgot I had a little brother left behind. I should have come home. But after the … incident with the women in my bed—"

"When you hid in the guest rooms for a week?"

Richard nodded. "After that, I could not bear the thought of going back. So I stayed with the Ridleys. Their father was happy to host an heir to an earldom, and I let him. But if anyone abandoned you ... it was me."

Perry stared down at his boots, reluctant but compelled to speak the words that had clung to him for years. "You saved me, Richard. When Father died, and you took over—you gave me the one thing I had never had. The ability to choose my life. Leaving for school ..." He broke off, overcome.

Richard swallowed. "I am glad to hear that. I only wish I had known all this sooner."

Perry rubbed discreetly at his eyes. "Would we have been ready for this conversation before now? I think ... it took Sophia, and your choices, to bring us here. Without them, I do not believe I could have spoken of it."

Richard nodded thoughtfully. "No, I was not in any position to help until I met Sophia. But, Perry ..."

Perry froze, not daring to move lest his brother ask the question he dreaded.

"Is there more to this recent behavior? I understand your pain over Grandfather, but ... this performance at the ball, the dramatics—it feels like something deeper is troubling you."

Perry dropped his head, the heat rising furiously in his face. He knew he was crimson from ear to collar, and he hated how telling the reaction was.

"I do not know what you mean," he muttered into his wrinkled cravat.

Just then, his stomach betrayed him with a loud, accusatory growl.

Richard blinked. "Have you eaten today?"

Perry shook his head, still staring resolutely at the floor.

"Then we shall find you something to eat before we address this mysterious nothing that causes you to blush like a lad caught kissing the vicar's daughter."

Despite himself, Perry huffed a quiet laugh and rose to follow his brother. He could not yet meet Richard's eyes, but he took comfort in the shared silence as they walked toward the kitchens. Whatever came next, they would face it as brothers.

EMMA AND BETTY shared a room at a quality coaching inn, recommended by the earl to the coachman of the lead carriage. Richard had insisted that Betty act as chaperon for the journey, and Emma had agreed to have her maid share the room—both for propriety and the added security. A woman staying alone at an inn could attract unwanted attention, and this way, they would both be safe.

It had nothing to do with her need for distraction.

Having a plan gave her a small sense of peace. They were making excellent time, with fine weather and smooth roads easing their return to the countryside. The rhythm of travel, the familiar sights of hedgerows and rolling fields, provided solace to her bruised heart. Yet when left too long to her thoughts, her mind drifted in unwelcome directions —imagining Perry in the widow's arms. Lady Slight, arching and sighing where Emma might have been. Perry pressing kisses over alabaster skin that was not her own. His hands, his mouth ... giving to someone else what she had only just begun to discover.

She sighed, eyes closed as Betty brushed out her hair, the bristles pulling gently through her curls to ready them for bed. It was not her place. Not anymore. And she must stop thinking of it as though it had been. Perry did not belong to her. He belonged to no woman. Least of all to a country girl with modest means, a modest dowry, and dreams that had overreached their limits.

Emma bit her lip. Would she ever look at another man and feel something again? Perry had been her first stirrings of real interest. Yes, he was handsome—extraordinarily so—but it was more than his striking features or his easy charm. He had made her laugh. Challenged her mind. Shown her how to relax and enjoy the moment. And somehow, in the short time they had spent together, he had seen her. Not just the awkward girl in borrowed gowns, but the woman beneath who ached to be understood.

He had been good for her. Until he was not.

What was he doing now? Her heart winced to think of it. Most likely ... wrapped up in someone else's arms, lips on someone else's skin. She clenched her jaw. Enough.

When she finally climbed into bed, she stretched long across the mattress, grateful for a full day in the carriage if only for the fatigue it brought to her limbs. Sleep, however, might not come easily. Not with her thoughts so quick to wander back to London ... back to him.

There was to be an assembly in Rose Ash at the end of July. Perhaps she might attend. It could do no harm to meet a few local gentlemen. If nothing else, it would be a distraction. And who knew? She might one day find someone honest and kind, someone who could challenge her mind and win her heart. Someone new.

Her pride might be bruised, but her future remained intact. And perhaps, somewhere out there, there was a gentleman who would one day share her love for the country, and estate matters, and the simple, contented life she had once imagined for herself.

She smiled faintly, pulling the covers up to her chin. Yes. One day, she would stop comparing every man to the London bachelor who had stolen her heart like a thief in the night. But not tonight.

Tonight, she simply missed him.

CHAPTER
SIXTEEN

"Are you reading a book on mathematics, Balfour? Never say you are attempting to do something useful with your brain?"

July 1816, Lord Julius Trafford to Peregrine, on his twenty-first birthday.

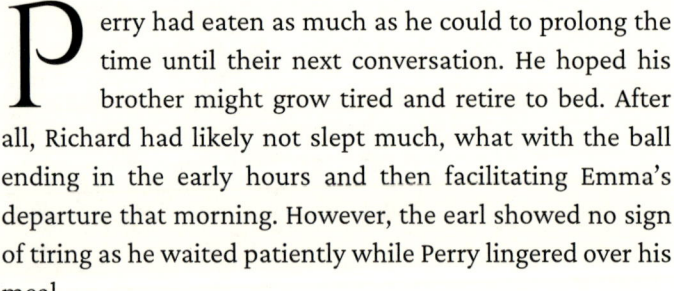

Perry had eaten as much as he could to prolong the time until their next conversation. He hoped his brother might grow tired and retire to bed. After all, Richard had likely not slept much, what with the ball ending in the early hours and then facilitating Emma's departure that morning. However, the earl showed no sign of tiring as he waited patiently while Perry lingered over his meal.

"Halmesbury advised me it is better to have difficult discussions on a full stomach and after a good night's sleep," Richard finally remarked, breaking the quiet. "But with your recent evasions, I can only ensure the food."

"Why must we talk about this?" Perry asked quietly.

"Because I care about you," Richard said, without hesitation. "I cannot let this continue, not when I see it is hurting you. We settle it tonight, little brother. I may have waited too long to offer my ear, but you shall have it now."

"I did not ask for it," Perry muttered.

Richard gave a lopsided shrug. "You asked for it the moment you made a public mess of things with a young woman we both care for deeply. Tonight, you will tell me what troubles you."

"And if I do not?" Perry asked, more weary than defiant.

"Then I shall ask again tomorrow. And every hour I am not otherwise occupied, until you relent."

Perry's chest loosened at the words. He would never say it aloud, but his brother's insistence—his determination to listen—felt like affection. True, familial affection. Richard had always been his one constant since their father's death, but this level of attention ... it was new. And it was comforting.

It was the kind of care Richard gave to Sophia and to Ethan. Perry had never been the recipient of that kind of patient concern.

Except, perhaps, from Emma.

He sighed heavily, the sound catching in his throat. Emma had waited for him in his room that night, offered him her strength, her comfort. And he had known, even then, that he would betray her with cruelty. At the ball she had worked so hard to prepare for.

I truly am despicable.

Now Richard would make him confess—and then he, too, would see how unworthy Perry truly was.

Would I rather it be Halmesbury? No. It had to be Richard. It had always been Richard.

"What should be Richard?" the earl asked, frowning in confusion.

Perry winced. "Did I say that out loud?"

"You did."

"I was thinking I would rather talk to you than Halmesbury."

"Halmesbury already told me it must come from me," Richard replied. "He said it is not his place. That I am perfectly capable."

"He is right."

Richard stopped walking and turned to look at him, a hint of surprise in his expression. "Truly?"

Perry nodded, managing the ghost of a smile. "I imagine he gave you instructions on how to go about this, but you are doing an excellent job of taking me in hand."

"Huh." Richard looked amused. "Well, that is good to hear. I shall remind you of that if you try to squirm away later."

"I think I am ready," Perry said, more quietly this time. "I need help, Richard. I want to make it right, but I do not know how."

Richard tilted his head, watching him closely. "There is something specific troubling you, then? Not simply the memories of our father?"

"There is enough there to haunt a lifetime," Perry admitted. "But no. What burdens me is something I did. Not something he did."

Frowning, Richard resumed walking down the hall. They entered the study together and each took their usual seat, Perry's gaze settling on the deep green wallpaper that transformed the room to a sanctuary instead of a tomb.

He took a deep breath. "Will you forgive me what I am about to tell you?"

Richard gave a soft chuckle. "No matter what it is, Perry, I can almost guarantee I have done worse. You are in no danger of being judged tonight."

Perry cleared his throat. "When I was fourteen, I met a young woman in the village near Saunton Park. She was blonde, delicate, and she smelled of gardenias."

Richard's brow furrowed. "She reminded you of our mother."

"She did. Her name was Laura. She was kind. She listened to me. I thought Grandfather had abandoned me. Father was..." He paused, steadying himself. "He had taken a disturbing interest in shaping me into a man, and I was miserable. Laura worked in the shop, and I began slipping away from the manor to see her. She never treated me like I was strange. I would scrounge for coins, just to buy some trifle so I had an excuse to visit and talk with her."

"She helped you feel human again."

Perry nodded once. "One day, Father came looking for me. I did not hear him come in. He found me at the counter, speaking with her. And the look in his eyes ... I knew he had taken notice. So I stopped going. I thought I had drawn his attention away. After a few weeks, I believed I had succeeded."

He looked down into his lap. "But I had not accounted for my fifteenth birthday."

Richard groaned softly and leaned forward, bracing his elbows on his knees. "He had some twisted notion of what manhood should look like. Forgive me, I think I shall pour us a drink."

"You no longer drink."

"I can make an exception. And Sophia will agree that some memories deserve it."

He walked to the sideboard, poured a single measure of

brandy into two glasses, and returned, handing one to Perry before reclaiming his seat.

"I apologize for interrupting. The horror of my twelfth birthday was revived quite thoroughly when those bawds were planted in my bed."

Perry winced at the memory. He was glad he had not been present that day.

"So, what did the Earl ... of Satan ... do?"

Perry smiled faintly at his brother's quiet encouragement. Richard had never adopted the moniker that Perry used for their father, but he allowed it tonight—and that small concession meant more than Perry could say. His chest ached, a deep, physical pain from the strain of recalling a night he would give anything to undo. He lifted a hand to rub the tension away.

"He arranged for Laura to be in my room that night. As a ... gift."

Richard frowned. "Arranged? You mean—she was willing?"

"She was not. She was a maiden. But when I walked into my bedroom on the night of my birthday, there she sat, trembling and weeping ... and our father was lounging across the room in my armchair."

Richard downed the rest of his drink in a single swallow and shot to his feet, pacing like a storm rolling in. "He did not. Tell me he did not."

"He did," Perry said quietly. "He threatened to ruin her —have her dismissed, cast out of the village, even arrested. Then he offered her coin to stay and ... comply. From the way he told it, she stood no chance of refusal."

"What did you do?"

"I told him I did not want any such gift. That I would see her safely home. He said I had no choice."

Richard made a harsh sound, turned, and hurled his glass into the fireplace. It shattered in a brilliant cascade of sparks and glass.

"You have been doing that quite often lately," Perry remarked, his tone dry.

"It is only the third time," Richard retorted, exasperated, "and this has been a rather dramatic year!"

"May I?"

Richard gestured grandly with a wave of his hand. Perry stood, tossed back the brandy, and then flung his glass in a powerful arc toward the hearth. It shattered with a clean, satisfying sound. "Huh. That does feel rather good."

"There is a time and place for such things," Richard agreed with a faint smile.

Perry's smile faded. "Richard ... if I tell you the rest ... will it help? Will I feel lighter for it?"

"My experience this year tells me yes. Telling someone helps. But we shall not know what more is needed until you finish."

Perry sat again and stretched his neck side to side. Then, with a breath, he continued. "I tried to think clearly. I thought—I still might get her out. So I agreed to give us time. But he refused to leave the room. He stayed, seated like a judge, saying he would oversee my education as a man. That he had failed with you, and would not fail with me."

Richard's expression twisted in grief. "He became that far gone?"

"He had been unwell for years, but near the end, he was entirely changed. But his nature had always been ... distorted. This only made him more volatile."

"What did you do?"

"I pretended to go along. Told him if I was to do this

properly, it must be with brandy, much to his approval. I fetched his bottle, brought it to him and encouraged him to drink up while pretending to drink with him until he passed out."

"Oh, Perry ..."

When Perry looked up, there was a sheen in his brother's emerald eyes.

"I am so sorry," Richard whispered. "I did not know. I never imagined he would ... I would have come home, I would have—"

"You would have come home and been forced to do the same to someone else. A housemaid, a tenant's daughter ... even someone's wife. He would have found someone to hurt. It was better that you were not there."

"Did you ..." Richard could not finish the question.

"No. But she was frightened. I calmed her, hid her in the attics, and then gathered everything I could—coin, trinkets, even items from your rooms I could sell without drawing suspicion."

Realization dawned in Richard's eyes. "You were careful not to take anything a servant might be blamed for."

Perry nodded. "I had planned to run away myself more than once. I already had the bones of a plan. I rode into Saunton, sold everything I could, and collected enough to pay for her escape. I got her back to her home to pack her belongings, then put her in a post-chaise bound for Cornwall, where she had a cousin. I begged her to disappear. To forget the village. To start anew."

"And you?"

"I faced Father's fury. But whatever I endured, it was not what she would have faced had I failed."

They sat in silence. Perry waited, watching his brother, unsure what he would say next. Despite Richard's earlier assurances, surely this revelation crossed some line ...

But after a long while, Richard exhaled and raked a hand through his hair, leaving it wildly tousled. "I do not see shame in that. I see bravery. I see a young man saving a young woman in the only way he could."

Perry blinked, unsure he had heard correctly.

"If you had not stepped in, she would have been ruined. You did everything in your power to stop it."

"He would not have noticed her if not for me."

"He would have chosen someone, Perry. He had the night in his head—he only used her because it amused him to drive the blade in. But the plan, the depravity—that was his alone. And you did not allow it to play out."

Perry rubbed his hands over his face. "Truly?"

Richard leaned forward, firm and kind. "Yes. I shall have my man of business seek word of her. But no matter what you learn—remember this. You were a boy with no power who stood between a monster and a girl, and you stopped him. You should not carry guilt. I am proud of you."

Perry's throat tightened, and he nodded once, afraid to speak. For the first time in years, something in his chest eased.

He was not alone.

He never had been.

Perry nearly wept in relief. "Truly?"

"Brother, you acted with honor. I am certain if we were to find this Laura, she would say a young lad of fifteen rescued her from a terrible fate."

Overcome, Perry nodded, blinking rapidly to keep his composure. Richard was right—just speaking the truth aloud had brought unexpected lightness to his chest. "Thank you, Richard ... for listening."

Richard's smile was gentle. "Of course. Now, what do you intend to do about Emma?"

Perry dropped his gaze, studying the shine of his Hessians. "I love her, you know?"

"I do. She is a rare and wonderful young woman."

"I am not worthy of her."

"You are far better than you believe yourself to be. And let us not forget, Sophia married me when she ought to have run the other way. Yet somehow, love prevailed. Women—remarkable women like Sophia and Emma—have the gift of seeing not just who we are, but who we might become. They teach us to be better men, kinder men. They teach us to love. And as far as this family is concerned, Emma is a saint. So I am quite confident you can win her back ... provided you have not done the unforgivable."

Perry hesitated, then remembered the very thing that had consumed his thoughts—until tonight.

"The unforgivable?" he asked.

Richard winced. "You did not join the widow in her bed, did you?"

Perry blinked. In truth, he had nearly forgotten Lady Slight entirely. "I was in her bed only because I passed out. When I awoke, I still had my trousers on."

Richard gave a glance at said trousers and raised a brow. "Given the condition of those trousers, I believe you."

Perry glanced down and grimaced. "Yes, well. Thank you, I suppose."

"There is something else I have been meaning to tell you for some time," Richard said, his tone shifting. "When Grandfather visited me at Oxford, he informed me that he had created a trust for Shepton Abbey."

"His home? What of it?"

"I inherited a half-interest when I turned five and

twenty. And as of your birthday the other morning, you now own the other half."

Perry blinked. "I ... I do?"

"I attempted to tell you many times," Richard said with a slight smile. "But every time I mentioned Grandfather, you would claim a pressing appointment and vanish like smoke. Eventually, I decided to wait until the papers were signed and the thing was done."

"Oh. That is ... good news, I suppose?"

"You misunderstand. I want you to manage it. It lies near Rose Ash and needs thoughtful stewardship."

"I have no notion of how to manage a property."

Richard sighed in mock despair. "You have charm, wit, and more intelligence than you claim. The estate earns income, but Johnson, my man of business, says it could thrive with the right improvements. The region is primed for wool production, and mechanization would benefit both tenants and owners—but the locals are wary. It will require someone with a persuasive nature and a little fire."

Perry gave him a flat look. "You mean someone like Emma."

"Exactly," Richard said with infuriating cheer. "She has a gift for land management. You have a talent for persuasion—if not always used wisely. Between you, the estate would flourish."

Perry groaned. "This is Sophia's idea, is it not?"

"She may have hinted. I may have listened. And now that I have had the idea myself, I claim full credit. Sophia will be delighted, and as you know, when Sophia is happy, the entire household benefits."

"I have not even convinced Emma to speak to me again, and you are plotting our future?"

"I am an optimist." Richard grinned. "Consider it. And

do not scowl. You always scowl when someone suggests you might do something worthwhile."

Perry huffed. "You might have mentioned this earlier."

"I had the documents ready on the morning of your birthday. But someone was too busy stomping about and refusing presents to hear me out."

"I was not stomping."

"You were rather dramatic."

Perry crossed his arms, but a smile played about his lips. "Is there more?"

"There is capital waiting to be used and a steward in place—he is capable, if somewhat lacking in imagination. It could be your project. Yours alone."

Perry tried to remain unaffected, but the idea burrowed deep. A place of his own? Work to occupy his days? A legacy that might—just might—appeal to a certain young lady with wild curls and a keen mind?

Before he could speak, Richard added, "If you mean to make amends, you must begin with a grand gesture. Something that shows her you are sincere. Something that proves you are worthy—even in your unworthiness."

Perry sighed. "Must you enjoy this so much?"

Richard's smile was downright gleeful. "It is not every day that my wayward little brother is bested by a clever country miss. How could I not enjoy it?"

Perry muttered something beneath his breath.

"Now, now, Perry," Richard said in a mild tone. "Do not let your lady love hear you curse. You are meant to be reformed, remember?"

Perry shook his head, but inside, something quiet and warm had begun to grow.

Hope.

CHAPTER
SEVENTEEN

"Twins, Balfour? You disdain interest in a matching set of songbirds who step the boards of Drury Lane?"

July 1817, Lord Julius Trafford to Peregrine, on his twenty-second birthday.

Emma stared down at the page covered in ink blots, then at her hand smeared with errant ink, and frowned. If Perry were here, he would say—

"Look at you, making a mess."

She stilled. The memory of his voice was so vivid, it felt as though he were in the room. Her head snapped up, her heart thudding painfully.

"Perry!"

The exasperating desire of her heart stood in the doorway, looking sheepish and out of place, with guilt written all over his handsome face.

"Indeed."

Emma stared, stunned. The duke had predicted Perry would follow, but she had not dared to believe it—not truly. She had felt too fragile to hope.

"Did he? Halmesbury always was an insufferable know-it-all," Perry muttered, with a crooked smile.

Oh heavens. She had spoken aloud again.

She was torn. She wanted to fly across the room and throw herself into his arms. Or strike him with her ink-splattered blotter. In the end, she settled on the safest middle ground: dry sarcasm.

"What can I do for you, Mr. Arrogant?"

Perry chuckled. "That seems fair."

"I think so. You took your time."

"I left the morning after you, but we were caught in a rainstorm, and the roads turned to mud. The carriages were bogged down for three days. You, of course, had the finest conveyances at your disposal."

Emma folded her arms. "And the evening before you left?"

He met her gaze. "I spoke with the earl. We had a long conversation about my misspent youth—and how often I act the part of a bounder."

Relief washed over her. "And the evening before that?"

"I drank myself into oblivion, out of shame and sorrow for what I had done to you. I passed out. Mostly clothed."

Emma breathed in deeply, her head spinning with unexpected comfort.

"I am not sure ... I ... What ..."

"Forgive me," Perry said gently. "I want to be honest with you, Emma. I must admit that, although I was mostly clothed, I was in Lady Slight's bed. Trafford and Ridley carried me there from the drawing room."

Emma blinked. "Oh. Why were you not fully dressed?"

"I had spilt wine on my waistcoat and shirt."

"A disaster of an evening, it sounds like."

"That is precisely what it was. When I awoke, she and I argued—over you. She asked that I never darken her doorstep again."

Emma stared at him, trying not to smile. "That is ... good."

Which brought her to the question that mattered most.

"So ... why are you here?"

He dropped his gaze to the floor, suddenly uncertain. "To apologize. To explain myself, if you will allow it. I know I do not deserve your understanding. But I owe you the truth."

Emma stood, hesitant but curious. "Very well. Let us sit by the fireplace. I cannot close the door, but we shall not be easily overheard."

He nodded and waited as she crossed the room and perched on the edge of a green armchair. He took the seat opposite, folding his hands in his lap as he stared into the unlit hearth.

"It is not a pretty story," he began, his voice low. "But you deserve to know the truth."

Emma inclined her head. "I am listening."

A heavy silence followed as Perry stared into the grate, struggling to find his words. Emma clasped her hands tightly, sensing the tension radiating from him. This was not the time for accusations or hurt feelings—not yet. She had longed for understanding, and now he was offering it.

At last, he spoke. "My father ... was not simply unkind. He was a cruel man who took pleasure in tormenting others. After my mother died, he turned that cruelty upon me."

Emma's chest tightened. She remembered the shadows

that had crossed Perry's face when certain topics arose—now she understood. The expression she had seen so many times was not flippancy. It was pain. And fear.

She held her breath as he continued, revealing how he had adopted sarcasm and distance as a shield. How he had become glib and reckless because it kept him safe. How his father's behavior had shaped him in ways he did not fully understand until he met her.

And then he stopped, glancing at her with uncertain eyes.

Emma took a long breath. "Your father was monstrous."

Perry gave a quiet laugh. "Indeed. I regret, more than I can say, that I allowed my past to poison what was growing between us. There is more I could tell you, but it is of a more personal nature. And perhaps best left for another time. I only wanted you to know that meeting you ... disrupted everything I thought I knew about myself. You see, I did not mean to care for you, but I could not help it. And once I realized how deeply I did ... I panicked."

He met her gaze fully. "I told myself I had to protect you. That I would ruin you if I stayed. But what I did at the ball—that was not protection. That was cowardice. And I am so deeply sorry, Emma. If there is any way you might forgive me ..."

Emma was silent for a long moment, her throat thick with emotion. He had come all this way, carrying the weight of his past, just to speak these words. Just to try.

"I cannot pretend I was not hurt," she said softly. "You wounded me deeply. But ... I understand you better now. And that makes a difference."

A tentative smile touched his lips. "Then there is hope?"

She gave the faintest nod. "There might be."

He exhaled, the tension draining from his shoulders. "That is more than I deserve."

Emma's lips twitched. "Yes. But I have been known to be generous."

His smile widened, and for a moment, neither of them spoke. They simply sat across from each other, the fireless hearth between them, a quiet understanding beginning to bloom in the silence.

~

Mr. Davis was a stocky man of medium height, with the black hair and sharp eyes that he had passed on to his eldest daughter. He also shared Emma's keen intellect and fierce loyalty to family.

Thankfully, he remained unaware of the precise nature of what had occurred in London, a truth for which Perry was immeasurably grateful. All the gentleman knew for certain was that his eldest child had returned home in low spirits, and that the man who had escorted her to Town under promises of care and propriety now stood before him, requesting permission to call. It had taken some persuasion—no small feat given Mr. Davis's clear displeasure—but in the end, he had consented to an evening visit, on the strict condition that Emma welcomed it.

Perry had been relieved beyond words when she did not immediately show him the door. Instead, she agreed to speak with him in the library. Their conversation had been tentative, the silences long, but Emma had listened. That alone meant everything. He had made his apology—earnest, unpolished, and full of regret—and while she had offered little in return beyond quiet understanding, she had not turned away. She had not judged. She had not retreated.

And she had invited him to dine with her family.

It was more than he had hoped for, and he returned to the inn with a lighter heart than he had carried in days. His boots were still caked in mud and his clothes travel-worn, but he had a purpose again. He entered the taproom to find Trafford and Ridley waving him over to a scarred wooden table near the hearth.

He joined them gratefully and ordered an ale and a meal to tide him over until supper.

"Did the bluestocking receive you?" Trafford asked, his drawl a clear indication that this was not his first ale of the afternoon.

"She did. And that is Miss Davis to you, Lord Insolent Oaf."

Ridley chuckled into his tankard. "I wish I had been there for the first volley."

"You were there, you inebriated cad," Trafford grumbled. "You just could not hold yourself upright long enough to notice."

He turned back to Perry, eyes narrowed with dramatic suspicion. "Remind me again why we are in Sleep Ash?"

"Rose Ash."

"Same thing."

"Because," Perry said patiently, "you are to assist me in my grand gesture. I cannot do it alone."

"I still do not understand it," Trafford declared. "You have repeated the plan multiple times, always in that superior tone that makes me want to kick over your ale. I am tired of rain and mud and sheep and trees—and frankly, I am tired of you. When this young lady of yours sees what you have concocted, she will be just as weary."

Perry shook his head with a wry smile. "One day, you will meet a woman who brings you to your knees, and then you will be glad you had friends foolish enough to come to your aid."

Trafford made a face. "Let us hope I remember not to parade a provocative widow on my arm while cutting her in public when that day comes."

"I have apologized."

"And yet we all must suffer your penance," Ridley added cheerfully. "But I will say this—I do not enjoy seeing a young lady treated with anything less than respect. I am here to see that you make things right."

"And to enjoy the spectacle," Perry murmured.

"That too."

"I, for one," Trafford said, leaning back in his chair, "am looking forward to the moment the Davis family watches you make a complete fool of yourself. It shall be a memory to cherish."

Perry laughed, though nerves twisted tightly in his belly. For all his practice, for all the hours spent rehearsing his plan, he could not deny the thrum of anxiety beneath the surface. But for Emma's smile—for the chance to restore the pride and confidence he had so thoughtlessly damaged—he would endure every moment.

Even if it meant humbling himself in front of the entire Davis family. Even if it meant risking his heart in such a public manner.

EMMA GLANCED out her bedroom window and caught sight of the Saunton carriage pulling into the drive. Her heart gave an unsteady lurch, though she told herself it was simply nerves. Turning to Betty—her young maid with a cheerful face spattered with freckles and thick brown hair that never stayed pinned—she urged, "Please hurry, Betty, or I shall be disgracefully late."

The hair tonic had indeed coaxed her hair into lush curls, but Emma found it intolerably slow going. She ought to already be downstairs to greet their guest, but as it was, she would be the last to arrive.

They worked together quickly, Betty circling her to tug and smooth the folds of her gown while Emma craned to peer at her reflection, adjusting where needed. Despite their hurry, Emma found herself hesitating. She lingered at the mirror, adjusting a nonexistent crease, brushing invisible dust from her skirts.

She was ... shy. It was the only word for it. After all that had transpired in London, to now be awaiting Perry in her home—under the scrutiny of her family—left her unsettled. She did not know quite what to expect from him. He had apologized, yes, and his regrets had felt genuine. But what came next? Was he here to court her?

Or to say goodbye?

The memory of their shared intimacy—the kisses, the whispered words in the dark, the stolen moment in the music room—rose unbidden, and Emma flushed. No, Jane had not been privy to all of it. Her younger sister had missed more than she had witnessed, for which Emma was grateful.

She gave herself one last glance in the mirror. Her deep blue velvet gown was modest and appropriate, yet it still brought out the striking contrast of her dark hair and pale complexion. Appropriate for supper at a small country estate, but finer than anything her family would wear. After the London ball, she was acutely aware of the disparity in their worlds. Perry would no doubt arrive looking effortlessly elegant—his cravat just so, his linen fresh, his coat brushed to perfection. He would even dress down in the most fastidious way, probably with his best buckskins.

Impeccable with everyone but me.

Emma sighed at the thought.

Yet even in recalling the sting of that humiliation, her heart softened. The Duke of Halmesbury had been kind. Gentle. He had urged her to listen if Perry came seeking forgiveness—and he had. Not only had Perry traveled through mud and storm to reach her, but he had also bared his heart in a manner that had clearly cost him much. And she had seen the rawness behind his words.

He was trying. And that mattered more than she had expected.

Bluster would serve no purpose now. She had been raised in a household where grudges were inefficient—there were simply too many siblings to hold one for long. Arguments were had, then settled. One said one's piece and moved on. Even if frogs were involved.

And so she would see what he had to say for himself tonight. She might be cautious, but she was not closed.

"Thank you, Betty." She squeezed the maid's hand and left the room.

Descending the stairs, she slowed as the entryway came into view over the banister. Her breath caught, her steps faltered.

At the foot of the stairs, her family stood assembled, her father looking wary, her mother warm but watchful. The boys were freshly scrubbed and dressed neatly—Oliver and Max shining from their bath, and Thaddeus standing solemnly with little Maddie's hand clutched in his. All their eyes were fixed on the guests.

Guests?

Perry stood in the vestibule flanked by two men.

Two very fashionable, very tall men.

One she recognized from Balfour Terrace—the one with the rumpled blond hair and lazy drawl. Lord Trafford, if she recalled correctly. And the other, whose wit had been drowned in drink the last time she saw him, must be Mr. Ridley.

They looked absurdly out of place in the cozy hall of Rose Ash Manor, all three men dressed with elegance and ease, as if they had just stepped out of a London drawing room and not six days of country travel.

Emma swallowed hard. Her stomach twisted.

"Em—Miss Davis," Perry greeted, catching himself too late. Her father stiffened, his disapproval unmistakable.

Emma could only manage a faint smile in reply.

Perry cleared his throat, looked to his companions, and gave a quick nod. The three men stood straighter, turned toward her ... and began to hum.

Emma's eyes widened.

And then, to her astonishment, all three burst into song.

> *Let Bucks and let bloods to praise London agree*
> *Oh the joys of the country my Jewel for me*
> *Where sweet is the flow'r that the May bush*
> *   adorns*
> *And how charming to gather it but for the*
> *   thorns*

Emma barely dared to breathe. They were serenading her? The popular Dibdin aria that they sang was unexpected—*The Joys of the Country*. She attempted to ascertain if they were singing in jest; the song being an ode to rural life while secretly poking fun at the nuisances of such. Yet they did not seem to be making sport as they sang the lively lyrics. Was this intended to be a reverent gesture?

> *Where we walk o'er the mountains with health*
> *   our cheeks glowing*
> *As warm as a toast honey when it en't snowing*
> *Where nature to smile when the joyful inclines*
> *And the sun charms us all the year round when*
> *   it shines*

Despite her best efforts to ignore them, the twins were attempting to hold back their mirth, hands clapped over their mouths while their eyes watered with the strain. Thaddeus had dropped little Maddie's hand in order to plug his ears with his index fingers, while their youngest sister's mouth hung open, her eyes wide in amazed horror at the spectacle unfolding.

> *Oh the mountains & vallies and bushes*
> *The pigs & the screech owls & thrushes*
> *Let Bucks & let bloods to praise London agree*
> *Oh the joys of the country my Jewel for me*
> *The joys of the country my Jewel for me*
>
> *There twelve hours on a stretch we in angling*
> *   delight*
> *As patient as Job tho' we ne'er get a bite*
> *There we pop at the wild ducks & frighten the*
> *   crows*
> *While so lovely the icicles hang to our Cloathes*

From the corner of her eye, she could see that her father stared at the ceiling, his lips quivering with a threatening gale of laughter while her mother gazed at the front door as if she contemplated running off into the early evening. All that protected Emma herself from guffawing like a jackass was the sheer surreal shock of it.

> *There wid Aunts & wid Cousins and Grand-*
> *mothers talking*
> *We are caught in the rain as we're all out a*
> *walking*
> *While the Muslins and gauzes cling round each*
> *fair She*
> *That they look all like Venuses sprung from*
> *the Sea*

Emma flushed at the bawdy lyrics. She and her family had heard the aria many times, but being singled out and serenaded by three gentlemen from the city highlighted the naughty meaning of the lyrics. She squirmed with the awareness that her parents stood right beside her, restraining laughter at these theatrics. Emma bit her lip to prevent any reaction from crossing her face, but tears of mirth threatened when the trio of ... tenors ... began the chorus once more.

> *Oh the mountains & vallies and bushes*
> *The pigs & the screech owls & thrushes*
> *Let Bucks & let bloods to praise London agree*
> *Oh the joys of the country my Jewel for me*
>
> *Then how sweet in the dog days to take the*
> *fresh Air*

MISS DAVIS AND THE SPARE

*Where to save us expence, the dust powders
   your hair
There pleasures like snowballs encrease as
   they roll
And tire you to death, not forgetting the Bowl*

*Where in mirth and good fellowship always
   delighting
We agree, that is, when we're not squabbling &
   fighting
Den wid toasts & pint bumpers we bodder
   the head
Just to see who most gracefully staggers to bed*

*Oh the mountains & vallies and bushes
The pigs & the screech owls & thrushes
Let Bucks & let bloods to praise London agree
Oh the joys of the country my Jewel for me*

As the song drew to a close, Perry fell to one knee at Emma's feet, his head almost at bosom level as he gazed up at her in adoration.

She frowned down at him, nonplussed, doing her best to bite back the giggle that threatened to spill from her lips as he threw his arms wide and belted out the last line at the top of his lungs.

The joys of the country my Jewel for me!

CHAPTER
EIGHTEEN

"Please, I beg of you, please never sing again! Hum, if you must, but never, never sing again."

July 1818, Richard Balfour to his brother, Peregrine, on his twenty-third birthday.

~

At the final, enthusiastic rendering of the song, shoulders shook and faces reddened as her family did their utmost not to dissolve into laughter. Max lost the battle and howled like a braying ass, which meant his twin followed suit. Both boys doubled over, clutching their bellies, while helpless mirth overcame them.

Her father gasped for air, steadying himself against the wall, his shoulders shuddering. Her mother's lips were pressed into a thin, white line as she struggled to maintain composure, looking as though she had forgotten how to breathe. The entire room shimmered with stifled amusement as each occupant fought to collect their wits.

Emma turned her gaze on the rogue still kneeling at her feet, her expression one of wonder. "Uh ... thank you?"

"You are welcome!" Perry beamed up at her, flushed with exuberance and clearly not at all regretful for his assault on their ears.

Emma glanced briefly at her family, who were still snorting and wheezing with laughter, and then addressed the two gentlemen who had flanked Perry during his display. "Mr. Ridley and Lord Trafford—"

"That is Lord Oaf to you, Miss Bluestocking," Trafford interjected with a rakish grin.

Her father stiffened at the slight, but Emma ignored him, determined to maintain civility. "—you are musically gifted, and it was an honor to hear such marvelous tenors in our home."

Mr. Ridley gave her a warm, gracious smile, vastly improved from their first encounter when he had been so soused. From the kindness in his eyes, Emma felt reassured that this had not been some elaborate jest made at her expense. Both men bowed politely.

"They are excellent tenors," Perry agreed cheerfully from the floor, one hand still braced on his knee. He made no move to rise.

Emma pursed her lips, half-tempted to let him remain kneeling forever. "Mr. Balfour, I hate to be the bearer of bad news ... but you are not musically competent."

He nodded solemnly. "Quite true."

"You are aware of this?" she asked, genuinely uncertain.

"I am," he replied with no trace of embarrassment, which prompted another soft wave of chuckles from her family.

"Then why—may I ask—have you regaled us with this ... unusual rendition of Dibdin's aria?"

Perry's green eyes twinkled. "It seemed only right that I reveal, in the most humiliating and public fashion, my most distressing personal flaw." His gaze flicked meaningfully toward her family, a silent apology for the night at the ball when he had humiliated her so publicly. And just like that, Emma understood.

Her thoughts flew to Lady Slight and the cruel taunts at the ball. To Perry's confession that morning, and his heartfelt apology. To the very real vulnerability in his voice now—and the assault her ears had just endured.

"You are correct. Tonight, you have revealed your most unfortunate trait. I am not sure any of us shall recover."

"Hear, hear!" Trafford chimed in with mock solemnity.

Perry grinned. "A most regrettable and, I fear, memorable performance."

Emma could not help herself—she laughed, the sound bubbling up from somewhere warm inside. The last remnants of pain seemed to drift away on the joyful absurdity of it all.

"It is not entirely my fault," Perry continued with exaggerated dignity. "My father did not believe music was a worthy pursuit for a gentleman. Richard once attempted to correct the oversight, but after five minutes in the music room, he fled, claiming his ears were bleeding."

Trafford and Ridley nodded gravely. "It has been an excruciating week, traveling with Balfour and rehearsing," Ridley confirmed.

Emma smiled softly. "Your father had much to answer for."

"That he did. But tonight is not about him. It is about you." Perry reached up to clasp her hand. She noticed her father tense, but her mother gently touched his arm, and he relaxed.

"Miss Davis," Perry said, his voice low but steady, "there are no words to describe how a country jewel slipped into my soul and stole the heart from my chest." He tapped over his left breast. "And while I can never undo my past foolishness, I can attempt to atone for it, in word and deed."

Trafford mumbled something about irreparable idiots, but Emma barely heard it.

"You are wit, and beauty, and joy," Perry continued. "Despite my many shortcomings, I hope you might consider my offer. It has come to light that I am in possession of a substantial estate near Rose Ash. And so, I ask— will you accept the position of mistress of Shepton Abbey?"

Gasps sounded around the room. Even her parents, new to the region, had heard of Shepton Abbey.

"You mean to live in the country? A city buck like you?" Emma asked, breathless.

"I do. The city has lost its shine without you in it. If the lady does not come to London, then I shall come to the country and attempt to become worthy of her."

Emma's heart swelled. A thousand emotions danced within her—hope, joy, disbelief. Could this really be happening?

"Like Edward Ferrars in *Sense and Sensibility*!" Thaddeus piped up, starry-eyed. Emma's heart softened further at her little brother's romantic idealism.

"You wish to marry me?" she asked, just to be sure.

"I do." Perry leaned in, voice quiet. "I hope I have humbled myself sufficiently for you to forgive my ... imprudent deportment?"

Emma leaned closer, matching his tone. "You have.

Especially since you brought Lord Oaf. Word will travel far and wide of your deplorable lack of talent."

Perry chuckled softly, and she straightened, drawing in a breath.

"In that case," she said aloud, smiling down at him, "I accept, Mr. Balfour."

Cheers erupted. Her family surged forward to embrace her, each hug warm and brimming with delight. And through it all, Emma held fast to Perry's hand.

For once in her life, everything felt exactly as it should be.

Perry reflected that his grand gesture had been a grand success. Emma's good spirits had been restored, and the dinner had been lively. She had glowed with renewed confidence, and Perry was deeply gratified to see the damage he had wrought to her self-esteem now eased, if not wholly erased.

Even Trafford had surrendered his usual cynicism to enjoy hearty country fare, relaxed etiquette, and simple pleasures in the drawing room afterward. Mr. Davis had remained with the women and children after the meal, rather than withdrawing as gentlemen often did, and Perry had been charmed by the warmth of the Davis household as they passed the evening with music and parlour games —though he was firmly admonished not to sing.

Thaddeus had solemnly complimented Perry's dancing skills despite his "lamentable lack of musical gifts," which he took to be high praise from the earnest young lad.

Come morning, Perry sat with Emma and her parents to finalize arrangements. As agreed with Richard, the Davis family would join them at Saunton Park for a wedding in the chapel in just a few days, ahead of the impending house party. Now that Perry had declared his intentions, he and Emma had no desire to delay. He discussed marriage terms with Mr. Davis, who had grown markedly more genial since witnessing Perry's musical humiliation. Apparently, any man who would publicly debase himself for the love of his daughter was considered worthy enough to enter the fold.

It touched Perry more than he had anticipated—this warm welcome into a loving family. He finally understood what had overtaken his older brother months earlier when he had taken Sophia's hand in marriage. In gaining Emma, Perry would gain five younger siblings and new parental figures who lived only a short ride away. It was almost too much to take in, and the thought of raising a family among such loyal, kind-hearted folk brought an unexpected lump to his throat.

Mr. Davis even offered insight into the mindset of the Shepton Abbey tenants—a valuable resource, given the upcoming modernization plans. That practical support only deepened Perry's appreciation for the unexpected blessings of his impending marriage.

After two days in Rose Ash, Perry was more than ready to escape coaching inns. With great satisfaction, he assisted the Davis family into their carriages before joining Trafford and Ridley in the Saunton coach. As he settled into the familiar leather squabs, he sighed deeply and allowed himself to imagine married life with Emma.

"I must admit," Trafford said, watching the countryside roll by, "Miss Bluestocking is quite comely. I begin to see the appeal—especially after spending time with her family."

"Keep your eyes off my jewel," Perry replied with mock

menace. Still, he found himself wondering if even Lord Oaf might one day settle down. That Trafford had agreed to journey into the wilds of Somerset and make a public spectacle of himself had revealed more heart than Perry might have guessed. And Ridley, who had abandoned a promising widow for the cause, had shown himself a true friend.

Perhaps they, too, were nearing the ends of their careless bachelorhoods. Perry would not mind being the first to walk a new path, if it meant inspiring others.

"I did not know you intended to move to Shepton," Ridley said, arching a brow. "Will you spend any time in London?"

"As little as possible."

Trafford straightened, aghast. "Is that a line for the country mouse?"

Perry let the quip slide. "I shall be engaged with the estate. I think it wise to avoid London's entertainments while I adjust to married life. Emma need not endure awkward encounters with the ghosts of my past. Richard and Sophia have had their share of scandal since marrying, but I am not bound to Westminster as my brother is."

Trafford shuddered. "You are becoming domesticated."

Perry's mind drifted to late evenings with Emma—chamomile and ink stains, laughter over tenant ledgers, soft kisses beneath patchwork quilts. "Aye. And I welcome it."

Trafford groaned. "It is one thing to take a wife, but to rusticate?"

"You are always welcome at the abbey," Perry offered. "If you need respite—or if you need to hide from a particularly disgruntled paramour."

"No one will think to look for you in Somerset," Ridley added, chuckling. "It is a brilliant hiding place."

"Exactly," Trafford muttered, slumping back. "Only a black day would drive me so far. I have drunk enough ale to last me a decade. I need wine. Fine, rich wine."

"The wine will flow at Saunton to mark the celebrations."

"Thank heavens," Trafford replied, hands to his face.

They arrived at Saunton Park later that afternoon. The earl had sent a missive the same morning Perry left London, instructing the staff to prepare for both the Davis family and the upcoming house party. The guest wing had been opened for the newcomers, while Trafford and Ridley were shown to the bachelor hall.

Perry met with the senior staff to finalize arrangements for the ceremony and the wedding breakfast. The next afternoon, he stood on the manor's broad stone steps, watching the procession of carriages from London. The Saunton arms were emblazoned on the first few, but it was the familiar gilded coach of the Duke of Halmesbury that made Perry's breath catch. Two more ducal carriages followed behind.

"My sister must be here," Ridley murmured behind him.

His cousin and the duchess had come. They had traveled all this way to attend his wedding. The warmth in Perry's chest was swift and profound.

Richard stepped down from the lead carriage. Perry hurried to meet him. "Richard—what is this?"

"Halmesbury insisted on accompanying me when I shared the news."

"You knew I would succeed?"

Richard shrugged. "I told him you were terribly persuasive when you wished to be."

Perry blinked. "The duke canceled plans to attend my wedding?"

"He did. He and Annabel are staying through the house party. You have made quite the impression."

As Perry tried to absorb that, Sophia and Ethan disembarked, followed by Jane Davis. The introductions began, and Halmesbury crossed to thump Perry's shoulder.

"Congratulations, Peregrine."

Perry raised a brow. "You may call me Perry, Halmesbury."

The duke paused, his gray eyes considering. "Congratulations, Perry."

Perry grinned. "Richard, do we have the license?"

Halmesbury tapped his coat pocket. "The Archbishop sends his regards."

"You secured the license yourself?"

"I did. He owes me favors. I thought it time to collect on one."

"I thank you. It means more than I can say."

Inside, the drawing room soon swelled with sound and laughter. Oliver and Max entertained their guests by mimicking Perry's tone-deaf serenade. Ridley bounced his baby nephew, Jasper, on his knee while Sophia and Annabel exchanged amused glances. It was boisterous, joyful chaos.

Across the room, Emma glanced at him. Her eyes, dark and knowing, caught his. And held.

He ached to be near her, but not under the watchful eye of her father. No, he would behave—for one more night. Tomorrow, she would be his wife. His partner. His beloved bluestocking.

He could wait.

Just one more night.

~

Emma studied Jane, concern etched across her brow. "You are still not sleeping? Did you speak with the physician Sophia recommended?"

Jane gave a careless shrug. "There is no need. It is only excitement."

Tilting her head, Emma narrowed her eyes. "I wish you would consider seeing either the physician or an apothecary. It is unlike you to struggle with sleep. Even when we moved from Derby, and the entire household was up at all hours from the anticipation, you slept without trouble. I recall envying you at the time."

Jane pulled a face and changed the subject with a pointed cheerfulness. "Now that you are to wed—as I predicted, mind you—it is my turn to find a beau. The countess mentioned several eligible landowners are arriving on Friday for the house party. I am sure to meet a gentleman who captures my heart the way Perry has captured yours."

Emma smiled softly. "Is that important to you—that he be a landowner?"

Jane paused to consider the question. "I suppose it is. It just seems the epitome of success, does it not? For a young lady to marry a man with land. But honestly, I do not know what sort of gentleman would truly suit me. Perhaps someone young and fun?"

"Perhaps," Emma allowed. "But it is worth considering what kind of life you wish to lead. The man you marry will greatly influence the course of your future. I wanted to be with Perry, but while we sparred in London, I questioned whether we could reconcile our differences—especially since it would have meant settling in Town. His decision to take the reins at Shepton Abbey played a significant role in my decision to accept him. It shapes what our future will look like, and I have always known I was destined to be involved in estate management in some form."

Jane's brow puckered. "I do not know what I am destined for. I have never thought beyond meeting a man I loved and raising a family together."

Emma reached across and gave her sister's hand a light squeeze. "Perhaps now is the time to think about it. Before the house party begins and charming smiles cloud your judgment. Consider what you truly desire for your future—so when a suitor does appear, you will know whether he is truly a match."

Jane huffed, though without heat. "Good heavens, Emma. You are such a pragmatic bluestocking. Are you truly saying you might have turned Perry down if he had no satisfactory plan for the future?"

Emma nibbled her lip, then turned her head to glance across the room at her betrothed. Perry caught her gaze and offered a quiet, affectionate smile. Her heart lifted.

"Perhaps I would have risked it regardless," she admitted. "But I am relieved he chose the path he did. It is an excellent opportunity—for him, and for us. I believe we shall be very happy at the abbey.

THE EARL BROKE AWAY from the lively group in the corner and approached Perry, who stood at the open window taking in the evening air. After so many years of solitude, it still astonished Perry to find himself surrounded by relations—relations who wished to spend time in his company. He was grateful, deeply so, but it would take time to grow accustomed to the hum and bustle of such familial closeness.

"How was your journey here, Richard?" he asked, as his brother joined him.

"Uneventful. We waited until the rain ceased before departing. You, however, must have been caught in it?"

Perry grimaced. "We barely moved for three days."

"Hmm ... and how long did it take to reach Rose Ash?"

"Six days. With Trafford whining the entire journey."

Richard chuckled. "He does like his creature comforts."

"I appreciated his support, but I confess there were moments I wished to shove him under the carriage wheels."

They both turned to observe the spoiled lord now in deep conversation with young Thaddeus, who looked very serious while Trafford appeared distinctly out of his depth. It was an unlikely but oddly endearing pairing.

"I have news," Richard said after a pause. "And I am hoping you will delay your departure for the abbey until the end of the week. There is someone you need to meet."

Perry arched a brow. "It would need to be someone rather remarkable for me to agree to remain under your roof amidst this many guests."

"A brother."

Perry stared. "What?"

"You recall our conversation in May, when we speculated that Father may have sired children we were unaware of?"

Perry swallowed, shifting to ease the sudden tension that gripped his spine. "I remember. I was not aware you had acted on that suspicion."

Richard nodded. "Johnson investigated discreetly. He found someone. I met with him before we left Town and persuaded him to join us for the house party."

Perry's stomach knotted. Another brother? On the one

hand, it meant he was not as alone as he had believed. On the other ... he thought of the boy's life. A bastard's life. He imagined the hardships, the isolation—what young Ethan might face as he grew older. Perry had struggled with being the overlooked spare. A by-blow would have faced far worse.

"Was it difficult," he asked quietly, "when you brought Ethan into your home?"

Richard sighed. "A few servants left. Some acquaintances withdrew. But I would make the same choice again without hesitation. I cannot abide disloyalty—especially to those who deserve our protection."

Perry nodded solemnly. His own moment of disloyalty to Emma still ached within him. He was grateful every day that she had forgiven him. That he had found the strength to right his course before it was too late.

"Why did ... our brother ... require persuading? Surely he would welcome a connection to an earl—and the support it could offer?"

"Barclay Thompson is successful in his own right. He had no need of our assistance, and no desire to claim connection to a man who never acknowledged his mother. It took every ounce of my persuasion—and his grandfather's support—to convince him to meet us. The prospect of advantages for his young daughter was the turning point."

"Barclay Thompson?" Perry narrowed his eyes. "That name sounds familiar."

"His grandfather is Tsar Thompson."

Perry's jaw dropped. "Tsar and Barclay Thompson? The architects?"

Richard inclined his head. "Just so. And Barclay is older than either of us. He would have inherited the title, had our father done right by his mother. It is a bitter legacy, but I hope to forge something better from it. I would appreciate it if you were here to welcome him. I should like him to see what our family might look like when it is not built on cruelty or lies."

Perry exhaled slowly, eyes wide with disbelief. "I suppose we can delay our departure until the morning after. I was a fool to think I had nearly no family left in this world."

"I regret that you were made to feel that way in your youth." Richard followed Perry's gaze to the tea table, where Emma sat with Jane, her smile radiant. "But you are making different choices now. You are rejecting his legacy. And I am proud of you, brother."

Perry's eyes lingered on the young woman who would soon be his wife. She looked up and met his gaze, her smile deepening, her expression tender.

"I am so pleased she agreed to be my wife."

CHAPTER NINETEEN

"I understand your trepidation, but it is imperative that I wed to protect the people who rely on me."

July 1819, Richard Balfour to his brother, Peregrine, on his twenty-fourth birthday.

∽

Emma shut the door to the hall and turned to Perry, her heart fluttering at the quiet intimacy now enveloping them. "Well, husband, we are finally alone. And wed."

"With our entire family likely speculating on exactly what we are doing now that we are finally alone."

Emma chuckled at his dry tone. "I think we might forget their presence if we go about this correctly."

Perry huffed a laugh. "I shall take that as a personal challenge."

He stepped toward her, sliding an arm around her waist and drawing her close. His green eyes softened as he lowered his head to capture her lips in a kiss that was both reverent and full of promise. Emma melted against him, her hands slipping up to rest against his chest as he deepened the kiss, slow and sure, as though he meant to memorize her.

They had waited for this moment through sleepless nights, aching hopes, and tender reconciliation. To stand here now, husband and wife, was overwhelming in the most delightful of ways.

His hands moved gently, cupping her face, brushing along her arms, as if he were rediscovering every inch of her. She sighed against his lips, and he smiled into the kiss.

She pulled back, taking his hand to lead him farther into the room. With slow, careful movements, she unfastened his cravat, her fingers trembling slightly as she slid the fabric free with Perry standing still, his eyes never leaving her face. Crossing to the bed, she reached out to turn down the counterpane. He laid her down gently, brushing a curl from her forehead before joining her on the mattress.

They lay there for a moment, side by side, simply staring at each other, hands entangled between them.

"I love you, Emma," he whispered.

Emma smiled, her heart full to the brim. "I love you, Perry."

Their mouths met again—soft, lingering, full of promise. Their hands caressed, unhurried and full of wonder. As the moonlight spilled across the counterpane, Perry pulled her into his arms and whispered against her temple, "You are my wildflower. And I shall never stop being grateful that you chose me."

EPILOGUE

"Happy birthday, my love."

July 1821, Emma Balfour to her husband, Peregrine, on his twenty-sixth birthday.

∽

JULY 1821, SHEPTON ABBEY

Perry woke at the soft knock upon the chamber door. Opening one eye, he watched as Emma slipped out of bed and padded across the room. Low murmurs followed as she accepted a tray from Betty and nudged the door closed with her hip. She set the tray on a nearby table, then turned back toward the bed with a smile lighting her face.

Still wrapped in the bed's warmth, Perry felt no great urgency to rise. He closed his eyes again, enjoying the lingering drowsiness—until he felt Emma's weight return beside him. She curled up behind him and pressed a teasing kiss just behind his ear.

"Happy birthday, my love," she whispered.

Perry smiled. It was a happy birthday indeed. He stretched lazily, preparing to pull her into his arms, but she scooted back out of reach, mischief gleaming in her eyes. Before he could coax her back, she placed a small wrapped box on his chest.

He stared at the gift in surprise. Birthday presents were not something he had received often in life—those he had once received from his father had typically come with cruelty attached. Most, he had returned or discarded as soon as he dared.

But Emma ... Emma gave nothing but goodness. And he knew, whatever lay inside this package, he would treasure it forever.

Sitting up against the headboard, he untied the ribbon with deliberate care. The paper fell away, revealing a small, velvet-lined box. Inside, resting in soft folds of fabric, was a delicate silver rattle, its floral engraving glinting in the morning light.

His breath caught.

His fingers trembled as he lifted the rattle from the box. He stared at it, wonderment blooming in his chest. "Truly?"

Emma's voice was tender. "I confirmed it last week, but I waited to tell you today—for your birthday."

She leaned in to embrace him, her eyes suspiciously bright. "In six or seven months, we shall welcome a new Balfour to the abbey."

"Oh, Emma ..." His arms wrapped tightly around her as he pressed his cheek to hers. "How did you hide this for a week? You must have been beside yourself."

"I was overcome," she whispered, laughing softly. "It

was excruciating not to tell you. But I wanted it to be perfect."

"It is perfect." He cupped her face and gently brushed away the tears gathered on her lashes. "You have longed for this with all your heart."

"I shall write to my family straightaway," she murmured, resting her head against his shoulder. "Mama and Papa will be beside themselves with joy."

Perry drew her fully into his embrace. His eyes prickled, and he blinked rapidly as he buried his face in her soft, dark hair. Life had taken a turn so beautiful, so full of grace, he scarcely knew how to hold it all.

A child. Their child.

"And so our family begins," he said hoarsely, the weight of those words sinking deep.

Then he stilled, realization dawning. "Your family will never leave once the first grandchild arrives, will they?"

Emma laughed into his shoulder. "You may as well prepare the guest rooms now."

He groaned, then chuckled. "Shall we have a cup of tea to celebrate before we venture downstairs? I imagine I shall need fortification."

"I think we must," Emma replied with a smile. "Besides, I am certain the earl will wish to hear the news."

Perry blinked. "Richard is here?"

"Betty just informed me," Emma said, returning from the door with a tray in her hands. "I had planned to breakfast with you here this morning, but it appears the servants prepared breakfast downstairs after learning of the earl's arrival."

"Then we shall drink our tea here before I return to my rooms. I am certain my valet is waiting by now."

"It is later than we usually rise," Emma said with a teasing smile, "but we were rather ... occupied."

Perry grinned. "It is not my fault the new night rail was so alluring."

"I purchased it with your birthday in mind," she replied pertly. "I wanted this year to be special for you."

"No matter what you had done, this would have been special." He reached for her, pulling her close and pressing a sound kiss to her lips. "Come here, wife!"

Less than an hour later, Perry descended the stairs in high spirits and found the earl enjoying coffee in the breakfast room. Gathering a generous plate from the sideboard, Perry seated himself across from his brother.

"Good morning, brother."

Richard smiled over his cup. "Happy birthday, Perry."

"Is that why you are here?"

Richard nodded. "It occurred to me that I have not visited you nearly enough this past year. After listening to myself lament that fact, Sophia reminded me your birthday would be the perfect occasion. She shooed me out before dawn. We leave for the King's coronation in a few days, so this was my only chance to come."

"Interrupting nothing important, I assure you—" Perry began, but stopped when Emma entered the room.

"Just his birthday breakfast with his wife," she said cheerfully.

Richard stood to bow. Emma waved him down, laughing. "No ceremony, Richard. We are family."

Perry beamed. "With more family on the way."

Richard blinked. "You do not mean—?"

"Your nephew or niece should be happy to receive you long before my next birthday."

Richard's expression softened, his eyes bright with emotion. "Well, that is very good news."

The three shared breakfast in celebration before Emma excused herself to write to her family. Perry turned to his brother once they were alone.

"All right. Why are you truly here?"

"I beg your pardon?" Richard asked innocently.

"You did not make the drive simply for breakfast."

Richard grinned. "You know me too well. I had two reasons for ensuring I made it here this morning."

"What is the first?"

"I received a report last month about the young woman from the village. Laura."

Perry froze, breath catching. "What of her?"

"It took time to find her—she severed all ties with the village, as you advised. But she was located three towns from where you sent her that night."

Perry exhaled, heart pounding. "And?"

"She married a baker a few months after reaching Cornwall. They have three children, and she is, by all accounts, content."

Relief washed over Perry. That was better than he could have hoped.

"And as predicted," Richard added, "you are the hero of her tale. They named their eldest Peregrine."

Perry blinked. "Their son?"

Richard barely suppressed his grin. "No. Their daughter. Apparently, Peregrine can be a girl's name, too."

Perry groaned and picked up a slice of toast, tossing it at his laughing brother's head, who caught it with ease.

"And your second reason?"

Richard's expression sobered. "The abbey has been

under your stewardship for nearly a year now. I wished to see the progress myself."

"I am pleased to show you."

After breakfast, the brothers rode out over the estate. Perry walked Richard through the upgrades and decisions made since he and Emma had arrived. They inspected the tenant farms, then a flock of young tan-faced Portlands, lambs frolicking among the ewes.

"I have not encountered this breed," Richard remarked. "Why Portlands?"

"Emma chose them," Perry replied with a smile. "They are hardy, lamb easily, and thrive on rough pasture. These fields were underutilized before. Now they serve a purpose while we assess other plans."

Richard grinned. "Never thought I would see the day you spoke so knowledgeably of sheep."

Perry gave a wry laugh. "My knowledge is surface-level at best. Emma says the fleece is fine and dyes well. I manage the relationships."

They returned to the abbey and settled in the library, where Perry preferred to work. Richard sipped his coffee before reaching into his pocket and placing a set of papers on the desk.

"Happy birthday."

Perry scanned the pages, brow furrowing. "What is this? Contracts? You are signing over your share of the abbey?"

Richard nodded. "Grandfather always intended it to be yours. I was included in the trust for legal protections, but he made me promise I would turn it over when the time was right."

Perry leaned back, stunned. "He said that?"

Richard smiled. "He spoke of how sweet you were. You brought him apples, flowers, chestnuts. He said you were our mother's son and deserved better than the fate of a spare. This was his way of giving you that."

Emotion thickened in Perry's throat. "This is ... more than I expected."

"It is what you deserve. You have earned it."

"Thank you, Richard. I do not take this lightly."

Richard cleared his throat. "One more thing."

Perry raised an eyebrow.

"Now that you are a proper landowner, your annuity ends. You are a man of independent wealth."

Perry barked a laugh. "We shall economize, then. Only three cups of coffee a day."

"As if," Richard said dryly. "Shall we tell Emma?"

"She will be thrilled. We are building a future—and a family."

They stepped out into the sunlit garden, where Emma was seated in her infamous straw bonnet, now feathered and as hideous as ever. Perry smiled at the sight of her, his wildflower radiant beneath the spring sun.

Richard made his announcement, and Emma's face lit up in pure joy. As Perry took her hand and bent to kiss her cheek, he breathed in her familiar scent—chamomile, wildflowers, and the sweetness of home.

He had never dreamed, on the day he left for the countryside over a year ago, that his life would transform so completely. But now, with his fair bluestocking by his side and the promise of a new generation ahead, he would not change a thing.

The next Dazzling Debutante will appear in *Miss Davis and the Architect*. **A sleepless debutante. A widowed architect. A lavish country house party might be perfect for new love to bloom.**

AFTERWORD

The included version of *The Joys of the Country* was transcribed onto music sheets in Jane Austen's own hand. I have not edited the lyrics but left them precisely as she wrote them. In her time, it was fashionable to capitalize important words, which are liberally sprinkled throughout the verses.

The description of the two flower girls is based on an account from the Victorian journalist Henry Mayhew in his work, *London Labour and the London Poor*, first published as a series of articles in 1851. His detailed account includes the physical descriptions of two young sisters, their lifestyle and earnings, and the generosity of their landlady, who supported them when the weather turned and impacted their ability to earn a living. I have taken the liberty of imagining flower girls in similar circumstances thirty years earlier, during the Regency era.

Portland sheep were first introduced to Calke Abbey in 1835 and were not widely bred during the Regency itself. However, King George III noted the delicacy of Portland mutton and demanded it be served whenever he visited the region. Emma's proximity to the Isle of Portland, off the coast of Dorset, accounts for her familiarity with the breed, and Perry's skill in negotiation secures her the outcome she desires.

As for Perry and his dark past, it is a sad truth that some children do not receive the kind of parenting every child deserves. This is something I came to understand deeply during my time working in drug rehabilitation. I met troubled youth whose decision-making had been shaped by their environments—by parents who drank too much, took too many pills, argued too often, and failed to realize that little eyes and ears were watching and learning every day.

Drug abuse and poor choices can be learned behavior. But—and this is important—it is never too late for a young man or woman to learn a different way. In many cases, what they need is a mentor, a guide, or simply access to people of good conduct so they can witness a better way of living. Setting a good example can influence others far more than most people realize.

Perry is raised as one of those unfortunate children. But Emma, the Davis family, and even Richard become the loving guides he never had. Though he initially envies the care and affection Ethan receives, Perry comes to recognize that when he is with Emma, he feels better, makes better choices, and realizes that a life with purpose is more fulfilling than his former idleness. This is a journey of growth that Jane Austen herself insightfully explored more than two hundred years ago in *Sense and Sensibility*, in which Edward Ferrars finds his way with the help of Colonel Brandon and a new purpose.

I hope you enjoyed *Miss Davis and the Spare* and the spirited, confrontational bond between Perry and Emma. **In the next book in the series,** ***Miss Davis and the Archi-***

tect, **will Jane Davis be the next Dazzling Debutante when she meets a man who loved deeply and lost?**

Only time will tell when we meet Barclay Thompson—a by-blow of noble blood who once married for love and now mourns the loss of his beloved wife. It will take a very special woman to heal his heart and help him, and his young daughter Tatiana, step into a brighter future.

About the Author

C. N. Jarrett started writing her own stories in elementary school but got distracted when she finished school and moved on to non-profit work with recovering drug addicts. There she worked with people from every walk of life from privileged neighborhoods to the shanty towns of urban and rural South Africa.

One day she met a real-life romantic hero. She instantly married her fellow bibliophile and moved to the USA where she enjoyed a career as a sales coaching executive at an Inc 500 company. She lives with her husband on the Florida Gulf Coast.

Jarrett believes in kindness and the indomitable power of the human spirit. She is fascinated by the amazing, funny people she has met across the world who dared to change their lives. She likes to tell mischievous tales of life-changing decisions and character transformations while drinking excellent coffee and avoiding cookies.

Stay in touch by signing up for the C. N. Jarrett newsletter!

ALSO BY C. N. JARRETT

DAZZLING DEBUTANTES

Book 1: Miss Ridley and the Duke

Book 2: Miss Hayward and the Earl

Book 3: Miss Davis and the Spare

Book 4: Miss Davis and the Architect

Book 5: Mrs. Brown and the Christmas Gift

The Meddling Duke: a Collection of Regency Romantic Short Stories

Made in United States
North Haven, CT
01 December 2025